the DANCE of FAITH

Praise for *The Dance of Faith*

'The story begins with endearing anecdotes and gradually moves into questions for deep introspection. The narration has a light touch, yet is profoundly thoughtful.'

—**Mani Ratnam**, film director, screenwriter and producer

'Seshasayee's gift of language, of turns of original phrasing, minting figures of speech, is captivating. But that gift yields place to his masterful understanding of life. From the carved truths on temple walls and in muezzin's calls, to the scarred realities of police lock-ups, greasy sculleries and railway sidings, he takes us through the furnaces of conflict, division and anguish to there, where seeker meets the sought.'

—**Gopalkrishna Gandhi**, author and former governor of West Bengal

'Consumed by the fervour of dance, but shackled to identities and labels, and indeed to the human need to belong, this is the story of how Zaheer found the sanctum sanctorum of his own god, Bharatanatyam. Seshasayee's deft telling of this life leaves us stirred, yet disturbed. And the uncomfortable and unanswered questions it throws up stay with us long after the last page has been turned.'

—**T.M. Krishna**, musician, author and activist

'The story is sketched in a very visual style, capturing the vibrant hues of Tamil Nadu, its society, art and religion. The protagonist Zaheer's unusual passion and personal beliefs, juxtaposed with his received faith, sociology and cultural locations, result in unfolding a great human story.'

—**Rajiv Menon**, filmmaker and director

the DANCE of FAITH

a növel

R. SESHASAYEE

HarperCollins *Publishers* India

First published in India by HarperCollins *Publishers* 2022
4th Floor, Tower A, Building No. 10, Phase II, DLF Cyber City,
Gurugram, Haryana –122002
www.harpercollins.co.in

2 4 6 8 10 9 7 5 3 1

P-ISBN: 978-93-5489-566-1
E-ISBN: 978-93-5489-568-5

Typeset in 11.5/15.2 Crimson Text at

Manipal Technologies Limited, Manipal

Printed and bound at
Thomson Press (India) Ltd

HarperCollinsIn

To my Amma and Appa, who revealed to me the beauty of the written word

The face glows with the light of faith, alongside flowing locks of dark hair. Every belief is candescent. I can be a Hindu one day, a Muslim the next.

—Amir Khusrau

Author's Note

This novel is an expression of my conviction that each person's faith is unique, and needs to be understood and respected as such; that no faith is superior to another; that faith is just one identity, and art is another; and that it's entirely legitimate to be a bundle of different identities, even if seemingly in conflict. Indeed that's the only way to connect the poles.

This novel is inspired by the real life of a person who does not wish to be identified. It is not a true representation of the person's life, as it has been fictionalized with various imaginary situations and characters.

PART I

Colours of Faith

one

Zaheer was overwhelmed by the noise and colours.

Thinaipatti, a sleepy village nestled in a fold of the Yercaud Hills, had woken up to the excitement of a rare temple festival. And along with it, to the cacophony of a myriad sounds and an explosion of bright colours.

Noise and colour: always the unerring measures of joy and merriment. This was to be the grandest festival in a long time …

The village, usually a dreary sight, was drenched in colours.

The red and black of political flags,

the religious green of mango leaves,

the swirling colours of the merry-go-round,

the candy shades of ubiquitous plastic pots,

the mangled hues of roadside filth.

And many more.

And there was the battle of noise too, with two rival record shops trying to out-wail each other. The incoherent music discs from the two shops were shooting out arrows of old film songs that came down as a rain of fractured sounds.

Zaheer had always been fascinated by colours.

He caught sight of the balloon vendor who was hoisting the pole of balloons, heralding the start of festivities.

Blue balloons, yellow balloons,

green balloons with blue streaks,

pink balloons that were ringed like intestines ...

Zaheer never understood how people could remain unaffected by the beauty of colours.

Especially his father. 'You want that wretched shirt? Why, that looks like a girl's blouse!' his father had said in shock, when Zaheer picked a shirt from the window of the only garment shop in the nearby town, while the family was out for shopping for Ramzan a few weeks ago. To Zaheer, the shirt looked like a sublime piece of art.

'Boys don't wear such colours,' declared his father.

'But gods do!' said Zaheer.

He had seen at his friend's house, pictures of the god Krishna wearing a bright yellow dhoti with red borders and zari dots, Rama wearing flaming orange and green. No mistake. The gods were fond of riotous colours.

'They are not our gods,' his father had ended the argument.

Anandhi Periamma, his aunt, did not see it that way, when Zaheer broached the subject with her a few days later. 'Of course gods like colours. In fact, they come in different colours. God Krishna is blue and Lord Rama is green,' she said, although she wasn't sure if Rama was blue or green.

'You mean, Krishna's skin is blue?' Zaheer asked incredulously.

'Yes. Actually, gods can change their colours too,' Anandhi said confidently.

She thought about what she had just said. (That's how it always happened: thinking after saying.) Gods can change colours, because they can change anything. They can then change themselves too. (Anandhi believed that a tiny elf stored one-liners from her favourite actor MGR's movies and her favourite song writer Kannadasan's lyrics in a treasure vault in her brain, and dropped them at appropriate times in the course of her conversations. She was often surprised with the profundity of her own statements.)

The street leading to the temple had been recently paved, just ahead of the local body election. On an uneventful day, the street lay like a lazy centipede with random shops and houses sticking out like spindly legs. Today, the street was busy and crowded, and the centipede appeared to be moving, albeit ungracefully.

Zaheer spotted his playmates among the children running around aimlessly. His buddy Tamizharasan was gawking at the misty pink swirls of cotton candy; Muniappan was running behind an electric blue BSA cycle, holding on to the 'carrier seat' with one hand, while struggling to pull up his oversized shorts with the other …

Zaheer had no interest in joining either of them.

He had an important mission for the night and he could not be distracted from it.

At the thought of his mission, Zaheer felt his pockets.

He had carefully kept a princely sum of two rupees. A rupee gifted to him by Salima Bivi, his grandmother, to enjoy the fair; another given by Anandhi Periamma—each unaware of the other's gift. This outwitting required some smart talk, but it was worthwhile since he needed the money for his mission.

The festival seemed designed to offer an eight-year-old infinite ways to transact pleasure with three rupees:

Two *kamarkat*s, a cotton candy and a rose sherbet;

a spin on the merry-go-round (new, motor driven) and a stick of ice cream, that came in two colours;

the tin box violin (although it came with a curse: that it would become tuneless in the hands of the buyer);

goggles with frames that came in different colours;

the long whistle, the sun caps ... and countless other packaged mysteries.

'Zaheer, shall I buy two cotton candies, one each?' Tamizh was yelling from the other side of the road.

Zaheer looked away. 'Say no, say no,' he kept repeating to himself. He had to turn away from Tamizh and the allure of all the fare on the roadside. He had to save the money for his secret mission that night. He had to tear himself away from all temptation.

Zaheer ran down the street to Anandhi Periamma's snack shop. He was required to give Periamma a helping hand, since the shop would get very busy with the festival crowd.

The 'shop' was a thatched roof of palm fronds, perched on the exterior wall of the Mariamman Temple, supported by a few casuarina poles. Anandhi believed that her entrepreneurial abilities were no less than her acknowledged culinary skills. When she sat in her shop in front of her stove and the bowl of batter, Anandhi fancied herself to be a business magnate. She had her own understanding of income, expenditure, profit, loss, customer care, etc.

Anandhi's enterprise flourished despite an impossible infrastructure. The most valuable movable assets of the business were the following, in ascending order:

Two benches, one with a prosthetic leg of bricks;

Three kerosene stoves, including a 'pump stove' with a brass tank, that was cleaned with a mixture of tamarind and respect every Saturday;

Four gleaming sets of stainless steel 'tumbler and bowl', strictly reserved for serving coffee to VIPs, the list of which was dynamic;

And a big, black-and-white photograph of MGR—the matinee idol, the messiah of the masses and the secret love of half the female population of Tamil Nadu.

(She also had a small colour photo of MGR, but that was not for public display. Her 'heart-throb' was carefully tucked inside her blouse over her left breast.)

Anandhi's moral right of ownership and possession over the fifty-odd square feet of land on which the shop stood, and the security of the 'movable' assets, was underwritten through the immoral (but customary) bribe of twenty rupees, paid monthly to the local policeman, who also claimed his share of four appams every morning as the unwritten part of the contract. 'Doing business is challenging,' Anandhi would explain.

Anandhi had always wanted to bequeath dignity to the shop with a 'name board'. She had designed it to the last detail in her mind (MGR SNACK SHOP, written in decorative letters, red in the lower half and black in the upper—the two colours of MGR's political party—with two red roses in the top right corner).

The policeman rejected the proposal.

He would get into trouble for ignoring such a naked act of aggrandizement, he pointed out, for a shop that was in unauthorized occupation of public land. Anandhi had to be content with the revolutionary leader beaming down enchantingly from the temple wall on her beguiled customers.

The shop was already crowded when Zaheer reached. Eight people were a crowd for that shop. The appam batter was obligingly morphing into pristine white lotuses, surrounded by the crusty grime of the cup-shaped iron pans.

Appam and stew was a signature dish of the shop. On a day like this, Anandhi would try hard to offer something new, like paniyaram and idiyappam, but her customers seemed to be stubbornly loyal to appam and the muddy glass of tea that only had the hot temperature to recommend itself.

Anandhi was undoubtedly a good cook, and an even better hostess. It was difficult to say for certain if it was the salaciousness of local gossip that drew people to her shop or the deliciousness of her snacks. Anandhi served both her snacks and the gossip with consummate finesse. She made few direct contributions to the discourse, particularly if it related to the shadier side of the leading lights of the village. As she did with her cooking, she would strategically intervene and stir the discussion to an interesting point or garnish the scandal with spicy titbits.

Anandhi herself had been the subject of a scandal in her early years, but that seemed to have only relieved her of any inhibitions to gossip; that was her way of getting even with those who had subjected her to ignominy in the past.

Zaheer noticed that Anbarasan, a young teacher at his school, was hectoring the crowd at the shop while waiting for his turn for the appam.

Anbarasan was a follower of the rationalist movement, once a strong force in Tamil Nadu but on the decline since the founder and first-line leaders had grown old or died. The rationalist movement had earlier waged a spirited battle against superstition, religious faith and the caste system, and had even gained political power in the state, through a surrogate party. The revolutionary fire, however, had died down over the years.

Zaheer did not like Anbarasan because he could never understand what he said.

'This festival is just an ugly reminder of the evils of the caste system,' Anbarasan spoke to the crowd in a raised voice.

No one showed interest.

'You all know the story of this temple, don't you?' Anbarasan raised his voice further.

No response. More chatter.

'What is the story?' Zaheer asked Anandhi, with curiosity.

'Let me tell you,' Anbarasan jumped in, encouraged at piquing someone's curiosity. 'Pattalathamman was a lovely damsel who lived about three hundred years ago in our village. She was from the high caste, but love knows no caste boundaries, right?'

'What's he talking about?' Zaheer asked Anandhi.

Anbarasan's message was targeted at the larger audience. He didn't bother to tailor his speech for an eight-year-old.

'So, she fell in love with this young man, who was of a lower caste, and they eloped.'

Anbarasan paused in some frustration as Anandhi served the next person in line, ignoring his turn.

'So, men from the girl's caste accosted the couple in the adjoining village and burnt them both to death. Burnt them to death, that's what they did. Just because the boy was of a different caste!'

People knew the story. It had, like the mist over the Yercaud Hills, hung over the village, unaffecting and distant.

'That was the year of the worst drought,' someone in the crowd added.

'What had drought to do with the torching of the girl?'

'The drought happened only because of the curse of the girl.'

'Who said so?'

'She came in a dream and said so.'

'Whose dream?' the teacher persisted.

'My grandmother used to say that everyone in the village had an identical dream on the same night. Isn't that a miracle?'

'Rubbish!' shouted the teacher. 'And the girl asked for a temple to be built to atone for the sin?'

Zaheer was intrigued.

'Is that true, Periamma?' he asked.

'That's what people say,' Anandhi said noncommittally.

Anbarasan seemed excited by the course of the conversation.

'So, Pattalathamman was transformed into "*Aatha*", the Mother Goddess! And a temple was duly built! Tell me, if she wanted only the temple, why does she still punish you with periodic droughts?'

'Because we had discontinued the annual temple festival. For nearly twenty years. The souls of the dead still live and they need annual appeasement.'

'The souls of the dead are very thirsty,' an old man added knowingly.

'That's right. And hungry. Every year we should have made an offering of a few roosters, if not goats.'

'You will have drought this year too, as that is what the Met department has predicted,' Anbarasan said. 'Frankly, you dumb guys deserve no better.'

'Last time we didn't offer a proper goat for sacrifice,' someone pointed out. 'It was Mariyappan's goat, and everyone knew that it had liver disease and was going to die anyway. We got punished for cheating Aatha. This time, if there are no lapses, Aatha will take care of us.'

'You are destined to live and die in ignorance and superstitions,' an unrelenting Anbarasan pushed on.

'You are talking too much!' At last, someone had got provoked. 'Watch out! You will be punished by Aatha and you will perish fibre by fibre!'

'Brother,' Anandhi interjected, as she felt that a physical scuffle was imminent. 'MGR was a rationalist, but don't you remember that, in one of his movies, he also prayed to his dead mother to bless him with success? All people, not only Pattalathamman, do become god, when they die,' she said emphatically, before quickly changing the subject.

'Zaheer, bring that lime pickle and place a generous helping on Anbu Thambi's plate. It goes very well with the appam,' she said.

The teacher sensed his moment to retreat.

~

'Did Rama and Krishna also die, before they became gods?' Zaheer asked Anandhi the following day.

They lived on this earth like all of us and died. But they were gods even when they lived,' answered Anandhi.

'So, some people can become god even when they live?'

'Haven't you heard the *Sumai Thangi* song? "*Manithan enbavan deivamagalam*",' she crooned in her shrill voice. 'If you are pure and good, you can become god,' she said and added as an afterthought, 'if you are pure and good, you are already god.'

~

The village sun was making a slow exit, seemingly reluctant to miss out on the merriment of the festival. Mercury lamps snapped to attention, like security guards woken up from slumber. This was the eve of the festival, when the guardian angels were invoked to keep the evil spirits at bay. The angels took their abode eagerly—on the bunches of neem leaves tied to the entrance doors of every house, on the black threads tied on the wrists of the temple priests, on the earthen pots with turmeric on their bellies, on drops of sprinkled water, and wherever else they were duly summoned. No one was allowed to leave the village once the angels had taken charge. Even the crowds pouring in from neighbouring villages would not leave until the festival was over at the end of seven days, after the guardian angels were duly and ceremoniously seen off.

'This is going to be a busy night,' Anandhi observed. 'Zaheer, don't run away. You better stay awake to help me,' she continued.

'You already have Selvi to help you. I am going to fall asleep,' Zaheer protested.

Zaheer was of course not going to sleep; he had his mission for the night and he didn't want to get stuck at the shop.

'I need all of you. This is going to be big business,' Anandhi said, rapidly dishing out appams to a swelling crowd.

Selvi, Anandhi's niece, was counting the glasses of tea she had made till then. 'Forty-three,' she said aloud.

Anandhi noticed that this year new competition had sprung up along the street, shops selling bondas, jackfruit bajjis, something that looked like fish chips …

She had stuck to appam, but business was still brisk.

'Seems like your business is roaring!'

Anandhi looked up. It was the owner of Kalaivani Nadaga Mandram, the *therukoothhu* street theatre group from Salem town.

'Welcome brother, you have lost weight,' she said cheerfully. 'So, what's the new play going to be tonight?'

'You stop making these same old appams, and we'll stage a new play,' the leader said with a little laugh.

'You are right, brother. I do try my best to do something different. But people don't seem to want change.'

'They trust your appam, like they trust my play, and they don't want anything new.'

'Yes, you alone have the power to destroy the trust and faith others place in you,' Anandhi said with great seriousness. She tried to remember the movie in which MGR had uttered those wise words, but couldn't recall its name.

The theatre group came year after year and staged the same plays, so, by now, Anandhi, like many others, could rattle off almost all the lines and sing most of the songs, including some blabber that went for lyrics. This time it seemed there was going to be some change, after all. She spotted a couple of new faces in the group.

'Zaheer, give them all some vadais, while I make the appams. So, brother, you seem to have a smaller troupe this year?' Anandhi asked the leader.

'Even with a smaller group, I can't run this company!' he replied. 'Your temple fellows haven't even paid my last year's dues. This will be the last show in this village. I am fed up.'

The leader, of course, made this complaint every year.

'Don't repeat the same *Nala Charithram* this year too, since this is your last show. The man who played the starving Chandramathi last year looked like he had just swallowed a whole horse!'

'This year we are staging *Arjuna's Thapas*; it's going to be a fabulous show!'

'I know, I know,' Zaheer said, jumping into the conversation. 'Arjuna is one of the five Pandava brothers. Isn't the Mahabharatam their story?'

'You are right,' Anandhi said. 'They are cheated out of their kingdom by their cousins.'

'I know, by the Kauravas. Hundred brothers! Periamma, were there really a hundred brothers?'

'You shouldn't ever doubt the epics. They are the eternal truth,' Anandhi said.

Anandhi made out that there were four male actors this year. Three who looked like the Pandava brothers, and one of doubtful identity.

'Shouldn't there be five brothers? There are only three here?' Anandhi asked the leader.

'For what I get paid, three are more than enough,' the leader said irritably.

'So, the Pandava brothers will be reduced to three?' Anandhi asked, puzzled.

'The other two will be just voices. In any case, they don't have much of a role in the Mahabharatam,' the leader said, and added, 'There are too many unnecessary characters in the Mahabharatam. Just adding to the cost when you stage a play.'

'Who is the fourth person there?' Zaheer asked, unable to contain his curiosity.

The leader turned to Zaheer indulgently. 'He will double as Krishna and Siva, depending on the scene.'

'Who is playing Arjuna?' Anandhi asked.

'That useless fellow with the crooked nose. Thinks he is MGR!'

Arjuna was lighting a beedi.

'Poor fellow! He has to stay up on the pole all night, until he sights the eagle,' Anandhi said.

Zaheer was curious.

'Stay up all night on the pole? What for?' he asked Anandhi.

'Oh that! You know Arjuna was doing penance and praying to Siva Peruman to acquire his boon. So, the actor has to climb up a pole, squat on a plank on top in *tapas* and keep praying to the Lord for the welfare of the village. If the person is truly devoted, god will send an eagle to signal that his prayers would be granted. The actor will climb down after that. That is the end of the play.'

'Periamma, is he supposed to act like he is doing tapas, or should he be actually doing tapas?'

'What's the difference?' Anandhi asked.

'What happens if the eagle doesn't come?'

'Thambi, listen,' the leader interjected, 'I have staged this play twenty-two times, in various villages. And there hasn't been a single occasion when the eagle failed to show up.'

Zaheer wasn't convinced.

Arjuna didn't appear bothered about this rather risky adventure. He was enjoying his leisurely smoke.

'Periamma, is Lord Siva more powerful than Krishna?' asked Zaheer.

'All are powerful. There are no greater or lesser gods.'

'Periamma, you told me once that Krishna was a great friend of Arjuna?'

'Yes. He was actually Arjuna's brother-in-law.'

'Then, why didn't Arjuna get the bow from Krishna? Why did he have to do penance for the boon from Siva?'

Anandhi ignored the question.

'Perhaps, they are the same god. They only change costumes,' Zaheer said.

A few customers laughed good-humouredly.

Anandhi couldn't make out why the gods were always playing such games. 'Get a glass of tea for that elderly man, he has been waiting for long,' she said, diverting the conversation.

The crowd was chaotically making its way to the small temple, and in the process, was spilling out to the flanks, right in front of Anandhi's shop.

Zaheer ran to the rear of the temple where the drama troupe had pitched its tent.

The play was not due until midnight and it would last until dawn. The Pandava brothers, in colourful faces and sequinned costumes, were slowly emerging out of the unimpressive mortal frames of the actors. He looked longingly at the brightly painted epaulettes which hung from the shoulders of the male characters, like the broken wings of some mythical bird, and the mirrored headgears.

'May I touch the crowns?' Zaheer asked the leader.

'Why my boy, you want to become an actor?' the leader asked. And added, 'Maybe one day, you *will* be an actor, not of wretched street theatre like this, but like MGR, a real movie star. You have fair skin and a beautiful face ... What's your name again?'

'Zaheer.'

The leader brought the cardboard crown and held it on top of Zaheer's head. 'Big for your head right now, but one day, god willing, any crown might be small for you.'

Zaheer felt a shiver run down his spine.

The village was soaked in religion. The festival was all at once an inebriating cocktail of soulful faith and crass commerce. The crowd pressing against the flimsy casuarina railings to catch a glimpse of the deity inside the sanctum of the Mariamman Temple comprised mostly women, middle-aged, many of them muttering prayers as they stood in line. Goddess Mariamman would have no doubt required an army of angels to assist her to deal with the wide variety of prayers, ranging from tracing lost goats to knocking out harassing mothers-in-law, from restoring wayward husbands to finding bridegrooms for eager damsels. Young men hanging around the temple in clusters, were not going to get distracted by the remotely rewarding religion; they were busy with the immediate task of fishing for mates (both temporary and permanent), preferably from neighbouring villages and plotting their next move and the night rendezvous.

Meanwhile, the bazaar had usurped the pride of place from the temple, with religion submissively providing the platform for commerce.

And there were the drumbeats, seemingly purposeless, providing the rhythm, as the village pulsated with excitement.

There was much more. The cinema, for instance.

Zaheer first saw the cinema poster a week ago as he and Tamizharasan were on their way home from school. His jaw dropped when he stumbled upon the poster in the marketplace. For one, it was in full colour, a rarity for Thinaipatti. Two leading ladies, Padmini and Vyjayanthimala, who had dominated Tamil cinema two decades ago, were now dominating the poster before his eyes. The 'King of Romance' Gemini Ganesan was ensconced by them, looking confused. The name of the film was *Vanjikkottai Valiban*. 'Don't miss the enthralling contest between the two reigning empresses of dance', the poster urged. Zaheer had in fact seen this same ad in the newspaper that his father regularly read.

While the black-and-white photographs in the newspaper, despite the smudged printing and weak ink, appeared fascinating enough, seeing the two heroines in splendiferous colour stirred his soul.

Zaheer stood frozen, enchanted by the beauty of the two women. The poster was no longer a two-dimensional piece of paper stuck on a bamboo mat. The actors were real. As he continued staring, Padmini and Vyjayanthimala were coming alive. He could now feel the gaze of the two women upon him, warm and caressing. He was melting like an ice lolly.

'What is happening to you?' Tamizharasan asked, concerned.

Tamizh had seen senior students in their school secretly share their hordes of movie bills, endlessly staring at pictures of bewitching, half-clad women. Till now, those things had never interested him or Zaheer, or anyone else their age.

'Tamizh, don't they look divine?' Zaheer asked.

'What does that mean?'

'Like the goddesses in the calendars?'

'No, they don't. Goddesses have four hands.'

Zaheer thought for a while. He preferred goddesses with two hands, the human variety.

For the next few days, Zaheer chose to walk home alone, giving himself enough time and solitude to savour the sight of the heavenly beauties, who would descend on Thinaipatti during the festival and possess his deprived soul. Zaheer had to see the movie, meet the stars on the screen. That was, at least for the moment, his life's mission.

The theatre group was leisurely putting up the stage in the centre of the marketplace. Zaheer's mission would keep him away from the play, but he could return to see the eagle appear in the skies during the grand finale, as that would happen only at dawn.

It was nearly midnight when Zaheer made his way to the movie theatre, which was almost on the outskirts of the village. There were continuous screenings of the movies until dawn, as the theatre also served as a night shelter to the migrant crowd from nearby villages.

The hooch outlets had been ordered to be closed during the festival, betraying official acknowledgement of their existence. With no other distraction, the crowd was closing in on the theatre like black ants on candy.

The theatre was a tent made of cloth of dubious texture and indeterminate colour. The poster that had mesmerized Zaheer was stuck on top of the entrance.

Zaheer had to snake his way to the ticket counter, carefully clutching the coins, amidst a chaotic and noisy crowd. The knocks and punches on the way did nothing to discourage or distract him from his mission. As he finally held in his hand the flimsy green ticket that secured for him a place in the front rows on the floor of the theatre, to watch for the first time in his life a movie—he felt that he was entering a new dream world, that was his own.

Zaheer hoped that no one from his family or any of his friends turned up at the theatre. He was aware that his parents would not approve of him seeing movies, let alone watching one all by himself. Anandhi Periamma, on the other hand, was a movie buff who watched every movie (especially an MGR movie) that was screened within a radius of twenty kilometres from Thinaipatti and devoured every scrap of news about movie stars (especially MGR). Although Zaheer knew that Periamma would be busy at her shop, he peered over the cloth screen that partitioned the male and female sections of the audience, to make sure she was not there. This was not out of fear, but only a determination to experience the dream world all by himself.

The start of the dream experience, however, was rough. Zaheer was pushed around before he managed to squeeze himself into a small place on the floor. As he scrambled to his place, he saw the slideshow of advertisements appear onscreen, which he first mistook to be the movie. The initial shouting and fisticuffs to get to their seats did nothing to dampen the enthusiasm of the audience which was now hooting and whistling to an advertisement for a popular aphrodisiac that promised heightened virility. The crowd was finally muffled into silence when the movie started with the bugle call of the Gemini twins, the mascot of the popular production house.

Zaheer managed to get a tunnel view of the bottom of the movie screen through the thick necks of two well-built men who squatted in front of him. What began to unfold in front of his eyes was truly breathtaking: there were big palaces, humble huts, sinking ships, small boats, rough seas, placid ponds, hurricanes, floods, fire, horse carriages, bullock carts, bad guys, good guys, crying men, laughing women, cardboard crowns, swords, spears, dark prisons, darker tunnels, soldiers in arms and men in masks.

And the two heavenly damsels. And their dances.

Zaheer was in a trance.

When Padmini crooned a folk tune, Zaheer's head spun around. When Vyjayanthimala winked at the hapless hero, Zaheer felt himself blush. The handsome hero on the screen was continuously being snatched up by one heroine from the other, leaving him rather indecisive and confused. Zaheer could not understand why the hero could not simply have both of them, as Zaheer's uncle Ahmed had cleverly done, under somewhat similar circumstances. In any case, both the ladies appeared eminently desirable. Almost two hours into the movie, it appeared that the hero could still not decide between the two. The two women had to take the matter into their own hands and proceeded to challenge each other to a dance contest, which was the high point of the movie. When the contest began, everything else that Zaheer had seen of the movie completely faded from his memory. This was the moment he was waiting for. Zaheer had never seen any dance like this. The two ladies were obviously furious, almost ready to physically strike and slap each other; instead, they danced, and as they danced, they whirled, swirled, jumped, slid, craned, crouched, stretched—all in perfect rhythm. The glitter from their crowns and the sparkle of their dangling earrings kept pace with the beats.

Padmini pirouetted in proportion to her anger. Vyjayanthimala drenched her rival in scorn with an arch of her eyebrows. Despite all the aggression and speed, grace and charm poured out of the dancers. Actually, it poured out of the screen and flooded Zaheer's mind. He gasped with the smothering of his senses by the beauty of the dance.

When the movie ended, Zaheer hurried to get out of the tent and back into the open. He felt that the spirit of the two dancers had possessed him. They had taken over his body and soul. In fact, they were no longer two women but had melded into one. Soon, there was no form for the spirit that possessed him. It was a sublime spirit of graceful movement, rhythm, beauty and joy.

Zaheer started dancing his way to the temple square, unmindful of the giggling girls, and sparing not a thought to the possibility that someone from his family would find him.

He forgot about the eagle.

Zaheer had arrived in his world, his dream world.

The Divine Love

(7th century CE)

'Godha, hang on to my arms. If you don't, you will get lost in the crowd,' Vishnuchittar called out to his daughter.

'What?' shouted young Godha. She couldn't hear her father over the noise and chaos.

'Why do temple festivals have to be this noisy?' Godha mused.

'Don't you know I like sound and noise?' Godha heard someone asking her. It was a clear voice that seemed to tunnel through to her ears.

Godha looked up at the temple chariot, which was at some distance. She saw the idol of Lord Vatapatrasayee decked in beautiful flowers and perched upon the throne in the chariot. She instantly realized that the Lord was looking at her.

'Oh! You startled me,' Godha told the Lord with fake anger.

'I don't believe that. No one can scare you!' the Lord smiled mischievously.

'I know You enjoy all the adulation You get, You bless those who call Your name out, but this noise is not all about You.'

'Doesn't matter. I am present in every sound of joy.'

'But people are not thinking of You, when they keep shouting.'

'No, they are not thinking of me, but are experiencing me when they are joyful,' the Lord said. 'So long as it doesn't hurt someone else. Godliness is all joy.'

'Yes, You are the Supreme Happiness!' Godha said.

Godha could see the Lord smiling at her.

'And Supreme Beauty!' she added, charmed by His smile.

'Beauty and Happiness are the same!' she heard the tunnel voice say.

Vishnuchittar wondered why his little girl was talking to herself.

two

Pattalathamman Temple was situated at the outskirts, about two kilometres away from the Mariamman Temple which lay at the centre of the village, and was the poorer of the two. In fact, it was no temple but a dolmen, with three corner stones and a cap stone. A female figure was sculpted along the inner walls and served to remind the villagers of the gory history of the woman who now waited to grant favours to the devout and punish the guilty.

The division of work between the two deities of the village was rather nebulous. However, it was generally agreed that while Mariamman, the elder Aatha, was relatively benign and granted boons to the villagers more generously, Pattalathamman, the younger Aatha, was more difficult to please and often unleashed her anger through outbreaks of disease or by blowing away the monsoon clouds. Her ire was not always general; it was sometimes specific to individuals and families. The villagers with their collective conscience singed with guilt over the violent end meted out to Pattalathamman in her human incarnation, readily legitimized her ill temper and attempted to appease Aatha with sacrifices of goats and chickens. Sometimes, the villagers tended to take her for granted. Pattalathamman had now elbowed herself to the centre stage, following a severe drought during the previous season. Aatha had made her point: She was no pushover. The annual festival, that had been discontinued for nearly two decades, had to be revived. The village got the message and chose to redeem its faith.

Pattalathamman's temple had been wrapped like candy to attract the less devout. A pandal of palm fronds stood over the dolmen like a giant spider, with festoons of coloured paper and mango leaves clumsily adding gaiety to its form.

The temporary spire made of wood, wrapped in foil, was gleaming in the evening sun, granting a certain primacy to the structure against the background of a dull landscape.

The temple was ready for the big day, but the goddess wasn't. She was waiting to regain her somewhat depleted divinity with the pouring of holy water that would be brought in a procession from the Mariamman Temple in an hour, with which her temple would also be consecrated.

A large crowd had gathered around the temple, waiting for well over two hours for the procession to arrive.

The sound contractor, appropriately so called, whose job it was to play music while people waited, had already played his inventory of six discs four times and was beginning the fifth round.

The women who had gathered at the temple, having exhausted their repertoire of local gossip were slipping into minor quarrels. The priest of Pattalathamman Temple was already restless, when Zaheer and Tamizharasan came running to the site.

Tamizh stopped near the priest, panting heavily.

'Don't start the rituals, don't!' Tamizh ordered the priest.

'*Adey!* Who sent you here to give me instructions?' the priest angrily asked.

'The President,' Zaheer interjected.

The President was the leader of the local administration, the largest landowner, the arbiter of all disputes and the titular head of the temple.

'Why on earth would the President choose urchins like you to send messages to me?'

'Because I run fast. I got the first prize in running at my school,' Tamizh said proudly.

'And why should I not start the rituals?'

'Because the procession hasn't started. Once it starts, we'll come and tell you. You can begin your rituals then.'

'What's the problem?'

'Don't know. Probably Aatha hasn't arrived.'

The priest was thoughtful.

'Aatha is truly angry!' he muttered to himself.

At the Mariamman Temple too, people were anxious.

The festival ritual required a 'low caste' male to be chosen, who, under public supervision, would follow a monk-like life for seven days and on the day of the main festival, be escorted to the temple with honours. He would be the medium for the goddess to provide benediction to the seekers and believers.

(When Anbarasan learnt about this custom, he was baffled.

'Why low caste?' he asked the temple priest.

'To atone for the sin of killing the lad who eloped with Pattalathamman, I suppose.'

'Is that an appeasement for the present or atonement for the past?' Anbarasan asked, expecting, of course, no reply.)

The chosen man, who had undergone the prescribed process of purifying himself, had been waiting impatiently for some hours now, for the goddess to 'possess' him. He was being drenched with pots of turmeric water, since a sanitized medium was required for the goddess to arrive.

The priest of the Mariamman Temple had tried every known ritual to coax Aatha to manifest herself. Yet, there was no sign of the goddess.

Zaheer had been watching the man with interest for the past week. The man stayed in a thatched hut, right next to Anandhi's shop, separated only by the entrance steps to the temple. Anandhi sent him some appams surreptitiously, though the man was not permitted to eat anything other than the daily rice offerings made to Mariamman, whose taste alternated between clay and chalk. Zaheer usually carried the appams to the man and became friends with him, as the man appeared glad to have someone to talk to. He was young and handsome and had a pleasant smile. He wore an orange loin cloth and did not appear to be embarrassed by the scanty attire.

The man was not allowed to go out of the hut except late at night, when he would go around the village beating a drum—it sounded like a funeral procession. When the man came out in the night, every house would get locked and children would be held back from casting their eyes on him.

'Why isn't anyone allowed to see him when he comes out at night?' Zaheer asked Anandhi.

'It's not the man; it's the evil spirits that he is driving out that you shouldn't see,' replied Anandhi.

'Why should you not see evil spirits?'

'Don't be silly. They will fasten on to you, if you see them.'

'But weren't the evil ones already driven away by the guardian angels?'

'Evil spirits are so evil that they often manage to hoodwink the guardian angels, since they are so nice.'

Zaheer thought perhaps the angels didn't deserve so much respect, given they were doing such a poor job.

Tamizharasan provided the answer when Zaheer shared his doubts with him one day.

'The man walks naked. That's why we are not allowed to see. I saw him through the cracks in the door.'

'Not even a loincloth?'

'Not even a loincloth.'

'Why does he walk naked?'

'To drive away the evil spirits. You see, the evil spirits can't stand nudity,' Tamizh clarified.

When Zaheer and Tamizh returned to the Mariamman Temple, they saw an anxious crowd surrounding the man.

'It's been more than three hours since the ritual began and Aatha hasn't arrived! Maybe this man committed some offence during his purification process. Did he eat meat? Wouldn't put it beyond him,' someone said. 'Why blame him? Anyone in the village could have offended Aatha! I actually saw a young girl and a boy doing dirty things in the orchard last night. If you care, I'll mention the names,' another jumped into the fray.

Anbarasan smiled at the irony of the situation. The village was atoning for the sin of destroying young love. And yet proscribing young love was part of the atonement!

'Don't waste time in idle chatter,' the President said, rebuking them all. 'Pour more turmeric water.'

More buckets of turmeric water were duly thrown at the man. The man was looking like a jaundiced apparition.

'Perhaps Aatha isn't quite happy about the arrangements,' another voice rose from the crowd.

'Which dog is saying that?' the President barked. He was already irritated as the delay in the visitation of the goddess was somehow seemed a direct affront to his authority. The nasty words that poured forth from him were fortunately drowned in the sound of the drums reaching a crescendo.

Drrrrrrrrrrrrrrrrr ...

The drummers were doing their bit to force Aatha to come out, hoping that she would be unable to bear the deafening noise.

The 'goddess man' was now beginning to sway. Only the whites of his eyes were visible. He was flaying his arms and his swing was getting more vigorous. The medium man morphed into Aatha at that moment.

Aatha had arrived. At last.

A loud cry of relief went up from the crowd.

Zaheer shuddered looking at the man. He had no resemblance to the friendly young man he had known, eager to receive Periamma's appams. He looked like a ferocious animal in a cage. The physical power of the man was unbelievable. He was trying to break free from the group of men who held him back with a thick rope. 'Why should the goddess be so fearsome?' Zaheer thought. Petrified, he clutched Tamizharasan's hands.

('Simple hallucination. A psychiatric phenomenon. How do I make these people understand?' Anbarasan meanwhile wondered.)

Women threw flowers at Aatha and lit camphor to welcome the goddess. They seemed to be very comfortable with the rather violent manifestation of the goddess. Loud prayers went up. They had to be loud enough for Aatha to hear over the drums and the noise.

The President seemed pleased, having successfully commandeered the goddess.

'Aatha, we are blessed,' the President said. 'We have been waiting for you to come and deliver us from the threat of another drought,' he began his speech.

The President was adept at giving welcome speeches to visiting political functionaries, and was proud of his oratory skills.

'Aatha, you know, we have been badly affected by last year's drought, and despite severe crunch, I spared no efforts to organize this grand festival,' he said.

'Rascal!' the goddess man said.

The President was bewildered. He looked behind him.

'I am calling you,' the goddess man pointed to the President. 'Do you think I don't know how much you swindle in your contracts?'

The President was taken aback.

'Aatha ... there is some mistake ... You are completely er ... misinformed,' the President stammered.

This was dangerous ground, Aatha had to be quickly diverted away from this subject. The President promptly gathered himself. 'Aatha, we are all your children. You are angry because we have not appeased you properly. But here we are, ready to atone for our sins. Tell us what we need to do to please you, and we will carry out your orders.'

Drrrrrrr. Drrrrrrrrr. Drrrrrrrrr ...

The drummers were now varying the rhythm. The rhythm used for waking up the sleeping goddess had to be different to the one for a talking goddess.

'You will do my bidding?'

'Sure, Aatha, isn't it the duty of the children to carry out ...'

'Cut out that nonsense!' the goddess man interjected. He swayed silently for a while.

'Come on, isn't it getting late?' a man in the crowd said.

'Rascal!' the goddess man shouted.

'Aatha!' the President's decibel level also rose. He couldn't afford more revelations in public.

'I am not talking to you,' the goddess man screamed. 'I am calling that fellow, Velu! Big Lord! He thinks I am wasting his precious time?'

The person identified as Velu froze in shock. He least expected that the goddess would identify him, especially since he was not even from that village.

'Shall I tell everyone what you did to that young girl, last new moon day, beside the Ayyanar statue?'

Velu rushed out of the crowd, fearing for his life.

The President decided to get a little tougher with the goddess. It was all right for Aatha to show a bit of anger, as all gods are entitled to, but uncovering private sins in public was not in the remit, however omniscient the goddess might be.

'Aatha, I told you we are all human and we do commit sins. Here we are seeking your pardon and your blessings. Tell us what more we need to do to atone for our sins. And let's get on with the job.'

Drrrrrrrrrrrrrrrrrrrrrdik.

The goddess man looked at the sky and shouted some incoherent instructions over the noise of the drums.

'What is the instruction from Aatha?' the President asked the priest anxiously.

The priest closed his eyes and appeared to listen to the possessed man intensely.

After some time, he said, 'Aatha would like one goat as sacrifice for each step she takes towards Pattalathamman Temple. That will be the minimum compensation for the sins of the village.'

The President did some quick mental calculations. Pattalathamman was nearly two kilometres away. Even if each step was long, it would not be more than a metre. That means, a thousand goats would be required for every kilometre, two thousand goats for the total distance! The President wondered if he had made some mistake. He spotted Anbarasan and asked him to confirm his calculations. 'You are right. The priest seems to be poor in arithmetic,' Anbarasan confirmed.

'You have made some mistake! We can't possibly find two thousand goats in a radius of fifty kilometres from here. Please suggest something more reasonable,' President demanded of the priest.

The goddess man was swaying.

Drrrrrrrrrrrrrrrrrrrrrrdik.

The goddess man turned to the priest and made gestures.

'Aatha says she will settle for nothing less than one goat for every twenty feet,' the priest interpreted.

The President was enthused. If the goddess was amenable to negotiating, he could drive a hard bargain.

'Aatha, you know that this has been a year of drought. Even though we wish to appease you, we don't have the means. Please give us three or four years of good rain and bountiful harvest, and then we can consider offering the sacrifice you desire. You must be more reasonable for the present.' Here the President paused. 'Perhaps we could offer five goats in all. Even that would be difficult, but we recognize that you are our reigning goddess,' he offered.

The goddess man continued swaying.

The President noticed that a few women in the crowd were beginning to sway too.

('Mass hallucinations,' Anbarasan reasoned.)

The drumming was sheer frenzy now.

'Aatha, you are beginning to manifest in many women now. We must settle your offerings quickly. Otherwise, there is a danger of more demands from all those possessed women and more confusion,' the President reasoned.

'They are all fake,' the priest declared.

But the priest also appeared to be keen to close the deal. 'Make it ten goats and Aatha will tolerate no more arguments.'

'Start the procession,' the President ordered.

The drummers burst into an ear-piercing beat. And the procession began.

Zaheer looked at the goat. It was decorated with a marigold garland and its forehead was smeared with vermilion.

The goat seemed to have a premonition of its fate. Like a martyr at the gallows willingly embracing death for a larger cause, the goat stood stoically. Zaheer met its eyes. He felt a churn in his stomach.

The next minute, the goat's head rolled down with a thud as the butcher's knife came heavily down on its neck. Zaheer let out a cry as a splash of the goat's blood landed on his knee.

'Why should the goat be killed for the sin of men?' Zaheer asked Anandhi Periamma that night.

'The goat, in any case, would have gone on the plates of men for their next meal,' she answered.

'If that is so, where is the sacrifice?'

Anandhi was quiet.

'Periamma, does the goddess really ask for the blood of innocent animals?'

Anandhi wasn't very sure.

'And will we have rains after the sacrifice?' Zaheer wanted to know.

Anandhi thought hard for an answer. Then she remembered a song that she had heard, that seemed to have the answer to Zaheer's question. She started singing in her shrill voice.

It's your faith that light will follow night,
Because so far it's proved to be right.
But tomorrow may be the apocalypse
When Sun is designed to finally collapse.

Ultimately good will win and sin will lose
The ancient ones used this clever ruse
To keep everyone in good check and order.
But to prove that theory has been much harder

Life spins on Faith.
Reason died yesterday. With facts.
Tomorrow is just about Hope and Belief.

Anbarasan had rehearsed it all in his mind. As he stood facing the police sub-inspector at the town police station, he was clear of the next steps.

'Dumb people believe animal sacrifice will bring rain! This is violation of the law, sir! You should have stopped this atrocity; it was plainly illegal. The police is abetting a crime!' Anbarasan packed a lot of force in his delivery, exactly as he had rehearsed.

'Do you know what causes rains?' the sub-inspector or 'Essai' jabbed his finger in front of Anbarasan's eyes.

'I am a teacher,' Anbarasan protested. 'I don't need to answer this question.'

'Ah, you are a teacher! So, you know everything about rains?'

'Well, rains happen through the evaporation of water and subsequent precipitation of water particles and the movement of these on a three-dimensional grid, when heavier moisture-bearing cumulonimbus ...'

Essai waved his hand. 'Do you know who created all these complex systems?'

Anbarasan stared back with contempt but remained silent.

'So, you don't know. You also won't know if prayers produce rains or not!'

'This is not about innocent prayers. This is about animal sacrifice.'

'There is no law against animal sacrifice,' Essai pointed out boringly.

'Yes, there is,' Anbarasan said. 'The Tamil Nadu Prevention of Cruelty to Animals Act of 1950.'

'There you are,' Essai said with a smirk. 'Law is only against cruelty, not against killing.'

'Killing is not cruel?'

'No. Not as per Indian Criminal Law.'

'Killing an innocent animal to wash your sin is cruelty.'

'How do you know that the goat was innocent and didn't commit sins?' asked Essai, impressed by his own cleverness.

'Sir, I will take this up politically. I will stage an agitation.'

Essai wasn't perturbed. He had enough experience to instantly assess the damage potential of any person who stood in front of him. Anbarasan was featherweight.

'Brother, listen to me. This is a religious matter. There will be a law-and-order problem if you attempt to do anything,' Essai paused. 'Then it will be my duty to take preventive action and take into custody any potential troublemakers. What did you say is your name? And what would be your father's name?' Essai pulled out a paper to write.

This had not been part of Anbarasan's rehearsal.

As Anbarasan came out of the police station in frustration, large drops of rain fell upon his face.

King Vallabadeva Pandian was worried.

The revenue of the kingdom was falling due to scanty rain and patchy farm output for the second year. It was almost the end of the month of Eyppassi, and there were no signs of rain. One more week of no rains, and the crops would wither. He feared that there could be a breakout of unrest.

'We will have to prepare to invade the neighbouring kingdom,' his clever minister had warned him. 'That will give access to their granaries, which are reportedly full.'

The minister added after some thought, 'The war will also divert people's attention away from the looming famine.'

The King wasn't very enthused ...

'Going to battle is the last resort,' he said. 'We should conduct special prayers at all the fifty-six Vishnu temples in the kingdom.' The King was a staunch Vaishnavite. He had been taught to believe that Vishnu was in charge of clouds and rains, while Siva was a rather distracted God, preferring to go about wandering in cremation grounds.

'And at the thirty-two Siva temples,' the Minister added, as he was a Saivite, and didn't want to cede territory to competition.

'And don't forget to consult Vishnuchittar at Villiputhur!' The King added, naming the revered Vaishnavite saint ...

'I have already done that, Your Majesty,' the Minister said. 'Vishnuchittar has a divine daughter, who keeps conversing with Lord Vatapatrasayee. She has promised to remind the Lord.'

'That's very good,' the King said with relief.

When the Minister walked out of the palace, he looked up to see dark clouds, that looked to him like the dark, powerful shoulders of Siva.

three

A split toenail. Ugly and dirty.

That was the first part of the anatomy of her husband that Anandhi set her eyes on. It was when her future husband and his family had come from a neighbouring village to shop for a bride ('That girl was fairer and brings more dowry, but this one will do more work, and be more obedient, so which is a better deal?').

Anandhi wasn't interested in raising her gaze. She felt depressed at the mere sight of the toenail. The bridegroom party mistook Anandhi's downcast eyes for shyness, a very valuable virtue in a girl.

And things had progressed fast from there.

'Our daughter is an excellent cook, her chicken curry tastes exactly like *amrutham,'* Anandhi's father said, in response to which the groom's father volleyed, 'Did you know that our son knocked down a thief in the cowshed single-handedly?' The boy's mother wondered whether Anandhi wasn't too plump and since girls tended to put on weight after childbirth, how would she look in her middle age? Stung by that impolite observation, Anandhi's mother, on her part, also wondered whether the boy's squint eye didn't indicate defective vision, and before the matter spun out of control, the marriage broker (who had high financial stakes in finalizing the marriage) hurriedly pointed out that it was far better to have plump and strong girls than slim and weak ones who might even die at childbirth and besides, a squint was a sure sign of good fortune, and in any case, the girl's birth star and the boy's birth star were such a perfect match on all ten counts, that such a thing happened only when the gods themselves had made them for each other. The broker suggested they settle the dowry after mutual consultations, which he expertly did in the next couple of days (with many a helpful lie) through which Anandhi was to receive a *thali* in four grams of gold (22 carat), one sari (artificial silk) and in return the bridegroom was to receive one milch buffalo (milk yield of four seers per day), a second-hand Atlas cycle, a silk dhoti (artificial silk) and miscellaneous gifts (which were detailed) along with, of course, Anandhi, adorned with one pair of gold *kammal* (22 carat), two pairs of bangles (gold covering), the net effect of the transaction resulting in Anandhi being assessed at a liability value of approximately rupees two thousand two hundred, which, of course nobody bothered to work out, immediately after which, the marriage date was fixed in consultation with the village priest, and the marriage was celebrated with thirty-four people attending, although the caterer billed for fifty-two, alleging that many people had more than one meal, which remained an unresolved dispute between Anandhi's father and the caterer. Anandhi found herself pushed into a hut with a solitary room, with a stainless-steel tumbler of hot milk (cardamom added) and a plate of betel leaves and nuts, bananas and guavas (guaranteed aphrodisiac).

'I don't like you,' Anandhi said.

She said this midway as her new husband was disrobing her.

She looked at the man she was married to, and she didn't like him. It wasn't only the toenail.

Her husband smiled stupidly. He kept looking at Anandhi and slowly undressed himself.

'Even now?' he asked expectantly, with his eager manhood in full display.

'More so.'

He lay by her side quietly, making sure his body wasn't touching her. Anandhi wished that he would say something. Something angry. But he just lay there. Macho heroes don't behave this way, Anandhi thought. Ahmed wouldn't have behaved this way.

'I like Ahmed,' Anandhi said.

Anandhi desperately hoped that the man would get up and thrash her for mentioning another man's name. Nothing of the sort happened. The man was not even looking at her.

After a while, he asked, 'In what way is he better than me?' Matter-of-factly. As though he were comparing buffaloes.

'Well, he has beautiful toes,' she said, instantly realizing that she had never seen Ahmed's toes. 'And feet, and strong legs and ...'

'And?'

Anandhi didn't answer.

After a while, he put on his clothes and fell asleep.

The scene of the first night repeated itself for a few nights thereafter, in silence. Like a movie being screened at the theatre every day. The end was always boring, with both of them dozing off.

Anandhi wanted to escape the mousetrap she had fallen into.

No one had asked her for her consent for the marriage, as no one was expected to ask for the consent of brides. Weren't brides too young and incapable of knowing what was good for them? In any case, everything leading up to the marriage had happened too rapidly. Anandhi cursed herself for not protesting in time and stopping the marriage. Perhaps she should have threatened to commit suicide. Perhaps she should have taken a small dose of rat poison, not enough to kill her, but just enough to froth a little at the corner of the mouth, just enough to scare the parents.

'I was an idiot,' she cried, and slapped her forehead hard.

She had been pushed into the wrong bus and she had to get off quickly. She wished she was thrown out. There was security in victimhood. Society always sympathized with girls who were thrown out of a marriage, even if they were declared inauspicious.

The neighbour woman might even spice up the tale with gory details of torture by imaginary in-laws, before she passed on the parcel to her neighbour. If gossip were to run its natural free course, Anandhi stood a good chance of being deified some years after death.

But victimhood appeared elusive with this husband.

Finally, Anandhi decided that she had to take the matter in her own hands.

Two weeks later, Anandhi and her husband stood in front of the village panchayat. There was an eager crowd waiting to see a sensational real drama play out.

'I haven't touched her,' the man said defensively.

'Is it true?' the headman of the panchayat asked Anandhi.

She nodded in confirmation.

'Maybe you have a problem. The village doctor should be able to help you,' the headman made a kind suggestion to the husband.

'No, he doesn't,' Anandhi said. 'I am the one seeking to terminate the marriage, because I don't like him.'

A few jaws dropped. Although the village custom did not prohibit women seeking dissolution of marriage, it was rare.

'Bitch! She should be thrashed!' someone shouted. 'This is why we should never take brides from outside the village.'

'That's true. Our girls would never do such a thing,' the headman agreed.

'So, let me not poison your well. Let me go,' Anandhi said.

'Call her father, he should be punished,' someone in the crowd cried.

'This has nothing to do with my father,' Anandhi said firmly. 'This marriage is neither good for my husband nor for me. If you people force me to stay in the marriage, then please take responsibility for fishing out my body tomorrow from the well behind his house.'

Anandhi hadn't thought about such a course of action, but it seemed a correct thing to say, under the circumstances.

'What do you want to do?' the headman asked the husband. The husband stared stupidly.

'I know what I want to do,' Anandhi said. 'I am returning the sari that my in-laws gave for my wedding.' She thrust a parcel in her husband's hand. He clutched it as though it was a gift from the gods. She looked at him with condescension and said, 'And you could keep all the dowry my father gave you.'

Anandhi turned back and left the place without waiting for the panchayat's verdict.

She felt like the heroine in a climax scene, who trounces the villain, delivering some power-packed lines before walking away from the scene.

Anandhi was impressed with her own courage.

Anandhi's courage seemed to melt away as she alighted at the Thinaipatti bus stop, a steel trunk in hand. Breaking the wedlock had been accomplished more easily than she had anticipated. During the few days of marriage, her young mind was totally consumed by the urge to flee. She had not thought enough about her life beyond. She had to figure out now where she would go from here.

As she tried to imagine her future, she began to panic. She thought of the reactions of people at her home and in the village. She would not be able to hide the truth: she had broken the marriage; she had not been sent away. She was the perpetrator, not the victim. She was evil, not innocent. Black, not white. There was no room for grey. 'How can you force a minor girl into a marriage?' 'What is wrong in terminating a bad marriage?'—none of that urban nonsense would fly.

What would her mother do? She would probably kill herself. That's what honourable women were supposed to do under such circumstances. Fathers killed wayward daughters and mothers killed themselves. That's how good movies would tell the story. Her father was not the killing type. He ran a grocery store and had borrowed heavily to conduct her wedding. At 5 per cent interest per month from the moneylender. And then there was the matter of family honour. Anandhi had three sisters, and their marriage prospects would be irreparably spoilt because of her rebellious act.

'All the girls in that family are of loose character,' the neighbours would say, tying everyone with a common noose. Was she of 'loose character'? Does breaking away from a bad marriage mean loose character? Would all the neighbours gang up to kill her to cleanse the village?

Anandhi began to feel she had made a terrible mistake. Maybe she should have learnt to live with the split toenail, after all. She dropped her trunk, collapsed on it and began to cry violently.

Then she thought of Ahmed.

She always thought of Ahmed as the MGR of Thinaipatti. Fair, tall and macho. In fact, three-dimensional Ahmed was decidedly more sensual than the two-dimensional MGR.

When Ahmed came to shop at her father's grocery, she became unsteady. His charm thrashed her like a wave rocking a small boat. She felt his wetness inside her.

Ahmed's visits to the shop became gradually more frequent and for trivial things. Once he came to buy a packet of Black Monkey tooth powder, came back to return it for Gopal tooth powder, and again returned to collect the change. She began to notice that he began to notice her. She applied extra coconut oil on her hair and plaited it tightly. Her father was baffled by the sudden disappearance of Gokul sandalwood talcum powder from the grocery shelf.

Ahmed didn't say much when he came to the grocery. Anandhi always giggled when he looked at her and she detected a mischievous wink in response.

Then, one night, it happened at the orchard.

It didn't take much effort on Ahmed's part. He gave Anandhi a 'come on, follow me' look and she followed him as if she was tethered to him with an invisible rope.

They walked, keeping a discreet distance between them, past the dying lights of the sleepy marketplace, past the temple from where the goddess kept a vigil, past the stinking fringes of the orchard and deep into its innards, which lay spreadeagled, ready to consume them, with the familiar ease of having devoured a thousand other such secrets of the village.

Under the black blanket of the night, they explored each other aggressively. Silently.

During the following weeks, Anandhi was distracted with fear and guilt.

Ahmed owned almost all her thoughts and dreams. As Anandhi savoured those vaulted memories, she was surprised with the many details that came out like an excavated ancient sculpture. Like the mild aroma of Ponds Dreamflower talc (wasn't he well prepared for the occasion?), like the thick wart on the nape of his neck, like the hollow smell of chicken on his breath ... When she ran out of details, she invented new ones, as her mind clutched tightly and didn't allow to let go of the memory of the night. Yet, she wasn't sure if she was in love with Ahmed.

Ahmed did not visit the grocery for many weeks after the orchard night. Anandhi felt a sense of relief. Her fear of facing her guilt was overcoming her body's craving for Ahmed. When they eventually met at the marketplace, there was pleasant awkwardness.

As Anandhi sat thinking, perched on her steel trunk, on the shoulder of the mud road that led to her village, one thing became clear to her. She had to jump into another marriage. Now. Like jumping from one boat to another, mid-sea. There was no habitable space in between. And it had to be with Ahmed. There was no other man in her life.

As she thought of Ahmed, memories of the orchard night came flooding to her mind. The same experience acquired new meaning. There was no longer any trace of aggression in his actions; instead, her mind was painting them with gentleness, love and breezy romance. Ahmed had to rescue her. Save her from being drowned. 'I love you, I love you, take me, please, save me,' she muttered.

Anandhi started walking towards the mosque, behind which, she knew Ahmed's family lived. As she heard the strains of the azan wafting through to her, once again, fear gripped her mind. She was walking towards a world that was alien to her. 'Aatha, take care of me, bless me to have a happy life with Ahmed and ...' Anandhi stopped the prayer abruptly, wondering if Aatha would help her marry a Musalman. She was not certain. 'Or will she punish me ...?'

Anandhi was walking out of a world that had protected her all these years. The vermilion world. With all its prescriptions of beliefs and customs, food and clothes. She was walking into a new world. A green world. With its own prescriptions of different beliefs, different customs, different food and different clothes. How would she be able to adjust to this new world? Anandhi suddenly remembered that her classmate Nuzrat was punished by her father for wearing flowers in her hair. Anandhi loved the scent of jasmine. She had nurtured a jasmine creeper in her backyard, that had just begun to flower. Enough for a small string on her hair. 'So, I can't wear flowers anymore!' she muttered to herself. 'And good Lord! Will I have to eat beef?'

As she neared the mosque, her knees were turning liquid. She had walked past the mosque hundreds of times to go to school. She had never spared a thought about what went on inside the mosque. Today, the mosque looked foreboding. The strange letters in the green board looked intimidating. Would she have to learn Urdu? She realized how little she knew about the green world and those who lived within it.

The vermilion world and the green world, two worlds, that have coexisted and yet are two worlds unknown to each other ... friends yet strangers, near yet far ...

Once again, Anandhi collapsed on her steel trunk, and cried.

Anandhi cried again later that evening, when Ahmed gently stroked her head and whispered his love into her ears.

She cried, when, in fact, she wanted to laugh. She had played a daring gamble with her life, jumping out of one boat with the slender hope that another would materialize in mid-sea, and it had! Thinaipatti MGR, the fair, handsome, macho man was in love with her! She felt light as a breeze, her fear vanished and was replaced by a feeling of triumph. In that moment of elation, the discovery that Ahmed was already married didn't matter so much.

'But I love you and I will marry you,' he assured her.

'How was I to know you loved me? You never spoke to me even once after the orchard night,' she complained.

'I loved you more after that night.'

'If you loved me, why didn't you propose to me earlier?'

Ahmed was silent for a while.

'Well, you are a Hindu,' he said.

Anandhi nodded. She did belong to a different world.

'But how can you love me, if you are already married?'

'Love is not divisible,' he answered profoundly, and added, 'Actually we are permitted to marry four times.'

'So, will you take two more wives?'

'No, no! You will be the only one in my life,' he assured her.

'How can I be the only one? You already have a wife.'

'Like you, I made a wrong decision.'

Anandhi felt closer to him. Fellow sufferer. Maybe a problem similar to an ugly toenail.

'I understand,' she said. 'But, why don't you get out of the marriage, as I did?'

'Where is the need?' he sounded surprised. 'Men can have two wives, women cannot. Men can choose to make love to one or both. Women cannot.'

'That's true, that's true,' she agreed.

'Besides, I earn enough. I can financially provide for my wife, because she would continue to live at home. That's all that matters.'

'That's true, that's true,' Anandhi said. For a moment, she wondered if this man would say the same if he fancied a third woman in future. 'Isn't that a risk every woman runs?' she consoled herself. At any rate, she had no choice.

Anandhi looked Ahmed in his eyes. He appeared sincere and straightforward. She felt reassured. Memories of the orchard night came rushing back to her again. And the mind played games. The same actions of the night acquired yet another meaning now: they were respectful, a whisper for permission, a pause for an invitation ... He was indeed a gentleman. She could trust him.

'But you will have to convert to Islam,' Ahmed said.

'What would that mean?'

'Well, nothing much, it will be a small ritual. Do you mind?'

'I don't know ... I am just afraid ...'

'Precisely,' he said. 'You are afraid, because you don't know. Once you get to know, you will find it easy.'

She thought for a while.

'Will I need to change my name?' she asked. 'Actually, I don't really like my name: Anandhi. What an old-fashioned name! Does anyone have such names these days? ... I don't mind Waheeda, that's a nice name. After the actress.'

'Yes, I also like Waheeda,' Ahmed said.

'You like the person Waheeda or the name Waheeda?' she asked sharply.

'Oh! You jealous girl!' he said, and patted her cheek playfully.

'Tell me, will I need to wear a burqa and eat beef?'

Ahmed looked at her intensely. 'Perhaps not. But, if you want me enough, you shouldn't think that these are big sacrifices,' he said.

'Is that all?' she asked. She was getting reconciled to the fact that the transition from the vermilion world to the green world would demand that she paint herself differently.

'Well, most importantly, I want you to truly believe in Allah.'

'How would you know if I truly believed in Allah?'

'No, I won't. But Allah will know. You will be punished if you don't believe in him.'

She remained silent.

'Even if I remain a Hindu and I don't believe in Allah, will I still be punished?'

'I guess so.'

Anandhi reflected on this for some time. 'I don't know anything about Allah,' Anandhi said. 'So, I don't know if I believe in him or not. If I am going to get punished anyway, what difference does it make whether I convert to Islam or not?'

Ahmed didn't quite follow the logic, but he liked her being thoughtful. Only up to a point—women should not be very argumentative.

'If you want to marry me, you have to believe in Allah,' he said firmly.

Anandhi circled her arms around his neck, 'I will believe in Allah to have you.'

Ahmed was pleased with her reply. 'Actually, it's not that difficult being a Musalman,' he said.

Salima Bivi, Ahmed's mother, thought otherwise.

~

'You are so fortunate to be born to me,' Salima Bivi would tell her children as though they had won a lottery to secure a place in her womb. 'Ours was the most respected Muslim family in the Deccan.' She was emphatic that her great-great-grandfather had been a minister in Tipu Sultan's court. Nobody bothered to verify the veracity of her statements.

'Your father was the most pious person in the state. He would have been a Haji, if death had not taken him away so soon. And he was so handsome, and so well educated that his parents could find no bride for him. That's why they had to bring me, a Deccani, all the way from Hubli,' she would say.

Salima Bivi's husband, if he was what she claimed, seemed to have distributed his genes amongst his three sons, as though he was partitioning family property. The eldest son, Wazir, had a strong inclination towards religion and he was on his way to become the mullah of the local mosque. Ahmed, the second son, was handsome and enterprising. The third son, Ismail, was the most educated and had recently taken up a job as teacher at the local school.

Ahmed was Salima Bivi's favourite son. Ahmed was busy most of the week at his meat shop in Salem, a city about sixty kilometres away from the village, but whenever he was back home, Salima Bivi felt as if she had been lit up with a powerful rod of energy. Ahmed would sit beside her, enquire about the needs of the family and would patiently listen to his mother's newly imagined glories of her ancestors. She felt a closeness to Ahmed that she did not feel with her other children. Perhaps she saw in Ahmed more of her dead husband than in her other sons. Ahmed's considerable financial contribution to the family exchequer no doubt helped.

It had been evident to Salima Bivi for some time now that Ahmed's marriage had all but failed. Ahmed's wife was her niece, whom she had carefully chosen for her favourite son. Though Ahmed had acceded to Salima Bivi's proposal and walked into the marriage, he showed no interest in his wife from the beginning. Despite Salima Bivi's clever and often overt efforts to bring the two together, the couple hardly spoke to each other, and when they did, it was as though they were transacting over a grocery counter. In the modest three-room house with a small courtyard, where the joint family lived, the distance between Ahmed and his wife kept increasing a few hundred miles every passing month. Salima Bivi hoped that locking them inside a room would be a sufficient condition for love, that eventually they would make a baby, and that the baby would make the marriage work.

That hope was shattered when Ahmed brought home Anandhi.

Ahmed knew that Salima Bivi, the tough woman that she was, would not consent to the marriage with Anandhi if she was asked. She would never understand that his youth craved intimacy that his marriage had failed to provide. Ahmed wondered if Anandhi was his intuitive response to his mother's constant manoeuvring to pull him towards his wife. If that was so, he felt justified. Anandhi had appeared as a spring from the earth, ready to quench his parched soul; marrying her seemed the logical course. He had merely to convey his decision to the family. He would take Anandhi home with him when he broke the news to his family so they knew it was a done deal.

As Ahmed entered his home with the air of a conqueror returning home, Anandhi stood hesitantly at the entrance, looking for a signal from Salima Bivi to permit her entry. Ahmed let Anandhi stand there, as a concession to his mother before he would let her know who the real boss was. Ahmed was aware of the potential impact of his decision on the family ties, but he would tackle that; a more generous provision to the family from his flourishing business would do the job. Ahmed wasted no time in building up the story for the climax. He simply conveyed his decision to his mother (and his wife, who was listening from the kitchen) matter-of-factly, as though he was talking about the purchase of a new two-wheeler.

No guilt, no excuses, no pleadings, no apologies. Marriage(s) will be his decision, not his mother's anymore. He was a man and he would decide for himself.

'Is this final?' Salima Bivi asked, after she had managed to recover from the shock.

'Yes, inshallah.'

Salima Bivi took a long breath. It was too late. She should have intervened more aggressively to save Ahmed's first marriage.

'I hope you are not going to give talaq to your wife,' she said hesitantly.

'Of course not,' Ahmed assured her.

Salima Bivi breathed with some relief.

'I will continue to provide for you and the family as before, inshallah,' Ahmed said.

'I know you will,' Salima said. 'But, if you had decided on a second marriage, could you not have found a Muslim girl?'

'Anandhi is going to convert to Islam,' Ahmed said.

Salima Bivi surveyed Anandhi closely for the first time. Anandhi had removed the *pottu* from her forehead, as a sort of peace offering. Salima Bivi was not impressed.

'But that's not the same as being born a Muslim. Besides, she is dark,' Salima Bivi said.

She was horrified by the realization that her fair (and therefore superior) stock was about to get polluted.

In Salima Bivi's eyes, the vermilion dye was deep in Anandhi's skin. No amount of green paint could conceal the undercoat.

'Anandhi will convert to Islam,' Ahmed said again, as though repeating this was an adequate answer to all questions on the subject.

As Salima Bivi struggled to absorb this news, Anandhi remained standing at the entrance. Slowly, a few neighbours, passers-by and a stray dog gathered around her to witness the staging of an interesting drama, as she was, for the second time in the day, the heroine of a soap opera. She had, however, an air of confidence, despite somewhat humbling circumstances, since Ahmed was looking at her as a protective deity from its sanctum.

After nearly an hour, during which the only noise was the weak wailing of Ahmed's wife from the kitchen, Salima Bivi addressed Ahmed: 'Call the imam and arrange for the conversion ceremony and the nikah.' She still did not look at Anandhi, who was by now sitting on the steps.

'But you have to keep her out of this house,' Salima Bivi added.

The nikah was swift and simple.

The family's standing and Ahmed's material status ensured that society gossip stayed muffled. Anandhi's parents made customary protestations and ostracized Anandhi temporarily, but her father was secretly happy with the unexpectedly generous *meher*, which came in handy to repay his debts. They chose to stay away from the wedding, fearing neighbours' wagging tongues, but allowed Anandhi's sisters to attend as a compromise. The sisters were excited, as they felt more emboldened to pursue their own adventurous liaisons, now that the elder one had shown the way.

Salima Bivi was keen to convert Anandhi to Islam as quickly as possible. The process began even before the nikah. 'She will be called Ayesha henceforth,' Salima Bivi decreed and thus managed not to utter the name Anandhi even once.

'I wanted to be named Waheeda,' Ayesha protested to Ahmed.

'Amma has chosen the right name for you,' Ahmed said. 'That's the name of the Prophet's third wife.'

'I thought I was only your second wife. Do you have one more?' Ayesha asked in panic.

'No, no, you are my second wife and there will be no more,' he assured her. 'Ayesha means life, and you are my life.'

Salima Bivi arranged for a moulvi to initiate Ayesha in Islamic customs and rituals. The moulvi was a kind old man and Ayesha took to him instantly.

He taught her to do *sana* and explained to her the meaning of the *surah*s.

'*Sajda* is exactly how we do *namaskaram* in our prayers,' Ayesha observed excitedly.

'What do you mean "we" and "our prayers"?' Salima Bivi admonished her.

'Yes, of course,' Ayesha corrected herself. 'This is how they also do it.'

'Allah is the only god and he is supreme. We don't have thirty thousand gods,' the moulvi said.

'Thirty-three crore,' Ayesha corrected him. 'But they are all the same god in different forms.'

'Oh, is that so?' the moulvi said.

'Yes, that's what Arunagirinathar says in the movie.'

'Who is Arunagirinathar?' the moulvi asked.

'Never mind who it is,' Salima Bivi interjected, 'this class is about Islam.'

'What does Islam mean?' Ayesha asked.

'Surrender. Absolute surrender to Allah. You live this life in accordance with Allah's will,' the moulvi explained.

'*Saranagati*, we call it,' said Ayesha. 'Sorry, they call it ... There is a beautiful song, *Saranam Saranam ...*'

'Cut that out,' Salima Bivi thundered. 'You can't seem to get that out of your system.'

'Sorry, I will try,' Ayesha said, 'but the two religions seem so similar!'

'I am trying very hard, but I keep harking back to the past,' Ayesha told Ahmed.

'Any way, we are going to have a separate home soon. You don't slip up when you are visiting my mother. Otherwise, I am not too bothered,' Ahmed said. 'No god pictures at our home, at any rate.'

'Can I keep an MGR picture?' she asked. 'He is not a Hindu god.'

'Most certainly not!' Ahmed said firmly.

Ayesha took full advantage of the concession that Ahmed extended. She slowly slipped back to being Anandhi in her home with Ahmed and morphed into Ayesha whenever she stepped into their family home. She performed *salah* five times a day and surprised Salima Bivi. She recited the surahs fluently and impressed Wazir. She also said her prayers to Mariamman, silently, from outside the compound wall of the temple.

four

Zaheer drew a light house on the letter *alif,* followed by a tiny boatman with an oar on the letter *ba,* and a tinier boatman with a fishnet on the letter *ta.* He was about to decorate the next letter *tha,* when the Arabic teacher landed a sharp rap on his knuckles.

'This is not a drawing class. This is Arabic class. Write the alphabets neatly,' he admonished Zaheer, while secretly enjoying Zaheer's sketches.

Salima Bivi was listening to the Urdu channel on her Murphy radio with one ear and to Zaheer's, her grandson, Arabic lessons with the other. Truth be told, she was listening to neither. The Urdu channel had to be the pervasive background score to the play of life at her home. No one at Bivi's home paid attention to what was being broadcast, not even when Lata Mangeshkar was defiantly singing '*Pyar kiya to darna kya*' or Ahmed Rushdi was beckoning across the border from Pakistan.

Salima Bivi always sat close to the radio, because she felt a compulsive need to soak her soul in Urdu, if only to cleanse it from the corrosive influences which were all around her.

Zaheer looked at his teacher and smiled. 'Aren't these letters beautiful! Every letter is hiding a picture, and I can see them all,' he said.

'Sure, they are beautiful, Khuda resides in them.'

Zaheer was writing the alphabets rapidly. He pronounced the letters as he wrote them. Some letters curled shyly and some others stood boldly, all forming an interesting tapestry of emotions on the paper. When the letters cosied up to form words, they spoke back to him with excitement. They whispered to him stories of deserts, camels and magnificent palaces.

Zaheer always had to start with the alphabets in his tuition classes. Even when he had progressed into words and sentences. 'You must get the exact shape. Scribbling is undivine,' the teacher had insisted.

Zaheer looked up again from his notebook. The boats were all charming, but the direction of the river was a trifle troubling.

'Ustad, why do we write Arabic right to left and Tamil left to right?'

Salima Bivi had a mind, like a bird in the nest, with a remarkable capacity to spring alive to the present from dreams of the past, at the mildest scent of threat. Especially if it was an affront to her cultural heritage.

'The right way to start anything is obviously from the right,' she pointed out. 'What hand do you use to eat?'

'Right,' Zaheer replied.

'That settles the issue,' Salima Bivi said, pleased with her cleverness.

Ismail didn't see his love for Tamil as a conflict with any of his other beliefs or non-beliefs. Religion and language remained happily unbundled in his mind. You could mix and match. Arabic was not always green and Tamil was not necessarily vermilion.

'Actually, Tamil is a much older language than Arabic,' Ismail pointed out after mustering necessary courage to contest Bivi's stubborn convictions. He had taught his students that *Tolkappiam*, the book on Tamil grammar, was written three thousand years ago.

'Rubbish!' Salima said firmly. 'Arabic is Allah's language. It is ageless!'

'Correct, that's the language in which Allah messaged to Muhammad, Peace Be upon Him,' the Arabic teacher added.

So, the gods also had 'mother tongue', Zaheer mused.

Zaheer was one of the very few boys in his class whose mother tongue was mentioned as Urdu, not Tamil, in his school 'calendar' although his mother spoke nothing other than Tamil.

'Is Tamil the language of Hindu gods?' Zaheer asked.

'Brahmins think all Hindu gods speak Sanskrit,' Ismail said. 'That's why the non-believers have sanitized Tamil, removing all Sanskrit words!'

'So Tamil is not a "holy" language?'

'I don't know about that. But Tamil came first,' Ismail said ensuring that the latter part of his reply was drowned out by the Urdu flood from Murphy.

'Which gods came first?' Zaheer asked.

'*Shahada!* There is only one god, Allah! *Allahu Akbar!*' the teacher replied.

Zaheer ignored his teacher's reply. 'Why can't they say which god came first, second and so on ? ...

'I wonder if gods talk to each other,' Zaheer said, addressing no one in particular. 'They all seem to have their own languages. It would have been so much better if they had all agreed on the same language. That way, we won't have so many languages. At least, I wouldn't have to learn this many ...'

Salima Bivi increased the volume of the radio. She listened this time: The broadcaster was explaining the recipe for Hyderabadi mutton biryani. Bivi salivated at the thought of the delicacy.

Everyone in the room was now being told to grind ginger and garlic into a smooth paste, add two cups of curd ...

'Now, which gods speak Urdu?' Zaheer asked.

'Enough of this chatter,' the teacher shouted above the radio, 'write the *surah fatiha ... Al-hamdu lillahi rabbil aalameen ...'*

As Zaheer chanted the surah while he wrote the lines, Salima Bivi, who couldn't have heard the chant with only her one spare ear, said with pride, 'His Arabic intonation is exactly like my father's.'

—

Salima Bivi was happy that Wazir had taken the family torch of religious scholarship forward, and she was keen that someone from the next generation should also be initiated into the tradition while she was still around. It was important that the family's heritage was firmly secured for another sixty years or so. She owed it to her dead husband. He had desired that the mullah of the village masjid should always be from the family. 'That will reinforce the respect and position for the family,' he would say. 'And Allah's grace,' he would add, as an afterthought.

Salima Bivi desired that the air around her carried her religion like a perfume. As she breathed in the air, she felt that the air was getting further cleansed with her pristine Islamic soul, and coming out purer.

'We should initiate Zaheer into religion,' Bivi declared one day.

Ismail didn't know why she chose to bestow this honour on Zaheer, while there were other contenders in that generation, but he preferred not to respond. He was afraid that the conversation would inconveniently turn towards his own indifference to religion. He was not regular with his namaz, rarely went to masjid and hardly knew the surahs. Salima Bivi had given up on him many years ago, but would choose to attack his vulnerability, whenever it suited her.

'I would have liked to send Zaheer to a madrassa, but this village unfortunately does not have one,' she said and added, 'One day, inshallah, we will have enough Muslims in the village and perhaps Zaheer will start a madrasa.'

After her declaration of the religious line of progeny, Salima Bivi moved quickly forward to arrange Zaheer's tuition in Arabic and religious texts at home, with a teacher who came from Ambur, a nearby town with a strong Muslim population. She took upon herself the mission to see Zaheer morph into a mullah. This was not a task that could be entrusted to Zaheer's parents.

She began preening Zaheer right earnestly, with a skullcap made of green velvet with a zari border.

'No one wears caps in my class,' Zaheer protested.

'Precisely why you should wear it,' Bivi said.

She made him run to the masjid at namaz times. She stood near the window, from where she could see the masjid, until she was sure that Zaheer had entered the prayer hall.

Zaheer loved to recite the Quran. He loved its lilting surahs. The stretch, the drop and the quiver of the holy words were captivating. He recited them as he caught little fish swimming in the rainwater gushing through the streets, he recited them as he washed his plate after a meal, when he was combing his hair, just, whenever he felt like.

Salima Bivi punched his ears when she caught him reciting the Quran at irreverential times and unholy places. 'The Holy Quran is not like Tamil cinema songs. You should recite only after *wudu* during namaz times and sitting on the prayer mat,' she would say but secretly feeling glad that Zaheer was getting interested in Islam.

'Before next Ramzan, inshallah, Zaheer should be readied for *Tilawat*,' Bivi instructed the Arabic teacher.

'What is Tilawat?' asked Zaheer.

'You have to recite the Quran three times at the masjid,' explained Bivi.

'The entire Quran?'

'Of course. You get the grace of Allah when you recite the whole of Quran. Thrice, five times or seven.'

Zaheer considered the proposal for a while.

'If I do that, will you allow me to go to Srirangam?'

'What is Srirangam?'

'I don't know. Ayesha Periamma said she was planning to go to Srirangam, wherever that is. I want to go with her.'

'Ayesha is planning to go to Srirangam? Isn't that where the big temple is?' Salima Bivi asked in utter shock.

'I think so.'

'You will do nothing of the sort!' Ismail shouted at Zaheer. 'Next time I hear you say this, I will give you such a wallop, you won't forget it for the rest of your life.'

'God talks to you in Srirangam. I want to hear god,' Zaheer said firmly.

'Hey Allah! Truly the devil has entered this house,' Salima Bivi cried.

'Some people misuse the freedom given to them!' said Ismail. He would never refer directly to Ayesha.

Salima Bivi made a note to talk to Ayesha about her unpardonable trespasses and her corrupting influence on Zaheer.

This had to be dealt with firmly.

Zaheer was spending increasingly more time at Anandhi's house.

Anandhi was a good cook. When Ahmed was not at home, she cooked vegetarian meals and Zaheer greatly enjoyed them. Her circle of fans began to grow from her immediate family to the neighbours. That was when she decided to venture into setting up her own snack shop. Soon her appams were getting to be popular in the village.

Zaheer had to help her with the grinding of the raw batter for the appam, but gratification was immediate. He would receive the first appam, which, with the onion and garlic chutney, tasted divine. There was always variety in the food at Anandhi Periamma's home, as she liked to experiment. The onion pakoras, the tamarind rice that shot its sharp, tangy taste right down the gullet, the ginger chutney that exploded like fireworks in the mouth; when Zaheer was not eating, he was thinking about these mouth-watering dishes.

'You are going to become a good-for-nothing glutton,' Anandhi would chide Zaheer.

At his home, presided over by Salima Bivi, the outcomes from the kitchen were invariably the result of utterly uncoordinated efforts of her daughters-in-law, who blamed each other for the mess, until Bivi stepped in to give her verdict of the guilt, which was wholly whimsical. Zaheer's preference for Anandhi's cooking was therefore entirely understandable.

Zaheer also enjoyed the free run of the place at Anandhi's house. With Ahmed being away most of the week at Salem, he had a lot more space for himself. Frequently, he was joined by Selvi, who played the role of elder sister to perfection. She taught Zaheer to play *pandi*, a hopscotch game played with boxes drawn on the sand, and invariably changed the rules of the game whenever she found herself losing. She initiated him into the secret that peacock feathers, hidden between the pages of a book, would replicate themselves. They played hide-and-seek, even if there were very few places to hide.

Zaheer was pulled by another very strong hook to Anandhi and her home: the chance to see every movie exhibited at the cinema tent.

Anandhi would shut her snack shop at dusk, as village life more or less followed the rise and fall of the sun. Whenever Ahmed was away at Salem, she would find her feet leading her to the cinema tent after the shop was shut. 'What can a lone woman do sitting at home?' she would murmur to herself, providing justification to her addiction. She was, of course, aware that a lone woman going to the cinema would be grist to the village rumour mill.

She needed respectable company. Zaheer was an eager accomplice after his momentous introduction to the dream world during the village festival.

The movies that came to the village were in the winter of their life, having spent their youth in more populous towns and cities. The 35 mm projector in the cinema tent shared its last days in appropriate company. Anandhi saw every movie (or almost every movie, as she kept away from some late-night ones, which were dubbed from Malayalam with suggestively evocative titles like *Rose in the Bed* and *The Drunken Damsel,* etc.) and she saw MGR movies as many times as possible. As Anandhi was always in an ecstatic mood after each MGR movie, she invariably bought Zaheer an ice lolly or roasted groundnuts on the way back home. Zaheer didn't care much about the story of the movies, but the dance sequences were another matter. Especially the dream scenes which were shot in Eastman colour, in which the hero and the heroine cavorted, usually in princely attire amongst rapidly moving clouds.

'MGR's heart is made of gold,' Anandhi would say, entranced, making no distinction between the actor and the real person.

'Someone said his legs are made of lead?' asked Zaheer.

'Which idiot said that?'

'Someone in the back row. He was saying that was why MGR was dancing so badly.'

'He must be a rogue who said that! MGR sings and dances like a god!' she said. She was so upset by the sacrilegious accusation that Zaheer was denied the customary ice cream that night.

Zaheer first heard about Srirangam when Pankajam, Anandhi's childhood friend, had accompanied them both to *Srinivasa Kalyanam,* a mythological movie about the celestial marriage of God Srinivasa to his lady love, Padmavathi.

Like Anandhi's husband, Pankajam's husband also spent most of his days in Salem. The nature of his job was never clear to anyone, but it was rumoured that it was somewhat grey in colour. Perhaps, to atone for this dubious livelihood, Pankajam devoted herself wholly to the world of god, temples and religion. She only read religious books or the first few pages of popular magazines, as they were always about religion. When the cinema tent screened religious movies, she never missed them. If it happened to be a mythological movie like *Murugan Arul* or *Sampoorna Ramayanam,* she even circumambulated the tent with folded hands.

'Wasn't that terrific?' she asked Anandhi, as they were walking back home after the movie.

'I didn't think so,' said Anandhi honestly. 'The actor who played the lead role had a face that looked like an eagle.'

'You should never talk ill of god,' said a shocked Pankajam.

'I am not talking ill of god. It's about the actor!'

'It's all the same,' Pankajam said. In her simple mind, there was no distinction between god and the actor, temple and the tent.

'And, particularly Srinivasa Perumal; he is a powerful god,' she added.

'The most powerful?' Zaheer asked. This was all very confusing. Are some gods more powerful than others?

'Almost. People say that God Ranganatha is even more powerful than God Srinivasa. He is sort of an elder brother.'

'You mean the god at Srirangam?' Anandhi asked.

'Yes, it's a huge temple at Srirangam. The temple is not inside the town. The town is inside the temple. Shops, houses, hotels ... all inside the temple compound.'

'Interesting! I should have gone before my marriage. I guess I can't go now,' Anandhi said.

Pankajam didn't reply. They walked in silence for a while.

Suddenly, Pankajam giggled, as she remembered something. 'You know what? Ranganatha has a Muslim princess as one of his consorts.'

'You mean God Ranganatha married a Muslim woman?'

'Oh yes! The Muslim princess he married even has a sanctum dedicated to her inside the temple.'

'Ranganatha couldn't find a Hindu wife?'

'Of course he had Hindu wives, four in fact. Ranganayaki, Uraiyur Kamalavalli, who was a Chola princess, Kulasekaravalli, a Chera princess and Andal.'

'One better than Muslims. They are allowed only four wives!'

'All of them fell in love with him, pining for him. What could he do? He always grants every wish of an earnest devotee!'

Anandhi thought of Ahmed. She too pined for him. And Ahmed granted her wish. Anandhi smiled at the thought.

'It's an interesting history,' Pankajam said. 'There was this sultan from Delhi who was plundering the temples in the south. I forget his name ... He plundered Srirangam and took away the idol of Ranganatha to Delhi. His daughter, to whom he gave the idol as a gift, became fond of the idol.'

'Lord Ranganatha in a zenana!' Anandhi laughed.

'Listen to the rest of the story,' Pankajam continued. 'Meanwhile, the devotees in Srirangam wanted to retrieve their

Lord from the Sultan. They travelled to the Sultan's court in disguise as minstrels.'

Zaheer had always wanted to go to Delhi. And Agra. By aeroplane, ideally.

'How did they go?' he was curious.

'That I don't know. But they managed to please the Sultan, who asked them to name a reward. They begged the Sultan to return the idol to them.'

'And he agreed?'

'Yes, he gave them the idol, without the knowledge of the princess. And when she learnt that Ranganatha had left her, she came running down to Srirangam.'

'You mean she actually ran from Delhi to Srirangam?'

'Don't ask silly questions. The princess was in love with Ranganatha.'

'You mean the idol or the person?'

'It's the same thing. If you keep asking silly questions like these, I can't tell you any story!'

'Oh! So it's a story?'

'No, no. Real! The Sultan was real, his daughter was real, her love for Ranganatha was real, Ranganatha's marriage to the Muslim princess was real, her sanctum in the temple is real ...'

'Oh!'

'Actually, this god is real,' Pankajam repeated with emphasis.

'Aren't all gods real?' Zaheer was confused.

'Yes, but Ranganatha is special. People have actually seen him get up from his serpent bed and come out of the sanctum!'

'You mean the stone idol just walked out?'

'Of course! Once he came out and a lantern-bearer happened to see him. So, he told the Lord, "God, if you come out like this, nobody will respect you. You shouldn't become too familiar! Go back to the sanctum and remain a stone idol." The Lord said, "You have a point", and went back.'

They all laughed, imagining god being bundled back.

'I would very much want to go to Srirangam,' Anandhi said.

'It would be great to see the idol walking out,' Zaheer added.

'Well, gods don't come rushing out to shake hands with you … it doesn't work that way … You have to be a true devotee. For many, many years … Pass all tests …' Pankajam explained.

'I am not a princess and I am only half Muslim! I hope I would be allowed to worship!' Anandhi wondered.

'Anyone with sincere faith will be allowed,' Pankajam assured her.

Besides mythological movies, Anandhi and Pankajam had another interest in common: palmistry. Pankajam had been married for eight years, but had not been blessed with a child. She assiduously studied all the rituals and prayers for childbirth prescribed in the astrology columns of popular magazines and began to practice them sincerely. She started keeping a record of all the vows and prayers that she had committed to perform in various temples, upon fulfilment of her wish. The pages were fast getting filled up with no sign of pregnancy.

That was when she chanced on a woman from the *kurava* tribe, who had come down to the village from the Yercaud Hills. The kurava woman was a soothsayer and a palmist. The big vermilion pottu she had on her forehead, her large deep eyes and betel-stained lips lent her a sense of authority and authenticity to her predictions.

The woman ran her wand over Pankajam's palm.

'Your wait is almost coming to an end,' she said. She brought Pankajam's palm close to her eyes, and shook her head in disbelief, after closely scrutinizing the lines. She broke into a song and slowly repeated the verse line by line for Pankajam to grasp the meaning. 'Do you understand the divine words?' she asked. Pankajam shook her head. She was too excited to make any efforts to understand. 'You will beget just one son, but he will rule the world and you will die like a queen mother at a ripe old age!' the kurava woman predicted.

Pankajam was overjoyed.

'But, I need to perform a puja for you during every *shashti* at the Murugan temple, so that the god could be well prepared to intervene, when the time comes,' she declared.

'Of course, I'll arrange to send you the money without fail,' Pankajam promised.

Pankajam ran to Anandhi to convey the exciting news. Anandhi, who was also childless and beginning to despair in recent months, rushed to meet the kurava woman.

The kurava woman assessed the jewellery on Anandhi and saw her eager eyes. She sensed that she had already hooked a relatively well-to-do customer.

'Where is the welcome offering of betel leaves, fruits and cash?' she demanded.

'You'd need to give me good news first and then I'll pay your fees,' Anandhi said, somewhat indiscreetly.

'You've got me wrong,' the woman chided. 'Lord Murugan conveys your future through me. He says the truth and doesn't trade good news for money!'

The woman pulled Anandhi's hand and stared at her palm. The woman once again started singing, but Pankajam noticed that the tone of her song was now different. It was not very joyful.

'The lines of your palm indicate that if you get a son before two years, you'll either live with a son or a husband, not both,' the woman said.

'There must be some mistake. Will you please look again?' a rattled Anandhi pleaded.

'There is no mistake. But, if you take care to wait, you'll be blessed with four children!' the woman conceded. 'And you'll have a very prosperous life too!'

Anandhi was confused. She didn't know if it was good news or bad.

'Two years will fly away quickly. You are still young. Just make sure you are careful!' Pankajam comforted.

Anandhi began to devise various plans to delay her pregnancy.

It was the day before the start of the month of Ramzan.

'Zaheer will start fasting this year,' Salima Bivi declared.

She said this while her one ear was still trained to the Urdu channel, which, at that precise moment was belting out, as usual, the recipe for Hyderabadi mutton biryani. The broadcaster's boringly uninvolved delivery of the recipe, now repeated hundreds of times, had been matched squarely with the thoroughly uninvolved listening of Salima Bivi, over an equal number of times.

Today was different.

'And, in celebration, we will cook Hyderabadi mutton biryani for iftar,' she added.

The family congregation was shocked.

'So, you are listening to the radio?' Wazir asked in surprise, when he recovered from the shock.

'But, all these years, we have never made Hyderabadi biryani in this house!' Ismail said, slowly pronouncing the words, with the reverence that the nawabi dish demanded.

Salima Bivi turned to her two daughters-in-law. 'This time for iftar, Hyderabadi mutton biryani it will be. And make sure you cook it exactly the way the radio is telling you,' she instructed.

'But I am not going to fast, nor do I want mutton biryani,' Zaheer said.

'Why not?' Salima Bivi asked, taken aback by his blatant insubordination.

'Nobody in my class fasts.'

'That's because there are no Muslim boys in your class.'

'There are five others in the school. None of them fast.'

'Young children need not fast,' Wazir added helpfully.

'It's good to train them from childhood,' Salima Bivi said. She pulled herself back a little, remembering that she had failed to instil the practice of fasting in her two sons, Ahmed and Ismail.

'Besides, I am not going to eat mutton,' Zaheer said.

'Why on earth?'

Zaheer did not answer. The goat that was sacrificed at the village festival was looking at him again like a stoic martyr. He felt the splash of blood on his knee.

It was the first day of Ramzan.

It was a time when religiosity blossomed like a seasonal flower. The fragrance of religion pervaded every cranny of Salima Bivi's home.

She woke up at three in the morning and preached to the sleepy household that waking up at that hour was an integral part of Ramzan. She pretended she had forgotten the Hadith where this was explicitly stated. Her two daughters-in-law, Ahmed's first wife and Ismail's wife, the non-protesting subjects of her kingdom, complied with her diktat. They cooked suhoor, which bore the scars of their suppressed anger and frustration, and served it before dawn.

Salima Bivi forced the meal down Zaheer's throat while he was still half asleep. Zaheer caught up on sleep during mathematics class in the morning, abetted by a benign teacher.

'So, you won't eat anything for the whole month?' Tamizharasan asked Zaheer, casually sucking a tender mango pickle. It was lunch break at the school.

Zaheer didn't reply. His stomach seemed to have fallen prey to a scorpion that was growing in size by the minute. He hated everyone at home who had conspired to starve him. He felt a strong urge to strangle Tamizh and snatch his meal.

'You want to share my curd rice?' Tamizh considerately asked Zaheer. 'No one will find out.'

'Allah will know if you attempt to cheat. If you feel hungry, think of Allah and pray that your hunger should go away. And it will!' Salima had assured Zaheer. 'But don't be a wretched weakling and break the fast,' she had warned.

Zaheer had been calling Allah from the time the scorpion began to gnaw at his innards, but his prayers didn't seem to have reached Allah.

'The gods test you,' he remembered Pankajam telling him. So this was probably Allah's test. Whether he was truthful to the promise he had made to Salima Bivi (or was it to Allah?), Allah would be looking to score him in this test. Zaheer ground his teeth. He was not a weakling. He would pass this test of Allah's.

Zaheer tore himself away from the assaulting sight of curd rice and tender mangos and ran back to his classroom.

An hour later, it felt like the scorpion had crept its way up to his throat. Anger was rising within him, in tandem with the scorpion. It did not help to remember that at the end of this ordeal, mutton curry awaited him at iftar. He wanted to throw up. Maybe the scorpion would be expelled too. Zaheer angrily pressed the pencil on the desk and it broke into two. He tore the sheets from his notebook.

His benchmate, astonished to see this unprecedented rage from Zaheer, hissed, 'Hey, are you mad?' He received a severe punch in the ribs.

When liberation came with the closing bell, Zaheer ran to Anandhi Periamma's house. He did not want to go home. What he craved at that moment was steaming appams with onion and garlic chutney. That was the only antidote to his hunger and anger.

When he reached Anandhi Periamma's house, he found her playing *thayakkattam*, a game of dice, with Pankajam, both of them chatting casually. This was very unusual. At this time of day, she should have been preparing dinner. Zaheer ran to the kitchen. The logs in the oven had been pulled out.

'Where is appam?' Zaheer shouted.

Anandhi looked up, startled. She had never seen this aggression in Zaheer.

A famished child wears hunger on his face. She understood.

'Oh, my little prince, you are hungry! But you have to go home for iftar,' she got up, and held him close. Zaheer pushed her off.

'I want appam. Now. This very minute!' Zaheer screamed.

'But today she hasn't cooked anything. Anandhi Periamma is fasting,' Pankajam said.

'What? Fasting?'

'Yes, today is *ekadasi* in the Hindu calendar, so I persuaded Anandhi to fast with me,' Pankajam said. 'If you fast today, you are sure to go to heaven.'

'I don't want to go to any heaven! Don't the gods have any mercy? I want food now!' Zaheer's screams hadn't softened.

'Pankajam, let's not preach to a hungry child,' Anandhi said and hurried to the kitchen. 'Zaheer, while I prepare the appam, have this,' she said, and opened a packet of chickpeas she had bought for her shop.

Later, when Zaheer was gobbling up the appams, Anandhi sat next to him, hugged him and kissed him on his head.

'Now go home and join the iftar. Don't tell anyone that you had food here.'

Zaheer had eaten enough and his anger had abated. He was now overtaken by a deep sense of guilt. 'Will Allah punish me?' he asked Anandhi Periamma.

'No, Allah understands. It's only humans who don't understand.'

Pankajam got up to go. 'So, will you come with me to Srirangam, coming Friday?' she asked Anandhi.

'Yes, I will. My husband is not coming back from Salem for a week, so I am free.'

'Very good. You will be stunned by the beauty of the Lord,' Pankajam said, as she was leaving.

Zaheer turned to Anandhi. 'Can I come with you?' he asked.

'Well, this is Ramzan and you are fasting. Your grandmother won't allow you to go to Srirangam.'

'She won't allow anyway.'

'That's true. She wants you to grow up as a devout Muslim. You cannot go to Srirangam.'

'Why can't I do both?' Zaheer asked.

'I need to go to Srirangam.'

Godha told her father Vishnuchittar matter-of-factly. She had just got up from her straw mattress with the break of dawn.

'You are getting to be lazy! Can't you hear the birdcall? The birds have been up and busy for quite some time now!' her parrot friend Sukhi chided Godha. 'You are unable to tear yourself away from the company of your Lord in your dreams!'

'Of course I heard the birds! They were all tweeting "Narayana, Narayana"! And did you hear the sound of churning of butter from neighbouring houses and did they not also chortle "Krishna, Krishna"?'

'Narayana has taken control of all your senses!' Sukhi chirped.

Godha could hear the shuffling of the hooves from the cowshed. Her cow friend Lakshmi always woke up at exactly the same time as she, a happening that was uncanny and unexplainable.

'I need to go to Srirangam,' Godha repeated to her father.

Vishnuchittar looked at his young daughter with wonderment. Her face was radiant with extraordinary beauty.

'Yes, child, we shall plan to go to Srirangam for Vaikunta Ekadasi,' Vishnuchittar said. 'Srirangam is the Very Heaven on earth!'

'But that's four moons away! I want to go now! Today!'

Vishnuchittar looked at his daughter curiously.

'Why the urgency?'

'Lord Ranganatha spoke to me in my dreams and urged me to come forthwith.'

'The Lord spoke to you?'

'You obviously don't believe me!'

'No, no ... I do, I do ...'

'The Lord is so charming, I simply cannot resist.'

'But I have some tasks that the minister has given me.'

'So be it ... I'll go alone.'

'You are still a young girl. You can't go alone!'

'Don't you often say that the King's reign is very good?'

'Yes, indeed!'

'And haven't you always said that the Lord keeps a caring eye on the devotee, without even a blink?'

'Yes, indeed!'

'If so, why would a girl not have safety and security on the road?'

Vishnuchittar looked at his bold and rebellious daughter.

'And, if you suspect that the Lord will not take care of me, you are grievously deficient in your faith.'

Godha went out to the cowshed. Lakshmi looked at her mischievously. Her udders were full and aching. Godha went to Lakshmi, gently touched her rump and bowed in obeisance. That was how a day ought to begin. Because blessings from the divine forces that were resident in that part of the anatomy of the cow were essential to steer your way during the day. Even the Lord at the temple started His day by looking at the behind of a cow. Godha untied a sleepy Vijaya, Lakshmi's calf, who sprang up to reach her mother's udders. Lakshmi licked Vijaya's forehead tenderly.

'If Vijaya is with you, you don't bother about anyone else!' Godha said, with mock anger.

'You had a whale of a time with your Lord last night,' Lakshmi winked.

Lakshmi always knew all her dreams. Godha wasn't sure whether Lakshmi also dreamt all the dreams that she dreamt, or merely knew of them.

Godha blushed.

'You are so jealous!' Godha poked Lakshmi in her ribs.

five

'*Varuvan Vadivelan ...*' Selvi sang, as she danced. The song of a forlorn damsel, yearning for the return of Vadivelan, her lover.

Her jewels were worthy of adorning a royal bride. Her eyes oozed romance through drooping eyelids. Her lips curled with eager invitation. Her pleated skirt of fine silk (which had the magic of changing colours to suit the mood of the song) swirled around, seemingly with a mind of its own. Her long, braided hair coiled around her waist like a mating snake. And her arms flung open anticipating the warm embrace of her beloved …

The dance reached the grand finale.

'*Varuvan Vadivelan, Vadivelan, Velan …*' Selvi repeated with an assertive stomping of the feet, driving away any doubt whatsoever about Vadivelan returning to fetch her.

And the huge crowd of onlookers broke into applause.

A sublime performance at a mammoth theatre.

That was the grand scene in Selvi's mind.

For the unimaginative, seeking documentary proof of life, the reality was that Selvi was dancing in Anandhi's small kitchen, with its strong smell of garlic and onion, that stayed permanently like litigant tenants.

Selvi was wearing a cotton skirt that had no distinguishable colour, because of the many washes that it had suffered. Her plaited hair's southern journey had ended well before her waist, in a pale-blue ribbon noose.

In Selvi's mind, there was no deficit in her looks or her dance, nor any inadequacy in the stage. She was performing magnificently. Like a diva. Never mind that her steps ignored the need for rhythm. Never mind that 'la la la' filled up the gaps in the lyrics, whenever the words fell out of her memory. Never mind that she did not understand half the words she was singing ... Do words even matter, when emotions are paramount?

She was the dancing queen, even if she was only thirteen, and she was on stage, enthralling a huge crowd of admirers.

That was it.

Selvi caught her breath as she ended her dance.

'Why didn't you clap when I finished?' she angrily asked Zaheer, her lone spectator, who was sitting cross-legged on the floor.

'Oh, I forgot,' he said politely. 'Did you notice that when you stomped, the brass vessel on the stool rattled?'

Zaheer stepped into the kitchen and jumped up and down. The brass vessel duly applauded.

'You lack the courtesy that even vessels have!' Selvi said.

'Sorry.'

'How was my dance?' Selvi came to the point directly.

'Who danced on that song in the movie?'

'Jayalakshmi.'

'Jayalakshmi would have done better,' Zaheer said, after a pause.

'Oh, I would have been just as good if I had the orchestra and the playback music, you know! Singing while dancing makes me breathless!'

'You don't move your neck.'

'What do you mean?'

'And eyes. You have to roll your eyes.'

'You speak as though you know all about dance.'

'And should you not end softly, like pining for Velan, rather than threatening Velan to come?'

Selvi stood dumbfounded.

Zaheer stood up and struck a pose. His head tilted slightly, eyes looking up to the sky, arms stretched in entreaty, legs crossed. '*Varuvan Vadivelan, Vadivelan, Velan …*' he cooed, emoting the longing of a damsel beseeching the beloved.

Selvi watched Zaheer with wonder, and then suddenly burst into laughter.

'Funny watching you dance,' she said, between snorts.

'Why? You don't think I was good?'

Selvi stopped laughing and looked at Zaheer for a while.

'You were really good,' she said. 'It's just that I haven't seen any boy dance. So, it was kind of funny.'

'What's funny about boys dancing?'

'Well, you are supposed to be wrestling or playing kabaddi or something like that.'

'I like to dance.'

'Boys are not supposed to *like* dancing.'

'Kamal Haasan dances.'

'He is a famous actor. Famous people like him can do anything. Ordinary boys don't do Bharatanatyam.'

'So, I have to get famous before I begin to dance?'

'I think so!'

'I can't become famous through dancing?'

'Girls have gone on to be famous through dancing.'

'But not boys?'

Selvi thought for a while.

'Actually, the god of Bharatanatyam, Nataraja, is male. So, I don't know why boys are not supposed to dance,' she said.

'Should I dance or not?'

'In Periamma's house, you can, but not outside, I think.'

Selvi's dance classes progressed from Anandhi's kitchen to her living room.

With Zaheer joining Selvi, it was not possible to dance in the kitchen, without their stretched hands knocking the vessels from the shelf, or hitting one another on the nose. Selvi insisted that standing on one leg, in 'Nataraja pose', was a qualifier for a dancer. When she couldn't manage the pose long enough, she changed her mind and said that it was actually the ultimate accomplishment. Zaheer and Selvi challenged each other, stood resolutely on one leg, and then losing balance, hopped and crashed on the floor, with Zaheer always managing to last a few seconds longer than Selvi.

'So, I should be your teacher,' he claimed.

The teacher–student roles were blurred.

They discussed all the dances they had watched in the movies. They wondered how Sridevi managed to keep spinning like a top in every dance, when they both grew dizzy in their fifth or sixth rotation. They snapped their hips like Sripriya and declared themselves better than the actress.

Selvi fluttered her meagre eyelashes and asked Zaheer if he thought she looked inviting.

'You are dancing like drumsticks. No grace,' said Anandhi, pouring cold water on their enthusiasm.

'Watch Jayalalitha on the screen and learn,' she advised. Jayalalitha, being the favourite heroine of MGR, no doubt influenced her judgement.

'I don't know who will teach me,' Zaheer wondered.

'I will,' Selvi said. 'I will teach you all that I learn in my school.'

Selvi went to a school in her village, which wasn't too far from Thinaipatti, that she was very proud of attending.

'That won't do,' Anandhi said. 'I can see Zaheer is talented. He should learn from a "proper" teacher.'

'Kamala teacher!' Zaheer exclaimed. She was the only dance teacher he knew of. 'Comes from Dharmapuri. But she will charge a fee for the lessons,' Zaheer said.

'Kamala must be a good teacher. Otherwise, why would people pay to learn from her?' Anandhi reasoned.

'But Periamma, Abba won't agree to pay fees for the dance class.'

'Don't ask your father. I will pay the fee.'

'You will pay my dance fees?' Zaheer was doubtful.

'Yes, I will. But you better make sure you learn to dance like MGR.'

'MGR?' Selvi wrinkled her nose. 'He dances horribly!'

'You devil! I'll break your bones if you say that again!' Anandhi tried to grab Selvi's pigtail, but Selvi ducked in time.

Zaheer knew better. 'I'll dance like MGR,' he said with a chuckle.

'Don't tell your father or Salima Bivi. They are pieces of wood. They don't understand art,' Anandhi said.

Selvi and Zaheer were both the artiste and audience for each other—they stoked each other's passion for dance.

All the dances that Zaheer had watched in the movies came rushing into his mind.

He dreamt the dreams of the heroines and danced their dances.

And his passion now spilled beyond Anandhi's house.

Zaheer often danced as he walked on the street, completely indifferent to the world outside. Except for Salima Bivi and his father. Whenever Zaheer came home, he would sternly order his mind to steer away from all thoughts of dance. The curves were straightened. The colours were whitewashed. He intuitively realized that his growing passion for dance would be ruthlessly crushed. Good Muslim boys recited the Quran, performed the namaz, listened to the Urdu channel and wore velvet skullcaps.

They certainly did not dance. At least in his village. If he was at home, he had to get into the skin of a 'normal' boy, as normal as an average, obedient, intelligent, tradition-honouring nine-year-old should be.

Zaheer's first public performance happened in his classroom.

That was the day Anandhi Periamma had given him ten rupees, encouraging him to enrol with Kamala teacher and formally learn dance.

He owed his debut, of all people, to his maths teacher, who had no familiarity with art in any form.

Zaheer's maths teacher was a habitual absentee. When he was absent, the students preferred to run out and play, and if that was not possible (because of the presence of Kamala teacher, whose role as a substitute was to confine the footloose children within the pen of the classroom), to throw paper balls at each other and on Kamala teacher. Sometimes they were outwitted and had to suffer the songs and dance of the girl students, in particular, of Kalaivani, who was learning from Kamala teacher, which gave her a kind of entitlement and a superior air, even if she lacked talent.

The maths teacher was once again absent, and Kamala teacher, who was once again despatched to 'control' the students, unimaginatively asked Kalaivani once again to 'entertain' the class and she, feeling important, once again, made a fuss about having to single-handedly bear the cross, and finally launched once again into her well-worn-out rendition of *Maraindhirundhe,* the Padmini dance item in a popular movie. Zaheer had seen the movie twice with Anandhi Periamma. He recalled the dance sequence vividly. He had played it in his mind tens of times. He knew where Padmini arched her thin eyebrows in surprise, where she curled her lips in taunt. Hers was an arresting performance. Here was Kalaivani delivering a pathetic version of it. Zaheer was irritated.

'You've got it hopelessly wrong,' he said.

'No, it's absolutely fine. You will see it hitting the target like a bullet,' the boy next to him said. He was busy making a paper rocket with a launch bow of a rubber band. He had assumed that Zaheer was commenting on the rocket.

'I am not talking about the rocket. It's about Kalaivani's dance.'

'Dance? Who cares?'

The boys didn't care and the girls were jealous. So, when Kalaivani finished her entertainment, nobody felt 'entertained' and nobody applauded. Kamala teacher, being the main sponsor, had to applaud, but did so rather meekly. There was another half-hour before the bell, and she wisely dropped the idea of asking for an encore.

'Who else can sing or dance?' the teacher asked desultorily.

'I will dance, teacher!' Zaheer jumped up and ran to the front of the classroom.

'You will dance? Seriously?' Kamala teacher wasn't sure if this was a prank.

'Yes, teacher. I will dance. On the same song!'

The classroom fell silent for a few moments. Boys were never called upon to 'entertain'. No one had heard any boy sing, let alone dance. This was strange!

Then the noise began.

The girls giggled. The boys booed. Giggling and booing. Booing and giggling. One fed on the other and the two melded into a roar of ridicule ready to consume the lone boy, standing shrunken in fear.

'Silence!' shouted Kamala teacher.

The noise subsided.

'Go ahead. Dance,' she ordered Zaheer.

The shame from the ridicule vanished from Zaheer's mind. The joy of dance took over.

In his mind, he had become the naughty damsel who was teasing her lover to come out of hiding. The twenty-square-feet space adjacent to the teacher's desk (the desk having been pushed to one corner to make room) transformed into the temple courtyard. His classmates appeared to have melted to one identity-less goo. A goo of Krishnan Velu Manimaran Saif Chandran Muthu Rajamaran Pugazhendi Muniyandi ... in the rear, with a border of Thangam Ponni Kala Vijaya Sigappi Devika ... in the front. Beyond the goo screen, Zaheer was looking at Padmini dance in the movie and he was following her movements closely, loyally, like her shadow.

When Zaheer finished dancing, Kamala teacher started a slow clap. A few girls joined in, and then a few boys, until most of the class was applauding.

Zaheer's cup was full.

He had done what he liked and his classmates seemed to like what he liked.

He walked up to Kamala teacher. There was a spring in his step.

'Teacher, I would like to learn dance from you,' he said.

Kamala teacher appeared taken aback.

'Are you serious?' she asked.

'Yes, teacher. I like to dance!'

Kamala teacher considered this unexpected application. It was tempting to accept the request, as she was in need of supplementing her income, what with a drunkard husband who was out of job. But she hesitated.

'I'll have to think about it,' she said. 'I haven't taught male students before.'

She had never appreciated male actors donning the role of females even in village plays.

'I will tell you next week,' she said.

The next class was Tamil, which Zaheer liked. Zaheer's father who taught senior students in the school, gave Zaheer lessons at home ahead of his class. Zaheer didn't know that he was a proxy in the rivalry that his father harboured against his Tamil teacher. When the teacher began a couplet from *Thirukkural,* Zaheer completed it. When the teacher started on a question, Zaheer shouted the answer. This only enhanced Zaheer's standing and diminished that of his teacher. At least, that was how his father saw it.

Today was different. Zaheer's mind was full of the damsel and her lover in hiding. 'Perhaps, I should have shown more anger,' he wondered. 'I must check with Selvi if my steps for the last stanza were correct'. Anyway, his classmates wouldn't know what he didn't. Not even Kalaivani. His classmates seemed to like his dance. The applause continued to ring in his ears.

He had to share this joy with Selvi, but she would not be visiting Anandhi Periamma's home for another few days.

When Zaheer came out of the school, unconsciously, his steps continued the rhythm in his mind.

That's when he heard his name being called out.

It was not a call. It was a bark. A threat.

Zaheer's stomach churned at the sight of a group of boys sitting on the culvert, abutting the road that led from the school. They were the notorious bullies of the school and the culvert was their hangout. Everyone knew them. Everyone including the teachers. The timid feared the bullies and the bold respected them. The leader of the group had a full-grown moustache and an adolescent beard. Predictably enough, he was the son of an even bigger bully. When the son was threatened by a teacher, the Father Bully threatened the teacher and put a full stop to such misadventure. Everyone knew how to deal with the bullies. By staying away from their attention.

And now, they were calling out to Zaheer.

Zaheer lowered his head and hastened past them.

'Hey! Look at the way he is walking!'

Zaheer ignored the jibe.

'Hey, *pottai,* come back,' one of them shouted.

'Drag him back,' another shouted.

Zaheer stopped and turned back to look. Pottai—sissy. That was the title he had earned for his dancing talent.

'Sissy, let's see you dance.' This was the leader. His tone was commanding.

Zaheer stood still, engulfed by fear.

The leader inched towards him.

'Darling, please dance for me,' he said, in a sing-song voice. 'Won't you do this for your dear friend?'

Zaheer started trembling.

'You are angry with me, darling?' The sing-song had acquired a menacing tone.

He put his arm around Zaheer's waist. With his other hand he gently lifted Zaheer's chin and brought his lips close to Zaheer's chin.

'Can I pull your shorts and see?' he whispered in Zaheer's ear. His hand slid down Zaheer's shorts.

'Let's see what a sissy looks like inside,' a voice from the culvert shouted.

Zaheer could feel the scorn from the leader's eyes boring into him.

'Please, please let me go,' Zaheer pleaded in a low voice.

The leader looked at Zaheer for a while, and slowly withdrew his hand.

'Please let me go,' the leader repeated mockingly.

A sharp slap landed on Zaheer's cheek. As Zaheer staggered from the force of the slap, the leader bent his knee and kicked him in the groin. The kick missed its target, as Zaheer fell on his back.

There was loud clapping from the crowd in the culvert.

Applause for Zaheer for the second time today. This time a clapping that crushed his heart.

Zaheer got up and ran in a daze. He needed the protective cover of Anandhi Periamma's love. With no restraint, he would cry loudly on her lap and wipe his shame out with his tears. Anandhi Periamma would understand. She would tell him not to worry about the world and encourage him to do what he liked. To dance. Was she not encouraging him to dance with Selvi?

Then it dawned on him that at this time of day Anandhi Periamma would be at the shop and her house would be locked. He couldn't obviously go to her shop. He couldn't risk breaking down in a public place. Would people not laugh at him when he cried? Boys his age didn't cry in public.

Zaheer ran towards his home. He would at least have the security of a private shelter, even if he couldn't get the love and understanding from his parents.

Home, when he entered, looked ominous.

The Murphy radio's unusual silence was deathlike. Salima Bivi was sitting beside the corpse of the radio, in mourning. Ismail was standing with his hands on his hips, like a big animal waiting to punish its prey.

'Hey! Come here!' Ismail shouted.

Although Zaheer had never felt close to his father, this angry person was unfamiliar.

'So, you danced in your class?' Anger and scorn. 'Take them in equal measure and mix them until you get a red-hot paste,' the Urdu channel would have said, if the radio was on.

Zaheer did not answer.

'Aren't you ashamed to be dancing like a sissy?'

S I S S Y ... Why does it hurt so badly to be called that?

'Don't stand there like a moron. Answer me!'

Zaheer said nothing.

'And you sang *their* songs? And danced *their* dances?' Salima Bivi choked on the words. 'Hey Allah! Have mercy on this family!'

'Did you or did you not dance?' The voices rose to force out a confession.

Zaheer did not answer. Abba knew the answer. Why did he need confirmation?

A sharp slap landed on Zaheer's cheek. This was the second slap of the day. On the other cheek.

'I am ashamed. You danced in the class. Like a girl!'

Zaheer wanted to say that the entire class had clapped in appreciation. He wanted to say Lord Nataraja was the king of dance. That Kamal Haasan danced. That dancing didn't mean being sissy. But Zaheer felt a revulsion in speaking. He did not want to talk to his father. Not to Salima Bivi. Not to anyone in that house.

'Hey Allah! Protect this family from ignominy,' Salima Bivi held her hands in *dua*.

'Nothing wrong with the family, except one person who is the corrupting influence,' Ismail said, avoiding naming Anandhi. Ahmed was a huge power centre in the family and nobody could afford to direct any charge against him. 'And this useless fellow,' he added, pointing to Zaheer. 'Next time I hear that you danced, I will chain you to this pillar. Mercilessly. Ruthlessly. Make no mistake. I would rather you mop the floor at home than let you dance. Like a girl.'

Zaheer's mind was empty. Then it was filled up with anger. It was a dead mind with angry stuffing. But it was an anger he could not direct against anyone.

six

It was late evening. The Dharmapuri bus station was in chaos. That being its natural state. Travel-worn buses, with their dirty radiator grills lifted immodestly, were dragging themselves into the station, as though in labour. As the heavy breath of the engines sputtered to a stop, they delivered their burden of weary passengers.

Some outbound buses were being given a ritual bath to rid them of the stains of vomit and other bodily fluids. Bodies purified, they set out like pilgrims on a yatra, carrying baskets of guavas, grapes and sundry fruits on their roof carriers.

Dharmapuri was the centre for the fruit trade in the state.

The retail litter of orange skins, spat out mango seeds and the like, and the wholesale mounds of rotten fruits and discarded baskets at the periphery of the station, stood out as insignias of that honour.

Bus conductors were shouting to announce the departure of buses to passengers, who already somehow seemed to know. Men were shouting to women to hurry up and women in turn were shouting to wayward children, who, in turn, were shouting to no one in particular.

Zaheer was not listening to any of the noises around him.

His mind was dull with pain. The ridicule of the bullies and the stinging words of his father soared inside him in waves. The slap that landed on his cheek was turning out to be the very definition of his father: scornful and angry.

His father had mostly remained in the background in Zaheer's mind. Much like the Urdu radio channel. Zaheer couldn't remember the last time that his father spoke to him or touched him with affection. He did help him with his Tamil lessons, but gave Zaheer no credit when he stood first in his class. 'See, how he has fared with my teaching!' Ismail would proudly inform Salima Bivi. Zaheer shared the same home with his father, breathed the same stale air inside that home, but without being close to him.

The slap had suddenly revealed his father. Zaheer had been shaken by the viciousness of the revelation.

When memories of his mother drifted into his mind, he also thought of the unwashed curtain of blue and red flowers that hung in front of Salima Bivi's bedroom door. His mother was also a sort of curtain, framed in unemotional routines. Not much else.

When he left home that evening, Zaheer had no idea where he would go. He just had to run away from home.

Escape.

Flee.

It had not occurred to him then that one did not simply flee. That one had to flee to 'some place'. He had to go 'some place' WHERE HE COULD BE HIMSELF. Anandhi Periamma's home wasn't that place. In Periamma's home, he could indeed dance as he liked and eat the best appams in the world. And he could go to movies and temples. He could be himself. But it would still be a cage. Salima Bivi, his father, the school bullies, would all be watching him from outside, waiting for him to step out of the cage. Waiting to beat him to shape, to be a 'normal' boy, a 'proper' Muslim boy. No, Periamma's home was not that 'some place'. He had to go to a place where he could be himself, without fear, without shame ... without being caged ... without being proscribed ... But where was such a place?

It was all very confusing.

The noise was subsiding at the bus station.

Zaheer noticed with a start that the traffic at the station had nearly come to a halt. A flush of fear drained him as he realized he would have to spend the night at the bus station. He had the ten rupees which Periamma had given him. He could buy himself a meal, but he would have to sleep on the platform. And then what?

Zaheer let out a sob.

A little boy, a few years younger than Zaheer, crept close to him. He stood staring at Zaheer for a while. The boy's parents sat a little further away, arguing loudly.

'Are you crying?' the boy asked him. Zaheer did not reply.

'Did your father beat you?'

Zaheer nodded. The boy looked at Zaheer with familiar understanding.

'My father also beats me,' he whispered. 'Whenever he is drunk,' he added, by way of clarification.

Zaheer felt a sudden gush of sympathy for a kindred soul.

'Is that very often?' Zaheer asked.

'Almost every day,' the boy said matter-of-factly. 'And you?'

The boy's mother got up to go and looked around for her son. 'Where the devil have you disappeared?' she shouted.

'My mother is not bad,' the boy explained in a hurry. 'It is just that she does not stop my father when he beats me.'

'That's equally bad,' Zaheer shared his considered view.

'But then she also gets beaten up,' the boy said.

Zaheer touched the boy on his shoulders.

'I have to go,' said the boy and ran behind his parents who were moving out of the bus station.

The boy gets beaten more often, but is running behind his father, Zaheer thought.

Had he made a mistake running away from home?

Zaheer remembered that his father had once taken him to a football match in Dharmapuri. His father had even bought him a white-and-red cap, that Zaheer kept with him for long, since he greatly liked the design. Zaheer found nothing interesting in the game, whereas his father was jumping and cheering loudly every time a goal was scored. 'Can't understand you!' his father had said to him with contempt.

'I am not his idea of a son,' his eyes welled up, as he muttered to himself.

And now the stomach was beginning to cry for attention: in the process, taunting him for being a bloody fool. 'You have nowhere to go! Forget about dance, just listen to your father and get a decent meal,' it said with great clarity of purpose.

'Hey boy, why are you sitting alone?' a voice called out.

A bus driver had noticed Zaheer. He was moving towards Zaheer. A burly guy with a moustache.

'Waiting for the bus,' Zaheer replied, half in fear.

'Where do you have to go?'

'Bangalore.' That was a spontaneous response. Now that he had mentioned it, it didn't appear a bad route towards the 'some place'.

'But the last bus for Bangalore has already left!'

'Yes, I just realized.'

'Where are you from?'

'Thinaipatti.'

'And you can't return, the last bus to Thinaipatti has also left!'

Zaheer was silent.

'And you are alone! What irresponsible parents! Do they have brains?'

Absolutely not, Zaheer wanted to say, but chose to remain quiet.

'What's your father doing?'

'Schoolteacher.'

'Schoolteacher? And he sends his young boy alone to Bangalore?'

The driver thought something didn't quite add up. He looked at Zaheer closely. 'You are not running away from home, are you?'

'No, no!' Zaheer shook his head vigorously. Perhaps he had spoken more than was necessary. 'I have been to Bangalore many times alone. My aunt lives there,' Zaheer said. 'I am ten years old,' he added.

The man looked around. He started scratching his groin.

'It's not safe to be alone,' the moustache had lowered its decibel level.

The man waited for an answer. Zaheer felt unsafe with the man hovering over him. He had to shake off this unwelcome intruder.

'I am not afraid,' Zaheer said.

'Why don't you come with me? You will need some place to sleep anyway.'

Zaheer shook his head. 'I will sleep here. And I will shout if someone bothers me,' Zaheer turned to look at the tea stall at the far corner of the station, that was doing brisk business. From the look of it, the shop was going to remain busy deep into the night.

'So, you will sit all night?'

'Yes,' Zaheer said resolutely.

The bus driver did some aimless wandering and returned.

'All right! Have something to eat at the tea stall. And then get into that blue bus and sleep inside. I will take care of you for the night.'

He walked away slowly, turning to look at Zaheer.

'Remember to get into the blue bus!' the man insisted.

After the man left, Zaheer counted the buses at the station. There were eight. They seemed a safe place to hide. And to sleep. Avoiding the blue bus, Zaheer crept into a red bus, curled himself on a rear seat and began to think about the 'some place'.

'All your wishes will be fulfilled,' the woman seated on the right of Zaheer was assuring the woman seated on the left, speaking past Zaheer, as though he were invisible. All three were seated on the last row of the bus that was speeding towards Bangalore.

'My husband says, don't believe in godmen, they are all cheats,' the woman on the left responded.

'Maha Baba is not any godman, he is god.'

'But gods are only in temples.'

'Sometimes god comes in human form.'

'How can you be so sure that Maha Baba is god?'

'Can ordinary men produce gold rings from thin air?'

'Only rings or chains too?'

'If he could materialize rings, he could materialize chains too. Anything, for that matter.' The woman was irritated with the irreverent question.

'Does he produce cars from thin air?' Zaheer interjected. This was interesting. Like the Lord who walked out of the sanctum.

The woman on his right ignored Zaheer and the question.

'My husband says it's all magic,' the other woman said.

'Rubbish! Can a magician cure epilepsy? I have seen with my own eyes when Baba touched a man with severe epilepsy, the man miraculously got up and walked straight!'

The other woman was undecided as to how to counter this new piece of evidence.

'Can a magician predict the future?' the right-side woman pressed ahead. 'Baba blessed me and said, "You will get pregnant within ninety days." Mind you, we were childless for seven years after marriage.'

'And you got pregnant?'

'On the eight-fifth day, I missed my period!'

The left-side woman was clearly on the back foot, with the assault of such irrefutable evidences.

'Make one visit to Munoor, have a darshan of Maha Baba, and I assure you all your wishes will be fulfilled.' The right-side woman was consolidating on her lead. 'He is truly god on earth, no doubt. I have seen a glowing halo around his head.'

'Well, we need some solution to our financial problems ... Two years of drought and we are at our wits' end ...'

'Maha Baba is the only answer ... But you should have complete faith. If you go to him thinking that he is a magician, he will just be a magician, no better!'

'I agree. We need faith. What else are we left with? But how do I change my husband? He has no faith in anything godly.'

'That's the problem with men,' the right-side woman agreed. 'My husband is no better. He was having this persistent problem of dry cough. I told him to smear some holy ash from Baba, which I had brought with me. He wouldn't listen. Then I mixed Baba's holy ash in his rasam or sambar without his knowledge and fed him for just eight days. Just eight days! The cough disappeared without a trace. Ignorant man! He thought that it was the cough syrup that was doing the trick. Only I knew that it was Baba's holy ash.'

The woman untied a knot from the tail of her sari, took out a pinch of holy ash from a small fold of paper. 'Keep this. It will do you good,' she said and dropped the ash into the outstretched palm of the other woman. She turned to Zaheer and smeared some ash on his forehead. 'Baba likes children. Whatever you wish, Baba will grant you,' she said. 'Make sure your mother takes you to Munoor, whenever she goes.'

'Oh no! He is not my son,' the other woman said with a chuckle.

'No? He has light skin like you, so I thought he was your son!'

'I thought he was accompanying *you*!'

'No, no, I am travelling alone. Funny, isn't it? Anyway, child, what's your name?'

'Zaheer.'

The right-side woman gasped, 'Sorry.' She reached out to wipe the holy ash from his forehead.

'It's all right,' Zaheer said. 'Baba likes Muslim children too, surely?'

'Yes. There are so many foreigners coming there. Faith cuts across religions, my child,' she said.

'And Baba will grant every wish?'

'Yes, but you need faith.'

'What if I want to become a dancer?'

'Dancer?' the woman looked curiously at Zaheer.

'Yes, a dancer.'

'Normally, boys don't take to dancing.'

'But I like to dance. Is that wrong?'

'You don't want to go to school?'

Zaheer was irritated.

'Why can't I do both?'

The woman thought for a while.

'You could become anything. You need to passionately desire that. And you need to have faith in Maha Baba.'

'Can I learn dance from Baba?'

The women laughed.

The right-side woman looked at Zaheer intently.

'You should surrender to him. With faith.'

'And you will find that you will meet the dance teacher you want. Pray to him. And you will one day become a famous dancer.'

The bus was pulling into Bangalore bus station.

'Munoor, Munoor!' a bus conductor was shouting for passengers to fill up the vacant seats in a bus. Zaheer jumped out and ran towards him.

Vishnuchittar had been named Periazhwar, the Principal Devotee of Lord Vishnu. The congregation of thinkers and philosophers had unanimously conferred the title on Vishnuchittar, at the end of a debate that had lasted for over five hours.

The King was mightily pleased with Vishnuchittar's scholarly performance at the debate, trouncing the Jain scholar from the Pallava kingdom, earlier that day in court. He felt that this was an auspicious event that signalled positive outcomes to his latent aspirations to overrun the shrunken Pallava kingdom some day.

'Periazhwar swami, you were brilliant,' the King said, his chest swollen with pride. 'You convincingly argued that rejecting all other gods and being devoted only to Lord Narayana is not a negation of other religions, but just an assertion of your own complete faith.'

'Your Excellency, The One which subsumes everything else is Narayana. If I have faith in the whole, I must have faith in the parts too.'

'Well said, well said!'

The King descended from the throne and prostrated at the feet of Periazhwar. 'Bless me with wisdom,' he said.

Godha wasn't too pleased.

'That was a wrong argument. Your opponents were too weak to contest it,' she said bluntly.

'What did you find wrong, my child?' Periazhwar asked.

'Well, we are not part of Narayana, we are not subsumed, until we surrender to be subsumed. We are His creations, created to serve and surrender at His lotus feet.'

The precociousness of his daughter astounded him.

'If we exist independent of the Supreme Being, isn't that a negation of the Supremacy of the Supreme?' he asked tentatively.

'That's an argument of the material world, subject to physical laws. In the spiritual world, creations come out of nothing, and could go back to nothing. Only, if we have the will to surrender, we go back to the Lord!'

Periazhwar looked at the baskets of gifts that the King had sent to his quarters at the palace.

'I don't deserve this,' he mumbled.

seven

The lunch was delicious.

'It is divine, that's why it's delicious. It has Maha Baba's blessings,' whispered the woman sitting next to him to her husband, who, wisely agreed.

It was especially delicious to Zaheer. This was the first hot meal he had had in the nearly thirty-six hours since he fled home. A free meal was even more delicious when the purse was as empty as the belly.

Zaheer was devouring the lunch being served at the huge dining hall, at Mahashanthi Mandir, the abode of Maha Baba in Munoor. It appeared that the impeccable white walls were designed to swallow all sounds. Zaheer wondered why everyone was eating noiselessly, looking almost sad and guilty. As though at a funeral. Back at his village, noise was another serving during a meal. A good meal demanded boisterous appreciation.

Zaheer belched loudly.

As he looked up, he noticed a young man seated across the aisle smiling at his indiscretion. Zaheer looked down with embarrassment.

Now, it was the turn of the young man: he belched. More loudly than even Zaheer.

In that shared moment of awkwardness, they both joined in a noiseless laughter.

'You enjoyed the meal,' the young man said to Zaheer, as they came out to wash their hands.

'You too,' Zaheer pointed out.

'Yes, the food is always delicious here. That's one reason why I come to Munoor.'

'For food? Not prayers? Not darshan of Baba?'

'Well, that too,' the young man said. 'But for a hungry person, food comes first, and only then god.'

'I, too, came here because I was famished,' Zaheer said. He was surprised that he could say this to a stranger unabashedly.

The young man looked around. 'I think a lot of people here find more joy in the meals than in prayers, but they won't admit it,' he chuckled.

'Are you alone?' the man asked.

Zaheer nodded. He hoped that the young man wouldn't ask more probing questions.

Ramulu was his name. From Eluru ...

He said he ran a watch repair shop. Zaheer noticed that he was very modestly dressed, but somewhat incongruously, wore what looked like an expensive watch with a golden strap. Much like the Seiko watch that Zaheer's uncle Ahmed would wear. Zaheer remembered that when Ahmed had bought the watch (he assured everyone at home that this was 'genuine, smuggled'), the children in the family were all given a chance to hold and fondle it for a few seconds. To Zaheer, a Seiko watch was always a masculine emblem. Somehow, it didn't sit well on Ramulu's wrist.

'Is it Seiko?' Zaheer asked Ramulu, hoping that it was not.

Ramulu looked at the watch, read out the letters of the brand slowly and then declared, 'No.'

'Did Baba give you this watch?'

Ramulu was amused by the question.

'Baba is not a watch factory,' he said with a laugh. 'Baba might produce watches from thin air, but I guess you have to be close to him to be blessed with his gifts.'

'Well, I am not looking for a watch,' Zaheer clarified.

Ramulu seemed a restless person. He was very familiar with the campus and slithered around the place easily. Zaheer was afraid that he would be lost in the huge campus without someone like Ramulu. But tailing Ramulu was like playing hide-and-seek, since he kept darting from one crowd to another. 'I come here for peace,' he explained, as though he was shopping for the item at Munoor.

Zaheer learnt that it was a special day at Munoor, a celebration of some festival. Ramulu didn't know the details and didn't seem to care.

As the day progressed, devotees kept pouring into the campus in droves. 'There will be one lakh people by the evening,' Ramulu said. It was a huge crowd, but curiously, there was no noise and merriment in this celebration, unlike the festival in Zaheer's village. There were flags and festoons, but no merry-go-round, no balloons, no kamarkat shops. Book shops and flower shops were there, but no small eateries.

Some groups of people were sitting in the vast lawns singing bhajans. In low voices, as though they were afraid to disturb god unnecessarily. There were others who were sitting in unexpected corners of the building with their eyes closed.

'Meditating,' Ramulu explained. 'They want to shut out the external noise to find god within them. God doesn't like noise.'

'What noise?' Zaheer wondered. 'They haven't seen anything like the Pattalathamman festival.' He was reminded of the ear-piercing 'drrrrrrk' of the drums, which heralded Aatha. His village gods loved noise. This place was different. This festival was for those who took life too seriously.

'Strange way to celebrate a festival,' Zaheer remarked.

Ramulu was pressing himself against a small crowd of people buying books on Baba. He didn't seem to hear Zaheer.

'Baba must be a strict person, the Kamala teacher type,' Zaheer thought, 'otherwise why would people be so silent and behave themselves so well?'

However, despite the silence, Zaheer could feel the excitement in the air. Devotees spoke in hushed tones about the special prayer in the evening. Maha Baba, the Living God, was going to conduct the prayers.

'Why does he have to pray to himself?' Zaheer asked in confusion.

'Well, he prays to other gods, like Rama and Krishna, and the devotees pray to Baba,' Ramulu explained, as though it should have been obvious to Zaheer.

'I understand,' Zaheer said politely, but didn't.

Devotees were rushing into the prayer hall to take vantage points. Zaheer learnt that Baba would walk through the aisle and randomly bestow personal blessings to devotees by touching their head or giving them holy ash. It was important therefore to find a place to sit close to the aisle, to stand a chance of receiving personal attention from the Living God.

Baba would also lead the bhajan and he would be followed by leading singers. 'Lata Mangeshkar is expected to come,' someone said. 'M.S. Subbulakshmi never misses an occasion like this,' said someone else. Every leading name in the music field was being mentioned in speculation.

'Do dancers also come here?' Zaheer asked Ramulu.

'Every famous person comes here. Dancers, actors, leaders … In fact, they are famous only because they come here,' Ramulu said.

'Does Kamal Haasan come here?' Zaheer wanted to know.

'I don't know,' Ramulu said. 'But many big actors do come.'

Ramulu had gone around the campus quite a bit and Zaheer thought that perhaps he was moving rather aimlessly.

Zaheer was beginning to get frustrated.

Earlier in the day, travelling to Munoor, fear had again possessed him. The money that Anandhi Periamma had given for enrolling in the dance class had brought him to Munoor and barely kept his stomach from complaining. He was scared to think of the next meal, of where he would sleep at night. Of the future. Every wave of fear left behind fresh doubts about his impulsive flight.

Until, that is, he alighted at the Munoor bus station …

Mahashanthi Mandir had infused new hope. There was warmth in the environment. Many people seemed to be living on campus. And living happily. He could see many boys his age moving purposefully, running errands. They wore white shorts and shirts and a look of seriousness to match. Ramulu explained that they were students, a lot of them orphans, and Baba provided shelter to them.

That was very encouraging. Perhaps Baba would also let Zaheer stay there. It was a nice place, though Zaheer didn't like the eerie silence. He wouldn't like to wear white, but perhaps Baba wouldn't mind him wearing colours … Baba must be aware that the gods themselves were fond of colour. And the food, of course, was delicious. Yes, he missed Anandhi Periamma's appams, but there was more than enough here to compensate. Famous actors would be coming to pray to Baba, and he would get to see them from close quarters. If there were singers, there would be dancers too. If he managed to convey to Baba his desire to be a dancer, Baba would perhaps arrange for a dance master to teach him. Perhaps Baba would simply touch him and he'd morph into an accomplished dancer? Like the story of Ahalya that Periamma used to narrate …

But first, he had to *meet* Baba.

Zaheer was impatient.

'When can I meet Baba?' he asked Ramulu.

Ramulu looked at him with amusement.

'You want to see Baba or meet him?'

'I need to meet him. I have something to discuss.'

Ramulu laughed loudly.

'Are you the President of India?' he asked Zaheer with a serious face.

'No.'

'Do you know the chief justice of Karnataka?'

'No.'

'Well, he waited for three days to meet Baba alone. He couldn't.'

'So is there no way I can meet him?' Zaheer panicked.

'Well, Baba sometimes meets very ordinary people like you and me. But most people are very happy just to have his darshan from afar.'

'I cannot go away without meeting Baba,' Zaheer said resolutely.

Zaheer had sneaked into the prayer hall, close behind a middle-aged couple, whom almost everyone seemed to recognize with awe. The couple was being escorted by an official from Mahashanthi Mandir and the crowd had respectfully shuffled to make way for them. As he unobtrusively moved behind the couple, Zaheer was surprised to find that, Ramulu, who had disappeared in the crowd for some time, was also behind him.

'They are very important people. Just keep close to them,' Ramulu whispered in Zaheer's ears.

'Who are they?' Zaheer asked.

'Big business. Very, very rich.'

Zaheer noticed that the lady was dripping with jewellery. Her fingers sported multiple rings, as if it were against the law to leave any finger unadorned. She wore a bright orange sari with zari lines that ran down like summer rains. Zaheer liked the sari, but didn't like the large, deerskin handbag the lady was carrying. It doesn't match her dress, she ought to have carried a flaming red handbag, Zaheer thought, or maybe something yellow.

As the four of them settled close to the rim of the aisle, the escort noticed with irritation the two stowaways behind the couple, but it was too late.

The huge hall was pleasantly cool, in contrast to the sultry July evening outside.

'Is this place always this cool?' Zaheer asked Ramulu.

Ramulu smiled. 'Gods are always rich. They can afford ACs,' he said.

The village mosque was always hot inside. The Mariamman Temple was worse. The bare-chested priest was always irritable due to the sweltering heat. All times of the year.

'Our village gods are not that rich,' Zaheer said.

Ramulu put his finger on his lips. 'Quiet.'

Silent gods and noisy gods. Rich gods and poor gods. Maha Baba was obviously very rich. And his gods were rich. Were Zaheer's village gods poor because the people were poor? Rich people make gods rich and poor people made gods poor … But aren't rich gods supposed to make poor people rich? It was all very confusing …

The bejewelled lady was mumbling some prayers with closed eyes. Now and then she would open her deerskin handbag and reverentially look inside. Zaheer was getting curious and dying to see what was inside. As she completed her prayers, she gingerly put her hand into the bag and brought out a heavy golden medallion. As she kissed the medallion, Zaheer caught a glimpse of the figure carved on the medal. It was Maha Baba. Why was she praying to a medallion, when the real god was going to be in front of them in a few minutes?

'Baba?' Zaheer asked her, by way of confirmation.

The lady nodded and proudly smiled at Zaheer. 'Baba himself produced this for me,' she whispered.

'So you are close to Baba?' Zaheer asked.

The woman ignored him.

She could be the one to take me to Baba, Zaheer thought.

'You know Baba well?' he persisted.

'I am blessed!' the woman now condescended to reply.

'Can you take me to Baba?'

'You can have a darshan of Baba when he comes.'

'That won't be enough,' Zaheer said. 'I need to talk to him.'

The lady was taken aback.

'That's not easy,' she said, 'but you could write him a letter.' Saying this, the lady helpfully handed him a small piece of paper and a pen.

That's when Zaheer noticed that almost everyone in the crowd was holding onto a folded piece of paper. It seemed a good idea to write letters to god. That way, you wouldn't omit to make all your requests.

'Will Baba be able to read all these letters?' he asked the lady.

'Baba doesn't need to read all the letters,' she said in an admonishing tone. 'Even without reading, he knows what you have written.' As an afterthought, she added, 'But I think it's important that he touches your letter.'

'And he will grant all the wishes?'

'Yes, of course, if you are blessed.'

'What does one do to get blessed?'

'I told you, write a letter, putting down your wishes.'

'Dear Maha Baba,' Zaheer began, but felt that Baba might mistake this for irreverence. He changed it to 'Most worshipful god ...'

Zaheer wanted to write only about his desire to be a famous dancer, but he found himself writing a long list of prayers that included the next meal, a place to stay for the night, a gory death to the school bully, nylon socks and brown shoes, a diamond ring … He wrote down a Seiko watch, scored it out and replaced it with a gold chain. It then occurred to him that he should first ask for some money. He put down twenty rupees, changed his mind and added two zeros to make it two thousand … That would be enough for some years, until he became a famous dancer …

The deep red curtains behind the mammoth stage opened, as if in obeisance.

As the stage burst into a flood of light, the entire prayer hall rose in an ear-renting chant, shredding the blanket of silence. '*Jai Baba, Jai Baba, Jai Baba,*' the devotees chanted.

Maha Baba entered.

Zaheer gasped.

He had imagined that Maha Baba would look somewhat like Hanuman from the *Sampoorna Ramayanam* movie. Supersized. Someone who could lift two adults in each hand.

Maha Baba was nothing like that. He was just a little taller than Zaheer. And frail.

Maha Baba raised his hand in a gesture of blessing and the hall instantly fell to silence.

Zaheer noticed that some people in the crowd, all adults, had begun to weep silently.

'Why are so many people crying?' Zaheer asked Ramulu.

'I think they fear that Baba will read their thoughts and find out their sins,' Ramulu said.

'If Baba were able to read their minds, why would they have to write letters?'

'Shh…!' the lady silenced them.

Baba was seated on an oversized throne that made him seem even tinier than he was. There were two ferocious looking large bronze lions on either side of the throne. It would have been interesting to see real lions that purred like cats at the feet of Baba, thought Zaheer.

'Did Baba transform real lions into those bronze ones?' Zaheer asked Ramulu.

'Maybe,' Ramulu answered. 'That would be a damn good story,' he added, with an ugly grin, which Zaheer didn't like.

Zaheer wondered if Baba could see each one in the audience. 'Can he really read minds without even seeing the face? Perhaps he can.' Tens of thousands of people in the congregation were no doubt conversing with Baba telepathically. Reciting their lists of requests. Zaheer had eleven requests.

Actually, demands. If his letter were to receive Baba's attention, in the midst of lakhs of such requests from devotees, he had to somehow ensure that Baba at least touched his letter.

From where he sat, the aisle was close enough. There were just two rows of boys, all clad in white, ahead of him. Zaheer would have to rise and reach out, but it could be managed. Zaheer shuffled closer to the aisle. He went through his list again. It would do for the moment.

Maha Baba began to talk.

Zaheer turned to Ramulu. 'What language is he speaking?'

'Kannada,' Ramulu said.

'Good Lord!' Zaheer was dismayed. 'I have written my letter in Tamil! Does Baba read Tamil?'

'He knows all languages,' the lady whispered.

The talk and the bhajan seemed to last forever. Baba was not a good singer but Zaheer was afraid of even thinking let alone voicing this. He didn't want to run the risk of Baba reading his mind, getting upset and refusing to grant his wishes. 'Baba is a great singer,' he kept repeating to himself. Zaheer tried to sing along because he had to drown the voice of the lady with the deer bag, who was singing horribly into his ears, but he soon gave up the fight.

Ramulu's sights were riveted on the deerskin bag.

At last, the moment that everyone was waiting for arrived.

The singing over, Baba drank a glass of water and wiped his lips with a white towel. There were a few people on stage, standing close to Baba, bowing deep in reverence. As Baba raised his hands towards them in blessing, he began to retch. And Baba threw up, cupping his mouth with a towel. A few seconds later, Baba took out a shining gold stone, the size of an egg, from the towel.

The crowd was ecstatic, as Baba held out the golden egg.

'It's a *shivlingh!* Golden lingh!' the lady with the deerskin bag cried out. 'Baba has produced a shivlingh from his mouth!' she excitedly said to her husband. The crowd went delirious.

'Shiv Shiv Shankar,' Baba chanted and the crowd echoed his cry.

As the crowd carried on with the chant, Baba descended the steps and walked towards the crowd. In his white robe that swept the ground, Baba looked ethereal. He appeared to float on the ground. This was far removed from Zaheer's idea of a powerful god, who could crush mountains with one clenched fist. He closely looked over Baba's head to spot the halo that the lady in the bus had mentioned but couldn't find any. He talked to himself that he must find the halo, and his mind eventually yielded and agreed that the halo was indeed there.

As Baba moved down the aisle, people threw themselves at his feet. Now and then Baba would stop, circle his hands in the air and produce holy ash. Those who received the ash distributed it to their neighbours with a look of supreme achievement. The joy of being blessed was getting transmitted through the trickles of the holy ash that was finding its way deep into the crowd.

'Baba, please, please let me receive your personal blessings,' the lady with the bag was muttering passionately, confident that her prayers would be heard by Baba, who was at least ten yards away. For some reason, she was muttering her prayers into her handbag, rather than to the real Baba in front of her. Zaheer propped himself up, ready to lunge forward to hand his letter to Baba.

Baba came near Zaheer. He slowed down his steps. For a few seconds, he stood looking straight at Zaheer.

'Letter, letter,' Zaheer shouted, with his hand outstretched. Baba didn't step forward. There was still some distance between them. There was no time to lose. Zaheer threw his letter towards Baba. If it touched Baba, it was as good as read. As his missile made its trajectory, midway, it was met with a white handkerchief from Baba that came floating like a dove. The kerchief gently landed, its ends touching the laps of Zaheer and the lady of the deerskin bag. It happened so suddenly that Zaheer couldn't figure if Baba had produced the kerchief miraculously, or he had had it on him already. Either way, this was a priceless possession.

'I am blessed!' the lady grabbed the handkerchief, tears rolling down her cheeks.

'It's mine,' Zaheer yanked the piece of cloth from the lady's hand.

'It's mine. Baba heard my prayers for a personal blessing.'

'I was the one who wrote him a letter,' Zaheer said, as though that should conclusively prove his entitlement.

The lady began to sob.

'Give it to her. It is hers,' the husband ordered Zaheer.

There was some commotion behind them. Baba had performed another miracle and the crowd was ecstatic. White robe-clad volunteers were pushing back people who were standing up to catch a glimpse of the miracle. 'This is a completely new miracle. First time,' someone was heard saying.

Zaheer did not loosen his grip on the handkerchief.

'Child, listen,' the woman said, in a conciliatory tone, 'I will give you money, and you give me the handkerchief.'

Just as she had finished saying this, she discovered to her horror that her bag was missing.

'Oh, my bag,' gasped the lady. 'Oh, my Baba medallion!' The lady began to sob violently, despite the restraints of the gathering.

That's when they noticed that Ramulu was also missing.

'You know what we will do to you if you don't tell us where your *dost* is?' the sub-inspector asked Zaheer, shaking him by the collar. His voice was harsh like a whip, but his eyes were strangely reassuring.

Zaheer had given the inspector all the details about himself. He had spoken in Tamil to prove his nativity, recited surahs to prove his religion, described his village, proven his lack of familiarity with Munoor town and promised on his mother that he had met Ramulu only at Mahashanthi Mandir.

'He is not my dost,' Zaheer said. He trusted the eyes and ignored the voice.

'Liar!' the husband of the lady with the deerskin bag shouted.

'Sir, please don't trouble yourself,' the sub-inspector said, his voice matching the eyes. 'We will take care of the case, sir. You please go and rest, sir.'

Sir was not going to give up that easily.

'Inspector, thrash him and you will get the truth. That's the only language these scoundrels understand.'

'No, no, please don't beat him,' the lady pleaded. 'Baba has designed this whole episode for some reason, I am sure Baba will come back to me.'

'You don't understand. There is no reason to be unnecessarily kind to thieves,' the man said.

'Don't you dare call me a thief!' Zaheer shouted.

'Baba will not leave me,' the lady said emphatically. 'I don't care what you police people do.'

'I am also a Baba devotee, madam. I am sure Baba will restore your bag,' the sub-inspector said.

Zaheer could see that Baba was blessing the inspector, from the desktop wallpaper.

'Jai Baba, Jai Baba, Jai Baba,' the lady chanted with closed eyes and folded hands.

There was the sound of a sharp slap behind him. Zaheer turned to see a burly constable dragging Ramulu in. He was handcuffed.

'Sir, we have caught the criminal,' the constable said, excited. 'It's Chinna, sir!'

'Oh, the old scoundrel!' the sub-inspector chimed, with the joy of reuniting with a long-lost friend. 'So, you are up to your old tricks within two months of your release?'

Chinna alias Ramulu said, 'Good evening, sir,' which seemed a trifle inappropriate, when one was handcuffed.

The sub-inspector got up and landed a slap across Chinna's face, a more appropriate way of greeting from the police.

'We have recovered everything, sir!' the constable said, and emptied his trouser pocket on the table. There was a wad of currency, an emerald ring and a mini silver liquor casket. The last piece aroused a curious look from the sub-inspector.

'Where is Baba?' the lady wailed.

The constable looked baffled.

'He's in your shirt pocket,' Chinna said.

'Oh, sorry, sir,' the constable said, and took out the Baba medallion from his shirt pocket.

The lady grabbed the medallion and placed it gently on her eyes.

'It's your strong faith, madam. I cannot explain this any other way,' the sub-inspector said with genuine feeling. He touched the feet of Baba in the photograph with gratitude.

'I told you that Baba had a divine design,' she said triumphantly. 'I got my Baba back, you nabbed the criminal … and … and …' she turned to Zaheer and asked, 'Where is the handkerchief?'

Zaheer took the handkerchief out of his pocket.

'Take this and hand over the kerchief!' the lady said, holding out a hundred-rupee note. 'It's Baba's handkerchief!' she explained, to the bewildered sub-inspector.

'And you get your money to go back to your home,' she said. 'How wonderfully Baba has designed the entire situation! Jai Baba, Jai Baba!'

'But I don't want to go back home,' Zaheer protested.

'That's fine,' the inspector said. 'You can stay there,' he pointed to an empty cell in the corner, 'and we will send word to your father to come and fetch you.'

Zaheer looked at the cell. Behind the bars he saw a rat scurry across the floor and disappear into a hole in the wall that appeared to have been plastered with shit.

Zaheer broke down and sobbed uncontrollably.

'Thank you, inspector,' the man said. 'I appreciate the prompt work done by you and your constable.'

'Sir, it's a privilege to serve you and madam,' the sub-inspector replied. 'Sir, if you'd put in a word with the commissioner, sir, I would be grateful, sir!'

'Of course,' the lady said. 'You got my Baba back.'

'So?' The sub-inspector gave Zaheer a long, blank look. When he recovered from his thoughts, he told Zaheer, 'If you wish to go back, I'll send a constable to escort you home, but your father will have to pay the constable's fare, since the government won't allow this expenditure.'

'I told you, I don't want to go back,' Zaheer said.

'I told you, if you don't want to go, I will inform the police station in Dharmapuri to direct your parents to come and collect you. In the meantime, you can stay with your friend in that cell.'

Zaheer looked at Ramulu.

Ramulu gave him a friendly smile.

'I'll go back home,' Zaheer said.

Periazhwar was stunned by Godha's question:

'Why do I need anyone to interpret my love to my Lord?' she had asked.

There were many scholars who had assembled to hear Periazhwar at the Vatapatrasayee Temple at Srivilliputhur.

'Everyone needs an Acharya, a Preceptor, to show the way to God, to show God,' Periazhwar had said. 'The Vaishnavite tradition holds an important place for the teacher.'

The assembled scholars turned with astonishment to see the young girl, Godha, question her father so boldly.

'We are all in darkness. The Acharya is like a lamp that shows the way,' Periazhwar reasoned patiently.

'Some can see the way, like me. I see the resplendent Lord as clearly as I can see you. I can hear the boisterous laughter of my Lord, even as I speak now.'

eight

The years that followed the return of Zaheer from Munoor were marked by an uneasy truce in the family.

When Salima Bivi heard about the blasphemous act of Zaheer's visit to Munoor, she felt as if her very soul had been besmirched. She was consumed by a punishing sense of guilt for having betrayed the trust of her ancestors. As a way of atonement, she tried to concentrate on the Urdu channel and almost stopped talking in Tamil. Nothing seemed to help. Salima Bivi was tormented. But she was careful not to bring up the subject directly with Zaheer.

Zaheer's parents had moved out of the joint family home to settle near the family's small farm, ten kilometres away. Zaheer's interactions with them became progressively infrequent, and on the rare occasions when he met his father, they did not speak directly to each other.

'Has he passed the exams?' Ismail would ask Salima Bivi.

Since Salima Bivi knew that she was not expected to reply, she would simply look at Zaheer, who would say, 'Does he think I failed? I scored eighty-two marks on average.'

'Well, if he concentrates on his studies without getting distracted by useless things, he could come first in the class,' his father would inform Salima Bivi.

Bouncing the conversation through Salima Bivi did nothing to shrink the distance between them.

Ismail noticed keenly how Zaheer walked and talked. He watched carefully if there was any hint of the effeminate in him. He sighed with relief when he could detect none.

'Does he play football?' he would ask Salima Bivi.

'I am not interested,' Zaheer would say aloud.

Ismail would shake his head in anguish.

Once, Zaheer found that someone at home had rummaged through his school bag without his knowledge.

Ismail made discreet enquiries with Zaheer's schoolmates and ascertained that he had not taken to dancing since he returned from Munoor. While that was reassuring, Ismail suspected that Anandhi might be secretly encouraging Zaheer to dance. For now, he chose not to confront her. He could not afford to offend Ahmed. It kept irritating him that Zaheer had not been punished for his rebellion, nor Anandhi for her influence on Zaheer.

Zaheer was unclear which had been the bigger act of rebellion, his dance performance in public or his slipping away to Munoor.

It was different with Anandhi Periamma.

'Baba produced a golden lingam from his mouth?' she kept asking Zaheer with wonderment, urging him to repeat the anecdote. Zaheer had grown enormously in stature in her mind, having witnessed a divine miracle. She embellished the story with sundry details, including a shower of golden flowers for a minute after the lingam materialized. She served the story with great flourish to her customers, along with her appams.

She even managed to get a photograph of Maha Baba, which found a place just below MGR's, on the temple wall behind her counter. The photograph was a useful conversation starter.

'Pankajam, we must go to Munoor, Baba is a living god,' she told her friend, who was unimpressed.

'When we can pray to Narayana directly, why should we go through intermediaries?' she asked.

'He is not an intermediary; he is god himself!' Anandhi clarified.

'Baba may be an aspect of god, like other godmen. Like Shankaracharya. But Narayana is greater than all of them,' Pankajam said. 'In fact, Narayana is the greatest.'

'Oh!'

'Some aspect of god descends on earth in the form of humans, in order to redeem the sinners. The beauty is that Narayana remains undiminished in heaven, although some aspect separates,' Pankajam explained.

Anandhi nodded, though she did not understand.

nine

'You are sure to win the first prize,' Selvi said, with the conviction of a clairvoyant.

That kind of profundity was pretty much the copyright of Anandhi. But Selvi was so much under Anandhi's influence, that she mouthed Anandhi's words like a puppet.

Selvi was referring to the inter-school dance contest at Dharmapuri, announced a few days ago. 'Prizes will be distributed by the Honourable Collector of Dharmapuri District' the promotion bill for the event had screamed in bold red letters, with the said honourable person shedding a discouragingly stern look from the centre of the bill.

'But Selvi, I stopped dancing four years ago,' Zaheer said.

'You never stopped dancing,' Anandhi Periamma pointed out. 'You are forever dancing in your mind.'

Zaheer knew that was true.

In the intervening years since he returned from Munoor, Zaheer became aware of an inner self, a *zaheer,* who seemed to exist almost independent of him. Like a mirror inside a mirror.

Zaheer could witness *zaheer* dancing gaily in his mind.

Zaheer would replay every dance sequence from the movies that Zaheer had watched. Not merely repeating but improvising, embellishing. *Zaheer* would dance to every movie song that Zaheer heard on the radio. *Zaheer* would dance to songs that seemed to spontaneously explode in Zaheer's mind, shutting out every other thought, sight and sound. *Zaheer* lived in dance, all the time, unless Zaheer's mind was occupied with some mundane demands of life. Sometimes, *zaheer* would squeeze himself into the open, with a lifting of an eyebrow, a tiny gesture of the hand, or a light rhythm in his steps. Zaheer would quickly hide *zaheer* from the public eye.

Zaheer did not care for the external world.

Anandhi Periamma had once told Zaheer that everyone had a soul that left the human body when one died.

'If you are blessed, you can actually see the soul which pretty much looks like a smoky, miniature version of the person, leaving the body through the nostrils when a person dies,' she told him.

Pankajam confirmed the statement and shared that she had actually witnessed the phenomenon when a saint had died at her village.

Zaheer wondered if *zaheer* was his soul. So his soul wanted to dance forever.

But that didn't explain how Anandhi Periamma knew of the existence of *zaheer*, since he was not yet dead.

'I met Kamala teacher in the market. She has agreed to get the school to sponsor you for the contest,' Anandhi Periamma declared a few days later.

Zaheer did not respond.

'Nobody from your school is contesting. She thinks that you have a good chance of winning.'

'Actually, I am happy dancing just in my mind,' Zaheer said. Or, with my soul, he thought.

Anandhi looked at him intensely.

'That's a lie,' she said. 'An artiste without an audience is like a mind without a body.' She wasn't sure that she had got that right. 'Or a body without a mind,' she hedged.

Anandhi and Selvi conferred and decided Zaheer should perform on the song *Varuvan Vadivelan*. 'He is very good expressing the longing of a maiden for her lover,' Selvi said.

'Yes, he was really very good with that number,' Anandhi agreed. 'His interpretation is unique.'

'Zaheer seems to be truly longing for something,' Anandhi observed.

'What else? To be a dancer!'

'Or is he seeking something through dance?' Anandhi wondered aloud.

Zaheer had danced to that song over a hundred times in Zaheer's mind. In the movie with the eponymous title, he had watched the dancer wandering around the temple, announcing with great gusto the arrival of the Lord. Zaheer had always felt that it would be more appropriate to depict the longing of a love-stricken maiden for the arrival of her lover. A hundred ideas had honed this improvisation in his mind. Selvi had caught glimpses of his ideas and she adored them.

'I think you should stick with your interesting interpretation,' Selvi said.

Zaheer did not reply. He was still unsure about his participation.

'I think we should get the song on an audio cassette and play it on the two-in-one, while you dance on the stage,' she said.

'Great idea! Not many people own a two-in-one,' Anandhi said with unconcealed pride.

'We have to ask Ahmed Periappa to get the audio cassette from Salem.'

Ahmed had brought home a two-in-one—a tape recorder cum radio—the possession of which defined a certain social status in the village. Ahmed's two-in-one had been duly smuggled from Singapore, and a bunch of cassettes of Tamil movie songs came free with the recorder. For that reason, the gadget had not yet been revealed at Salima Bivi's home. Ahmed was waiting to procure some suitable Urdu cassettes before the prized possession could be shared with the rest of the family.

Ahmed kept the two-in-one under lock while he was away in Salem for work. On days he was back at home, he would endearingly lower the gadget on his lap, sitting on the bed, and ask Anandhi to name her favourite song. Halfway through the song, he would snap it shut, accompanied by Anandhi's protest. 'Now you know, how it feels when you push me away when I am halfway,' he would chide.

There was much excitement when Ahmed returned with the *Varuvan Vadivelan* cassette. The purpose of the cassette had not been revealed to Ahmed, who was therefore puzzled, as to why Anandhi pushed him so much for it.

'Actually, it's an awful song,' he said with irritation.

Anandhi chose a tender moment in bed to persuade Ahmed to leave the two-in-one in her custody, before he left the following morning for Salem.

'Be careful not to overplay. The cassette wears out easily,' Ahmed said.

Zaheer realized that he was slowly luring himself to participate in the contest. With the very thought of the contest, *zaheer* was working overtime with ideas. With every new idea, with every new movement, excitement was building up. Zaheer could no longer bottle his creative ideas within himself.

'What do you think of this pose at the end of the first stanza?' Zaheer asked Selvi, when a new idea struck him.

'Very nice. But you should attempt to rehearse your improvisation only with the recorded music playing. Otherwise, you won't get your timing right,' Selvi said.

There was just a week to go before the contest.

'Where do we go for the costumes?' a worried Selvi asked Anandhi.

'What costumes?' Zaheer asked, puzzled.

'Why, you need skirts, a blouse, jewels.'

'And a wig,' Anandhi finished. 'We have to go to Salem.'

'I should dress as a girl?' Zaheer asked in dismay. Until that moment, this practical aspect of his performance had not occurred to him.

'Of course!' Selvi said. 'You didn't mean to play the forlorn damsel in pants and a shirt, did you?'

The implications of dancing dressed as a girl began to sink in. Zaheer was not sure if *zaheer* danced in girls' costumes or boys'. It seemed strange that he couldn't remember.

'Perhaps, I should withdraw from the contest,' Zaheer told Selvi the following day.

Anandhi who was overhearing the conversation, looked at Zaheer. She could see the pain in his eyes.

'Do you know the story of Mohini?' Anandhi asked.

Zaheer shook his head.

'Half the story is the usual stuff,' she said. 'Bhasmasura, an evil celestial being, performs a rigorous penance, praying to Lord Siva, and obtains a boon that anyone whose head he touches will turn to ashes.'

'Is it right for the Lord to let an evil person destroy anyone?' Zaheer asked.

'The gods' ways are too complex for us mortals to comprehend,' Anandhi replied.

'Perhaps you don't understand.'

'Perhaps,' Anandhi conceded. 'Let me continue. Immediately after getting the boon, Bhasmasura tries to burn down Siva himself. So, Siva runs to Lord Vishnu for help.'

Zaheer laughed. 'I can never make out who is more powerful, Vishnu or Siva! Sometimes Vishnu runs to Siva, sometimes it's the other way round.'

Anandhi ignored the interruption, and continued, 'Vishnu takes the female form, calling himself Mohini.'

'Abba would call Vishnu sissy.'

'Nonsense. Vishnu is Purushottaman, the ideal alpha male!'

'The ideal male cross-dresses?'

'Listen to the whole story. Mohini charms Bhasmasura with her dance, and at a moment when Bhasmasura lowers his guard, Mohini gets him to place his hand over his own head, and poor chap, the asura burns himself to ashes.'

Zaheer roared with laughter. 'They are clever, these gods!' he said.

'That's not the point,' Anandhi said. 'Gods cross-dress. They transcend genders easily as if they are changing clothes. Gods don't come in stereotypes. Humans are the ones hung up with stereotypes!'

'One law for the gods, another for us?'

'The gods have no laws. They don't need any,' Anandhi said. 'Just that humans shouldn't invoke religion to justify their suffocating laws!'

'Anyway, I think Abba has unfair rules.'

'Listen,' Anandhi said to Zaheer. 'I know you enjoy the thrill of being up on the stage and the sound of the applause.' After a pause she said, 'I also know that you are unclear whether you are afraid of your father or of yourself.'

Deep down, Zaheer knew she was right.

'Zaheer, now you should decide,' Anandhi said. 'Do you have the courage to pursue your passion and realize your dream or do you want to become a mullah, if your grandmother has her way? Jump over the well all the way or stay on the ground.'

Zaheer did not respond.

Zaheer spent that night in Anandhi Periamma's home. He couldn't be sure whether he was awake or sleeping, because *zaheer* was totally consuming his thoughts, with new creative interpretations of the song. Once, when he was half asleep, *zaheer* executed a rapid swirl, and Zaheer woke up with a pain in his ankle. He had rolled and dashed his ankle against the wall.

Zaheer perfected the choreography of *Varuvan Vadivelan* that night.

In the morning, Zaheer sought Anandhi out. 'When are we going to Salem for the costumes?' he asked.

Anandhi hugged him. 'This afternoon,' she said, 'Selvi will take you.'

The Kallankuthu street was narrow, lined with shops that sold or hired out drama costumes. Moth-eaten pomp was available on daily hire.

The wares of the shops were meant to transform mere mortals into powerful gods, albeit temporarily. But it was evident that the trade was in distress. Tin crowns sulked with peeling gold foils, the once-bright colours of kurtas were carefully hidden within their folds and the shaggy beards were matted with decades of sweat and grime. Every shop had its wares, looking like deprived ghosts, hanging out on display.

Selvi and Zaheer had marched up and down the street a few times, and while Selvi found almost everything attractive, nothing seemed good enough to Zaheer. Selvi was getting exasperated, when, in one shop, Zaheer pulled out a costume that lay hidden behind a stack.

'This maroon skirt looks good,' Zaheer said. It was a heavily sequinned skirt, and seemed the loudest piece in the street.

'That could be an expensive hire,' Selvi said hesitatingly.

'This is what I am going to wear,' Zaheer said firmly.

He had been watching *zaheer* dress up like a girl and dance during the last two or three days. And nights. Zaheer was not only getting increasingly comfortable with the idea of cross-dressing, he began to realize that he was actually enjoying it. The only trouble was, *zaheer* was changing costumes too often, sometimes right in the middle of the dance. When Zaheer set his eyes on the maroon costume, he recalled the image of *zaheer* with a similar costume. 'I will need a green blouse to go with that,' Zaheer said.

Selvi sniggered. 'You always like loud colours. I prefer lighter shades,' she said.

'Bright colours suit my fair skin,' Zaheer observed matter-of-factly.

'That costume will be a bit too big for you. I will give you a red one that will be just your size,' the shopkeeper told Selvi.

'Oh no, it's not for me. It's for my brother here,' Selvi pointed out.

'Then this is not the right costume. I have a boy's outfit too.'

'He is going to dress like a girl and dance,' Selvi said. 'It's for a dance contest. The Collector is going to give away the prize.'

The shopkeeper quickly collected himself.

'He will indeed look very good in a girl's costume,' the shopkeeper said approvingly, his experienced eye quickly measuring the contours of Zaheer's body.

'Thank you,' Zaheer said. *Zaheer* had already put on the costume.

'Since you are going to dance in the presence of the Collector, I suggest you go for diamond jewellery,' the shopkeeper enthusiastically said. The diamonds were, of course, synthetic stones that shone like specks of mercury lamps.

A set of 'diamond' jewellery, including a nose ring, a nose pendant, a *chutti* for the head, and sundry other pieces could be hired at the rate of twenty rupees a day.

'That's a bit too much,' Selvi said.

'Take it from me,' the shopkeeper said, 'anything less won't be impressive. Especially, when you dance before the Collector.'

'Don't forget the wig with the long plait,' the shopkeeper reminded them.

When Selvi proudly unwrapped the parcel of costumes, Anandhi wrinkled her nose.

'Where is that terrible smell coming from?' she asked. It was difficult for anyone to identify the source, because each of the items in the parcel had its own brand of foul odour. After some poking around, the wig was identified as the culprit.

Anandhi brought out a bottle of perfume that Ahmed had bought her some years ago. She had carefully preserved the bottle for an outing to Madras that had not yet materialized. She emptied the bottle on the wig.

'Ugh!...' Selvi retched. 'It's worse now.'

'Some chemical reaction,' Zaheer offered an explanation.

'We're going to have to wash it in boiling water,' Anandhi decided.

'We might as well wash the clothes as well. They stink to holy heavens!'

'But we have only one day! What if they don't dry in time?'

'Damp clothes are better than dirty clothes,' Anandhi said.

The wig and clothes had been washed and were dry by the morning of the contest. The clothes were limp, however, and seemed to have lost their will to exist without the grime.

Since the wig had been unaccustomed to any wash during its long life, it had reacted rather violently to the hot water wash. Strands of hair separated from the canvas on which they had been pasted. The wig ended up having bald patches, all at the wrong places.

'What do we do with the hair?' Zaheer asked. 'I can't put on this wig.'

'We will have to fix it with glue,' Anandhi said. 'It will be dry in an hour.'

Anandhi proceeded to boil a soup of flour that would serve as the glue.

By lunchtime, the costumes were ready.

'Face powder has to be applied on a foundation of Lacto Calamine lotion,' Anandhi instructed with authority. She felt like an expert, after a twenty-minute tutorial from Kamala teacher, who had the experience of putting a few of her disciples on stage. Kamala teacher had also helpfully lent half a bottle of said lotion, which was passed around with great respect. 'It's foreign,' Kamala teacher told them. Everyone smelt the bottle of lotion from a discreet distance and agreed that the smell was so good, it had to be 'foreign'. The pink talcum powder, which was laid in several layers over the lotion, caked up quickly, and when Zaheer smiled, the powder cracked around his lips and eyes.

The costume needed refitting.

'We need to open up the blouse a bit at the waist,' Anandhi said. 'The butt and the waist give away the man inside a woman's costume, not the bust, mind you, that's easily managed.'

The wig posed a new challenge. While the truant locks had all been forced into submission by the maida paste, it had acquired a new malodour, with the glue beginning to ferment rather early.

'It's stinking like hell! How can I dance with this?' Zaheer protested.

'Shut up!' Anandhi commanded. 'Fame doesn't come to the idle and the finicky.'

When the 'make-up' was done, Zaheer had morphed into a beautiful girl. Only the flowers had to be pinned on the braids. Anandhi decided to delay the decking until they reached Dharmapuri.

'I shouldn't cast my own evil eye!' Anandhi said.

'Why, the Collector himself might elope with Zaheer!' Selvi exclaimed.

Zaheer blushed.

Suddenly, the thorny memory of his father spitting out 'sissy' struck him. For a second, Zaheer wanted to tear away his costume and wipe off his make-up. His eyes welled up.

'Don't worry, your Abba is in his farmhouse. There is no chance of him coming here or to Dharmapuri,' Anandhi whispered in Zaheer's ears.

'Are you sure?'

'Absolutely,' Anandhi said. 'Besides, if you want to dance, you should cast away all these fears.'

Zaheer nodded. He was amazed at Anandhi's uncanny ability to read his mind.

It was two in the afternoon.

It had been arranged that there would be a convoy of three bicycles, Anandhi, Selvi and Zaheer riding the pillion, to take them to the Thinaipatti bus stand, from where they would board a bus to Dharmapuri.

'We will start by three,' Anandhi said. That would give them two hours to reach the venue. The contest was to begin by five.

'Let's start right away,' Zaheer said.

'In the afternoon sun, all the make-up will be washed away. Besides, you could have a few appams before you start, since we will have nothing to eat until late tonight.'

'No, we will leave now,' Zaheer said firmly.

Anandhi looked at him puzzled.

'The school bullies will be out on the road by three.'

The old and the lazy, sitting and chatting idly on the village roads, stared at the convoy with bewilderment.

A few called out to Anandhi, asking who the girl dressed up to dance was.

'She is the new heroine selected to pair with MGR!' Anandhi shouted back cheekily. 'I'll arrange free passes for you, when the movie is released.'

To a few middle-aged men, who ogled at the heavily made-up girl, she shouted, 'My daughter! I had to keep her hidden from scoundrels like you!'

The convoy had to go past the intersection of roads, from where the road to Zaheer's school lay to the right. The culvert, the throne of the school bullies, was a few yards into the road leading to the school. As the cycles approached the intersection, Zaheer turned to see the culvert. His stomach turned as he saw the bunch of bullies walking towards the culvert. They had obviously bunked their classes, earlier than usual.

A sharp whistle pierced the air.

'That's a cute consignment!' a voice shouted.

'Do you know the panchayat president of Bommidi, our neighbouring village?' Anandhi shouted back. 'It's his daughter. You do any mischief, you will have to count your bones!'

That was a gamble. If the bullies were looking for a fight, this would have been good excuse.

The whistling continued, but Zaheer noticed that the bullies were not pursuing them.

Anandhi, her tape recorder wrapped in a towel and carefully placed in a carry bag, Selvi with her shoulder bag that contained the bottle with the remnants of Lacto Calamine and the talcum powder (just in case the make-up ran out), and Zaheer—in whose mind *zaheer* was restlessly improvising new movements—made it to the venue of the contest after an eventful bus ride to Dharmapuri, during which, Anandhi kept introducing Zaheer to inquisitive fellow passengers with innovative new identities for him, with one young man casually brushing against Zaheer's padded breasts, the trio walking through the streets of Dharmapuri, with a street urchin pulling Zaheer's plait so hard from behind that the wig nearly came off, and finally Anandhi convincing the organizers that the dancer was indeed Zaheer, a male student in Class IX of the municipal school in Thinaipatti.

'Go and wait in the green room at the rear of the stage,' an organizing assistant directed the trio.

Anandhi hesitated. 'It won't be right. Girls might be dressing!'

'Or undressing,' Selvi said, with a chuckle. 'Imagine what would happen if they discovered that they had a boy in their midst!'

'I will stay outside,' Zaheer said.

When Zaheer's name was called out, *zaheer* having taken full possession of Zaheer's mind, started pushing himself out into the open with full force. When Anandhi nervously pressed the start button on the record player, Zaheer instantly pirouetted onto the stage, as though he had been longing for the cue all his life. He was completely blind to the confused audience who were wondering if they had heard the name of the contestant correctly, to the presence of the Collector who was busy with his own importance, and even to the whimsical amplifier, which was spitting out the song in bursts. Zaheer was simply the maiden in love, eagerly waiting for the arrival of the beloved.

Zaheer withdrew only when the song was completed.

That's when Zaheer looked at the audience and noticed with shock that his father was standing at the edge of the crowd. While *zaheer* exulted in the expression of his pent-up passion, Zaheer shrunk with fear. The whole exercise appeared ill-advised. He felt anger against Anandhi for letting him into the trap, anger against his father, in an entirely irrational way, and against himself and the whole world.

Only when Selvi hugged him and shouted 'congrats' did it register that he had won the first prize. His mind was still numb with fear.

'Your Abba has come to watch you. Someone in the village who saw us leaving for Dharmapuri had obviously tipped him off. But don't worry. Now that you have won the first prize, he should be happy!' she said. She didn't sound very convinced herself.

'Parents of the prize-winners, please come up on stage with the winners,' the organizer announced. As Zaheer climbed to the stage to receive the prize, he noticed from the corner of the eye that his father was following him.

'Congratulations! Your daughter danced exceptionally,' the Collector told Zaheer's father.

'My son,' his father said in a low voice.

'Oh, your son? Remarkable! He looked so convincing as a girl!' the Collector said. 'You must encourage your son to take up dance as a career.'

As his father turned to him, Zaheer's eyes met his father's. At that very moment, a puddle was forming at his feet.

ten

Strangely, the thrashing did not hurt.

The wig had spun off Zaheer's head with the third or the fourth slap on his cheek and was lying in the corner of the room, like a snake that had been beaten to death. The fake ruby jewel peeped out of the mangled wig, like an evil eye. Staring at it, Zaheer giggled. That little spill of noise was emasculating.

'Look at me!' Ismail screamed.

Zaheer looked at his father.

He looked particularly menacing. Like the Yali, with a lion head, an elephantine tusk, and an erect organ, the ubiquitous sculpture that he had seen on the pillars of the Siva temple in Salem. He had always disliked the Yali and could never understand why an ugly dragon had to stare down angrily at the devout in the temple. Ismail even had two protruding canines like the Yali, as he bared his teeth in anger.

It would be nice to have him suspended from the roof of the temple, Zaheer thought. And I will dance on the floor in front of him, making faces at him.

That thought brought forth another involuntary giggle.

And that triggered another round of thrashing.

This time, Ismail had unbuckled his belt and escalated the assault, the flick of the belt amplifying the fury. Zaheer swerved to avoid the belt and spun on the floor. The thick leather belt whipped across his shoulder.

'Go, get yourself operated!' Ismail hissed. 'Then you can dance in street corners.'

Salima Bivi choked.

The whiplash of Ismail's words tore deeply into her. Zaheer lay frozen, stung by the venom. There was only the sound of muffled sobbing coming from the curtain of ambiguous colours or from Zaheer's mother, he couldn't say which one.

Lying sprawled on the floor, Zaheer looked up. His mind's eye was playing a trick, interspersing the real with the imaginary. His father, the Yali in a lungi, was hanging from the top of the temple pillar, his eyes having rolled down a few inches from his sagging cheeks. And his legs flaying helplessly.

Zaheer gathered himself up swiftly. With a sudden energy that seemed to burst from the fountainhead of suppressed anger, Zaheer executed a fast dance manoeuvre, his favourite from the dance sequence of Padmini in *Vanjikkottai Valiban.* 'That's my response to you and your prejudices,' his gig screamed, mocking his father.

When Zaheer stormed out into the streets, with rivulets of the sweaty make-up descending on his cheeks, and unfastened blouse hanging on his straight, boyish shoulders, there was a new look of courage in his eyes.

'But you have to wait until you finish your school,' Anandhi Periamma told Zaheer, who lay with his face buried in her large bosom. 'And then you can go to Salem and do what you like.'

Zaheer had run across to Anandhi from his home. Although he didn't speak a word to her, Anandhi knew.

'I don't need to finish school to learn dance,' Zaheer countered.

'Yes, but dance can't provide you a living.'

'Dance will be my life.'

'You'll realize money is life. Simply money. Dance is an interest.'

'Dance is my passion.'

Anandhi sighed. 'Unfortunately, passion doesn't count to buy a meal,' she said.

Zaheer was silent.

'After you finish school, I guess you will have to do some diploma or the other, maybe stay in a hostel in Salem, and you could take to dancing as a pastime then.'

'That's three more years from now.'

'Yes, you have to keep your passion under wraps till then.'

'I cannot. It's consuming me.'

'I know,' Anandhi sighed. 'You will continue to dance in your mind. Nobody can stop that.'

Zaheer realized that even at that very moment, *zaheer* was dancing within him. Enacting the tragedy of a defeated protagonist.

Zaheer lay wrapped in Anandhi's warm embrace for long minutes, the hug that he had been missing for many months now. His eyeliners, that had flowed down his cheeks, were smudging her pink sari. The glass bangles in his arms were pressing against her back.

Anandhi's strong hands stroked his lower back. Zaheer did not want to lift himself from the puddle of that gooey affection. It felt comforting, although he knew that boys his age wouldn't like to be caught ever in that situation.

It just occurred to him that he couldn't recall hugging his mother ever.

That's when Ahmed returned home unexpectedly.

Zaheer coiled into himself in shock, embarrassed to have been caught in his feminine costumes.

Ahmed looked at Anandhi and Zaheer in puzzlement.

That night, Ahmed Periappa was a revelation to Zaheer.

It came as a complete surprise to him that Ahmed Periappa was aware of his interest in dance and that Anandhi Periamma had even kept him informed about his participation in the dance contest. Zaheer had had very few occasions to interact with Periappa in the past, although Periappa would now and then bring small gifts from Salem, which Zaheer imagined were at Anandhi Periamma's behest. Periappa had never shown much interest in the kids in the family, preoccupied as he was, with his mother and brothers, or with his friends in the village who often sought his help in their work-related issues. Periappa would occasionally pat his head perfunctorily, for no apparent reason.

As Anandhi described to Ahmed the events of the day, he listened to her without saying anything or displaying any reactions. It wasn't clear to Zaheer whether Ahmed Periappa was on his side or his father's.

'Go and have a bath in warm water,' he told Zaheer, when Anandhi finished her long narration.

It was after dinner, when Zaheer lay on the straw mat, still feeling very confused about his Periappa's reaction or lack of it, that Ahmed came and sat next to him. Zaheer had never felt Periappa's presence that closely. He felt a little awkward. There was a strong smell of meat in Periappa's body odour.

Ahmed ran his fingers through Zaheer's hair.

'You don't have to go back to your home, at least for some time. No one here is going to stop you from dancing!' he said.

Zaheer sat up.

'I'll tell your father,' Ahmed said.

Zaheer sprang up and circled his arm around his Periappa's thick neck. Ahmed gently kissed him on his forehead.

'You are my son from now,' he said softly.

Anandhi walked up to them and held both of them in her warm embrace.

Then she remembered the kurava woman's predictions. 'But it's almost two years now,' she comforted herself.

'I don't feel like a Brahmin girl,' Godha told Sukhi, her parrot friend. 'Mentally, I identify with the Yadava clan, the cowherds.'

Sukhi was busy cracking the almond seed. 'How does it matter?' she asked disinterestedly.

'Oh, it does,' Godha said. 'The Yadava girls had no inhibitions! They played with Krishna, felt Him, hugged Him ... They were not restrained by Brahmanical orthodoxy.'

'You too are doing exactly the same ... in your dreams.'

'Not only in dreams, you stupid! I am playing with the Lord day and night! Thank heavens you don't get to know that.'

'Of course, I know. I am astounded by your temerity.'

'You don't need courage to realize the purpose of your life, you need His grace!'

'All right, will you stop thinking about your Lord for a while and bring me my oil cakes?' Sukhi asked, happy to have cracked the almond shell.

eleven

Zaheer knew that prizes and trophies won by students at inter-school meets received a cursory mention by the headmaster in his mournful voice at the students' morning assembly. Usually, at the noisy assembly, the headmaster stoically allowed his announcements to drown in the din.

On the morning after the inter-school dance contest, Zaheer anxiously watched the headmaster's lips and noticed his name dribble out.

'zaheer of ninthst and ardbsection wontheinter school dance competition ...'

Zaheer felt relieved that nobody appeared to have heard the monotonous felicitation.

Except Kalaivani.

Kalaivani, the Peacock. Or, the Peahen with the Plumage and Pride. The only acknowledged dancer in the school. The one whose eyebrows remained permanently arched with conceit. The one whose eyes teasingly invited and then heartlessly repelled the lustful glances from a multitude of excited adolescents. And from a few wicked teachers.

'Congratulations,' she said, as she brushed past him when the assembly was dissolving.

Zaheer thought that he saw a flash of jealousy in those dark eyes.

Later that day, he changed his mind. Perhaps it was respect and not indignation he had noticed. A begrudging admiration?

When he lay in bed that night, those eyes nudged their way back into his mind. Interestingly, the fleeting few seconds of her look now appeared like eternity. The eyes appeared to convey a mysterious message. What was *that*? he wondered.

He didn't have to wait too many days for the answer.

It was late evening and the silhouette of the Yercaud Hills was a sharp etching against the ochre sky. As the last arc of the sun dipped into the horizon, the marauding army of mosquitoes, as if on cue, rose from the stagnant drains of the village, ready to kill and get killed.

That was also the cue for Anandhi to commence the closing rituals of her shop.

The lazy street dog that was Anandhi's most loyal customer punctually ambled into her shop, with his tail betraying eagerness to receive the customary crumbs.

Anandhi threw some burnt pieces of appams to the dog. There were a few cups of batter left in the pan, enough for four or five appams. It was her practice to proffer the last appams of the day to the goddess.

Anandhi considered Mariamman to be a minority partner in her enterprise, and the closing appams were her dues. Sometimes without chutney, if she'd run out, but Mariamman always understood. Or so Anandhi assumed, since the business was flourishing, and that meant Mariamman remained pleased. As she wound up her business for the day, Anandhi turned her head towards the temple and said her thanks to the goddess through the compound wall (that separated the shop from the temple), the irreverence of which too, Mariamman understood and duly pardoned. (Anandhi had not entered the temple since her morphing into Ayesha, fearing that Allah or Mariamman, or both, could be angered by the act). It was left to Selvi or Zaheer to run inside the temple and place the appams for a few seconds before the goddess, who was expected to alertly acknowledge and instantly bless.

It was when Zaheer was retrieving the appams from the goddess that he noticed Kalaivani at the steps to the sanctum. With folded hands and half-closed eyes, she was a vision to behold, a picture of utter piety.

'Oh, Kalai, I didn't notice you,' Zaheer said awkwardly.

'I didn't know you were supposed to offer appams to the goddess,' she countered.

'Not necessary. You can simply pray,' he replied.

Kalaivani stood looking at him.

Zaheer noticed that she was a bit taller than him. And considerably darker. (He was baffled as to why he was comparing himself with her.) Her rather flattish nose and poutish mouth were more than compensated by her large expressive eyes.

'Well, I actually came to see you,' she said.

'Oh, I am surprised, I thought you didn't much care for me,' Zaheer stammered.

'That's true, but this prize-winning business has changed my impressions about you,' her eyes said, somewhat condescendingly.

'What did you dance?' These were words from the pouty mouth.

'*Varuvan Vadivelan,*' Zaheer replied.

'Oh, I thought you would have chosen *Maraindhirunthe*! That's what you danced in the classroom some years ago.'

'You too danced on the same song.'

'Yes,' she said, 'but you're the one who got the applause!'

'And I am consumed by jealousy,' her eyes seemed to add.

'Well, the boys are applauding you all the time, whether you dance or not!' Zaheer said.

Now, pride quickly replaced jealousy in her eyes. She smiled in acknowledgement.

Kalaivani turned to the goddess and mumbled her prayers with closed eyes. She took her time in the quiet confidence that Zaheer would linger. When she opened her eyes, her gaze was still fixed on the goddess.

'I have been invited to dance at my cousin's wedding reception, about a month from now,' Kalaivani said, addressing the goddess.

'How wonderful!' Zaheer said.

She looked at him and her eyes struggled to convey something.

'Go ahead,' Zaheer said.

'Well, well, I don't know what to say ...'

'But you have come all the way to say something,' Zaheer said.

'Well, I ... I wondered if you could ... err ... teach me ... the way you dance to that song,' she said with some effort.

Zaheer tried to absorb the impact of her words.

Here was the peahen, of proud plumage, not only acknowledging his existence, but asking him to *teach* her!

'But you have been learning from Kamala teacher,' Zaheer said.

'Well, I have stopped the lessons for some time now,' she paused, and then asked again, 'Will you teach me?'

As if the scene weren't surreal enough, the solitary oil lamp in the temple was throwing mysterious shadows over the goddess, and in a curious way, rendering the stone idol (which was farthest from a human form) almost alive.

The moment was undeniably dramatic. Zaheer felt the situation required him to sound suitably theatrical.

'Well, whatever knowledge I have, I will throw open the doors to you,' he said with a flourish and added cautiously, 'but you know I am not a trained dancer.'

'Yes, I know, you are actually not a dancer,' Kalaivani said, 'but that's all right. I only need to know your movements; I will polish them thereafter.'

'That's not being very courteous.'

Kalaivani completely ignored Zaheer's protest and turned to leave.

As she stepped out of the temple, she added imperiously, 'We will meet tomorrow evening at the orchard after school,' leaving without waiting for an answer from Zaheer.

'Who does that queen bee think she is?' Zaheer later said to Anandhi, as he narrated their encounter.

'Queen bee,' replied Anandhi. 'That's what she thinks of herself!'

'I don't care for her,' he said.

'Very well! Now, pack up the vessels,' Anandhi said, as she emptied the leftovers into the dustbin.

The complaining clang of the vessels, as they were being dumped into the large canvas bag, betrayed Zaheer's irritation.

'Why does she think I will teach her?' Zaheer said aloud.

'Because you care about her. And isn't she right? You haven't been able to get her off your mind,' Anandhi pointed out.

Anandhi was right.

Kalaivani was buzzing around like a fly in Zaheer's mind. He felt irritated. He could not swat her away, much as he tried. They were intriguing, those eyes. Sometimes they were dark pools of conceit and arrogance. At other times, they looked eager and inviting. For a few fleeting moments, they even looked kind ...

'Forget her ... forget, forget ...' he kept saying to himself, in vain.

'But it would be fun to teach her,' Zaheer heard wide-eyed *Zaheer* say. And soon Zaheer realized that *Zaheer* was already trying out new movements with defiant enthusiasm.

It was difficult to sleep.

As Zaheer sat in the classroom the following day, there was a tug of war between his mind, which kept insisting that he didn't care for the girl, and his inner self, *zaheer*, which was excited with the prospect of a dance dialogue with a kindred spirit.

'It would be fun to dance in the orchard,' *zaheer* pointed out, 'and there would be company.'

'But she is full of herself,' Zaheer said.

'Remember it was she who invited you to teach her.'

'But she doesn't respect me.'

'She is not all that bad. For instance, she isn't as bad as your father.'

'Of course not.'

'So, why don't you teach her?'

'That's bad reasoning! I don't want to, and that's it.'

Zaheer had rehearsed in his mind what he would say to Kalaivani if she came to remind him of their rendezvous in the evening.

'I don't think you'll be able to learn,' he would say, 'one has to be creative and I just don't think you have it in you.' He tried various tonal variations, so as to sound dismissive but just short of being offensive.

Kalaivani spared him the effort. She was busy chatting with her friends the entire day and didn't even throw as much as a glance in Zaheer's direction.

Zaheer found the classes never-ending. As the closing bell rang, the combat between his mind and *zaheer*, began all over again. While it raged, he was surprised to find his legs leading him towards the orchard.

The orchard was big. Zaheer realized that Kalaivani had not mentioned where she would meet him.

It was not yet dusk and the orchard still wore the look of innocence it had during the daytime. People usually didn't enter the orchard, unless they needed to hide their acts, some acts less so, like defecating near the boundary, and others more so, which had to be carried out deep inside. Later in the night, when illicit activities unfolded under the dark caverns of its thick foliage, the orchard would turn an eager voyeur.

Zaheer tried to convince himself that he was there only to pluck some unripe guavas and tender tamarind, and definitely not to meet Kalaivani.

He wandered, plucked leaves, smelt them, plucked more and crushed them, picked up the overripe tamarind pods that had been shaken off the trees, tasted, and stung by the sharp tanginess, spat them out, threw pebbles at nothing in particular, pounded the thick trunks of the barren mango trees, chased a lazy mongrel, stared at two mating squirrels and was about to give up and return home when he heard the rustle of a nylon skirt.

Kalai swept in as though she were entering the stage itself.

Zaheer noticed that she had changed from her school uniform to a new dress. In her bright orange skirt and the yellow half sari, she appeared misleadingly holy, until one looked at her dark face, which had been freshly whitewashed with talc, and was decorated with a coquettish, teardrop bindi.

Zaheer felt flattered that she had dressed up for him.

'Let's begin,' she said sternly, as if to deny Zaheer any such presumptive pride.

'What—,' he started to ask, when she cut him short.

'You can sing and dance, and I will watch,' she said, 'I am a very fast learner.'

Zaheer, who had been longing for years to rush out from the confines of Zaheer's mind to touch the world, heard these words and burst out and began to dance. He was thrilled to see movements that had remained like frescoes in his mind take shape through his mobile limbs. Kalaivani was no longer important. He was dancing for the trees, the long shadows, the noisy parrots, the world around him …

The orchard rendezvous began to follow a daily rhythm.

Kalaivani always preferred to see Zaheer dance rather than dance herself. When he danced, she often busied herself collecting tamarind pods.

'At this season, they are not very sour. They are delicious with a pinch of jaggery,' she would say, carefully folding them into the ends of her half sari.

'You asked me to teach you,' Zaheer would say, 'and I don't see you inclined to learn.'

'I am watching your steps and I will later improve them with my own ideas,' she would reply, still busy tenderly cracking open the tamarind pods, to test if they were ripe.

Zaheer was irked by her superciliousness.

'She has no vacant space in her mind to learn; it's filled up with conceit,' he complained to Anandhi.

'Very well, don't waste your time anymore,' said Anandhi.

Kalaivani completely ignored him when they met at school. It was clear that she intended to keep the orchard meetings entirely clandestine. While it suited him, Zaheer was not sure if it was only her pride or something else that made her behave that way.

'I don't know why you complain about Kalaivani and then end up chasing her at the orchard every day,' Anandhi said.

'You have no idea what it means to dance without fear,' he said, 'and you have someone watching, even if only with fleeting attention.'

But, that was at the beginning.

It was soon no longer sufficient to find an excuse to dance. He needed more than his long shadows in the setting sun for accompaniment. It was interesting to get Kalaivani to pair him in the movements. He was excited whenever (which was not very frequent) she got it right and followed him accurately.

'If you are attentive, you'll get it right,' he pleaded with her.

'If you dance more for me than for yourself, I'll get it right,' she countered.

'I try my best to teach her, but she is not at all attentive,' Zaheer complained to Anandhi.

'So, don't teach her,' Anandhi said.

'Yes, I won't go anymore.'

The next day Zaheer went, protesting to himself.

Kalaivani was a painfully slow learner.

'I am raising my right hand, and you are raising your left,' Zaheer would say in frustration.

'Oh, how is this?' Kalaivani would respond, correcting her hand.

'Now you have got the foot wrong,' he would point out in desperation.

Sometimes he wondered if she was at all serious about learning.

A few days into their classes, the truth slowly revealed itself.

'I cannot dance today, I've hurt my leg,' she said. She pulled her skirt to show her knee, as she limped to sit under the guava tree.

'That's nothing, it's a tiny bruise,' he said.

'Can't you see my knee is swollen?'

Zaheer looked closely. He could see no swelling.

'Can't say. I will only know if I see the other leg.'

Kalaivani appeared very pleased with the response.

She eagerly pulled the skirt to reveal both the knees and a little more.

The dark skin above her knees winked at Zaheer mischievously.

'It's painful,' she said, as she gently stroked around the small red streaks.

Zaheer sensed a gentle stirring within him.

'Let's meet tomorrow,' he said.

She looked up. Her eyes spoke. Clearly. Unambiguously. Despite the creeping dusk.

'You are a bloody fool,' the eyes said. 'And you think I am talking about my stupid bruise.'

'I … I …' Zaheer stammered.

'Don't you want some fun?' Now, the knees spoke.

Zaheer touched her knee gingerly.

'I am very shy,' she said without the slightest trace of shyness.

As Zaheer slowly ran his fingers over the knee, Kalaivani appeared to slither into his being through the gentle touch. She was beginning to possess every cell of his body.

'I have to go,' Kalaivani pushed away his hand and rose to leave. She laboriously limped till the edge of the orchard and then walked away briskly.

'How is the knee?' Zaheer asked anxiously the following day. He fussed over the rapidly dissolving bruise and the imaginary swelling.

In the following days, his strokes on her knee got progressively stronger and longer.

It was no longer dance but the knees that were beginning to drive Zaheer to the orchard. Dance was of course very helpful to quieten *zaheer*, who was turning restless.

'You only have interest in knees,' *zaheer* chided Zaheer.

'Not quite, eyes too,' said Zaheer, trying to impart respectability.

Dance was indeed instrumental in getting their bodies to brush against each other. Zaheer discovered that he frequently had to put his arms around Kalaivani's hips in order to correct her posture. And the fingers found that they had to dig a wee bit more into her flesh just to hold her in position. He discovered many interesting movements that required him to press himself against her supple body. Dance was revealing to him new secrets…

Anandhi was amused.

'Isn't the wedding of her cousin over yet?' she asked, when she found that Zaheer's orchard trips had long become routine.

'It's over, but Kalaivani is training for another event,' Zaheer said.

'Watch out! You are too young!' Anandhi said, in a voice weighted by experience.

'It is just not an innocent prank of a mischievous boy!' Godha told Sukhi. 'Waiting avidly for all of us girls to rise stark naked from the river—would you call that innocence?'

Sukhi paused from cracking the almond nut.

'Well, serves you right for bathing naked in the river,' Sukhi admonished Godha.

'Does it entitle Him to take away our clothes from the riverbank?'

'I have no doubt you were actually enjoying Krishna's mischief!' Sukhi winked.

'Well, all the girls who were splashing around in the waters were eager to jump out naked and run to hug this prankster. I had to restrain those shameless females.'

'He is the most desirable in all the three worlds! He is the most adorable young boy, in this entire Universe.'

'Boy! He is a romantic hero, a philanderer, masquerading as an innocent little boy!'

'You pine for Him even if He deserts you for a minute, and yet, when He appears before you, you chase Him away!'

Godha sighed.

'How I wish I was alone. At the faintest whiff of sandalwood, that always heralds His approach, I would have rushed out of the pond and held Him in a tight embrace! But I couldn't trust Him, with so many beautiful lasses around.'

'It's the yearning of the souls, naked without the cover of earthly life, to become one with the Divine!' Sukhi said, as she shook off the water drops from her bath.

twelve

'If you keep looking at the mirror this often, it will reduce your lifespan,' Anandhi warned Zaheer, reminding him of the popular superstition.

(The diminutive mirror on the wall was a birthday gift to Anandhi from Ahmed, just big enough to frame Anandhi's face, which she felt was all that mattered.)

'Going by your score, you should have been long dead,' Zaheer retorted.

'Perhaps god accords a lower count for women, considering that they need to look at the mirror often,' Anandhi said. 'Like ten times for a woman equals one for a man?'

'That means god made men ten times better looking than women!'

'That's true, if you take Kalaivani and you, for instance,' Anandhi said. She spared no opportunity to signal her disapproval of Zaheer's interest in Kalaivani.

Anandhi could sniff out romance with a dog's precision. Lust, even more so. She could sniff pheromones at work between a man and a woman in a crowd of a hundred.

'That man, in the third row, the way he was exchanging lecherous glances with his neighbour's wife seated in the fifth row was downright scandalous,' she would recall to Pankajam, on their way back from the cinema. '*Narayana, Narayana,*' Pankajam would cry out, cleansing her ears with the name of god. 'It's a sin to talk like that about a married woman,' Pankajam would admonish Anandhi. That sharp observation from Anandhi would however be followed in due course by a sensational murder of the woman by her suspicious husband, that would shock the entire village.

Sometimes, Anandhi didn't even need to see the couple together to make her assessments.

'Your son seems to be in love, watch out,' she advised a customer one day.

'Are you saying some devil is trying to entice my poor, innocent lad?' the man asked.

'I can see love writ large in his eyes.'

'Impossible,' the man said, 'he is in the middle of a forty-one-day celibacy vow to make a pilgrimage to Sabarimala temple. He wouldn't dare think of a girl!'

'That's why I know. Celibacy for a love-struck youngster is worse than fasting,' Anandhi said. Sure enough, the boy and a girl from the village were found missing soon thereafter amidst rumours of an elopement.

It took Anandhi no time at all to sniff out Zaheer's crush on Kalaivani.

It was clear as day, that his orchard visits weren't about dance anymore. She was amused to notice Zaheer's sudden obsession with his looks. Her Pond's Dreamflower Talc was always in demand.

'You are fair-skinned. You don't *need* face powder,' she would say.

'Oh, it's for the sweat, not for the looks,' he would reply sheepishly, before carefully combing his hair with coconut oil and water.

Zaheer displayed an eagerness to flaunt his most colourful shirts. 'Thank god, Abba is not in the village, otherwise, he would have killed you,' Anandhi said to Zaheer one day, when he wore a shirt that looked as if a rainbow had melted on it.

'How would I look with a moustache?' he asked her dreamily, gently stroking the shy, delicate sprouts on his upper lip.

'Moustache, my foot!' she exclaimed. 'You were wetting your shorts not long ago!'

Anandhi was annoyed that Zaheer had picked Kalaivani, whom she intensely disliked, to have a crush on. In fact, Anandhi *loathed* Kalaivani, as only a woman can loathe another. That she knew little about Kalaivani, or the fact that she had seen her only a couple of times at a distance, did not matter in her intuitive judgement about Kalaivani.

'She is not a good type,' she warned Zaheer.

'What does that mean?' he demanded.

'Her eyes should tell you the answer.'

'Actually, she has very beautiful eyes.'

'They are deep, evil honey traps. I can see right through them,' she said.

'Honey, yes,' he said. 'Evil, no.'

She also worried about the location of their meetings, as she was only too familiar with the lusty juices of the innards of the orchard. 'That's a treacherous place,' she kept muttering to herself. That didn't prevent her from wistfully reminiscing about her union with Ahmed at the orchard. The memory of that escapade, even after all these years, brought nerve-tingling excitement to her. 'But then, I was a responsible girl,' she reasoned with herself, without much conviction.

'Why don't you take Selvi with you when you go to meet Kalaivani at the orchard?' Anandhi suggested, trying to sound as innocent as possible.

That was when Zaheer looked squarely in her eyes and said: 'Periamma, leave us alone.'

Hearing that, Anandhi choked.

'Oh dear, dear,' she cried. 'You are talking as though you are MGR!'

Until that moment, Zaheer was, in her reckoning, still a young boy, whom she could pull and hug. She wondered if she had misjudged. Did boys grow into young men at fifteen? Anandhi could never really be sure when precisely boys came of age. Was it when their voice broke? Or when hair peeped out of their chest? It was a different matter with girls, whose entry into adolescence was well celebrated at a social function and feast.

Anandhi was very troubled. She couldn't say if it was Zaheer's defiance or his liaison with Kalaivani that bothered her more. Her mind feverishly searched for a powerful statement appropriately grave for the occasion, but reluctantly settled for this: 'Learning stops for those who get entangled in love,' she told Zaheer, trying hard to recall where she had heard the lines. 'And, you haven't even started learning.'

Anandhi confided in Pankajam about her concerns for Zaheer.

'What is there to be worried?' Pankajam said, surprising Anandhi. 'Everyone invariably grows out of teenage crushes.'

Anandhi's mind leapt to the sanctum of Mariamman Temple. 'Aatha,' she prayed fervently, 'save this young boy from falling prey to that demon.' The matter was so critical that she instantly secured her prayer with a contract: 'I will offer two pitchers of milk, but please, please draw him away from the clutches of that devil,' she beseeched.

Anandhi didn't have to worry for long. Just when she had regained courage to do some straight talking to Zaheer, the orchard visits started to lose rhythm.

Kalaivani, having duly lost interest in learning, dancing and revealing a teasing knee, in that order, was beginning to tire of Zaheer. Being just 'knee' deep in romance was decidedly boring after a few days, with Zaheer lacking the initiative to progress any further anatomically. Besides, it was rather challenging to pretend to learn dance, and that too, for many weeks. For many days and weeks, Zaheer was left wandering in the orchard with no sight of Kalaivani.

Waiting for Kalaivani, he had learnt enough about the mating habits of squirrels:

He learnt to catch squirrels and hold them in his palm, to enjoy their squishiness, to identify the male and the female of the species when they jumped out, holding aloft their bushy tails like flag-bearing protesters.

He observed with fascination the foreplay, without initially understanding the purpose.

He was intrigued that four or five males chased a female, that the female appeared completely uninterested in anything as mundane as copulation, that the female suddenly changed her mind and beckoned the most aggressive and restless male to mount her …

He watched the unseasonal white flowers of the guava tree fatten at the belly like pregnant women, the smooth skin of the belly turning coarse overnight …

He saw the orderly serration on the leaves that god had patiently drawn on every single one like the homework of an obedient child …

The less he saw Kalaivani, the more Zaheer began to witness the beautiful dance of life in the orchard, its moods, its silence and its shame. When he danced all by himself, it wasn't *zaheer* oozing out unmindful of the external world, but it was Zaheer communicating to an engaged and expressive world. The orchard pulsated with the presence of life, when the leaves rustled and a mongoose sprinted across the grass. Kalaivani was slowly receding as the purpose of the orchard.

Anandhi was relieved that the adolescent infatuation had stopped at the fringes of the orchard and had not travelled into the caverns of vice.

'But, Kalaivani is a very, very nice girl,' Zaheer insisted, even though she had left him waiting in the orchard for many days by then.

'Nice girls don't meet boys alone,' Anandhi said, and instantly realized that she herself wouldn't pass the test of a nice girl by that standard. 'I mean, it's all right to meet men alone, if you are a grown-up woman, but not if you are this young,' she said.

'You are needlessly being harsh on an innocent girl,' Zaheer said. Anger was colouring the tip of his nostrils.

~

Anandhi was Ayesha that evening.

All that the morphing required was to wrap the white *thuppatti* around her sari and over her head, and not wear the pottu on her forehead. The toggle on the religion switches was simple enough.

Ayesha was grinding *maruthani* leaves on the stone mortar with the pestle, and the paste was collecting as shy green balls in a cup. She paused to look at her palms, which had turned deep orange with the dye of the leaves. She loved the smell of the wet leaves.

'Hmm ... this is very good quality maruthani,' she smelt her palms with great satisfaction.

Ahmed had begun to fret over the early sprouts of grey hair over his forehead and in his whiskers. Recently, he had indulged in a haircut at an expensive salon in Salem whose enterprising barber, running his fingers through Ahmed's hair, had asked if it wasn't time for him to think about colouring.

'Men colour their hair?' Ahmed asked in astonishment.

'Yes, in Madras and Bombay they all do. Many have begun to do it here too,' the barber had said. 'What's wrong in looking good? You are a handsome man, and it will be nice on you.'

'You think I am handsome?' asked Ahmed, eager to hear the compliment repeated.

'Sir, to be honest, you look like MGR!' the barber dutifully said.

Ahmed narrated this exchange with some pride to Anandhi, in the hope of hearing her approval of the enterprise of hair colouring. 'Since these are early days, no one has noticed my grey hair as yet, so it's a good time to start colouring,' he said.

Anandhi was aghast.

'Never heard of men dyeing their hair! You must be mad to think of it,' she said.

'Which law says men can't colour their hair?' Zaheer, who had overheard, said irritably. 'Why are men expected to look drab and boring?'

'Men don't like colours. They don't like what women like. Jewels, for example,' Anandhi said.

'Nonsense, some men do, and I can't see why they should be stopped,' Zaheer said.

'There are some rules. We should check with Wazir Periappa,' Anandhi said cautiously. Anandhi would often consult Wazir, her brother-in-law, what the religious prescriptions were with regard to many everyday matters. Wazir was always eager to guide. (There were difficulties sometimes, when Hindu and Islam practices were in conflict, but she made temporary choices that were convenient and ensured domestic peace.)

When Anandhi raised the matter of hair colour with him, Wazir smiled and pointed to his flaming red mop. 'Of course men can colour their hair; in fact, old men should use henna or maruthani.

Prophet (Peace Be upon Him), has actually observed that old men looked handsome with hair dyed yellow and orange.'

'Not black?' Anandhi enquired. She didn't think Ahmed would look good with orange hair.

'Never,' Wazir said. 'It is just not allowed to dye the hair black. It is the Hadith narrated by Abu Dawood,' Wazir elaborated.

So, it was settled that Ahmed would use maruthani.

'It is a confirmed Sunnah of the Prophet,' Ayesha reminded herself reverentially as she mixed the paste.

'My husband doesn't need this much maruthani to dye his hair. The balance is for you and me,' Ayesha told Pankajam, who was giving her a hand in grinding the leaves. The green paste would sit that night on their fingertips and palms like thimbles. When the dried paste withered away the following morning, it would have left beautiful orange stains on the hands.

'I don't want it. My husband will get furious,' Pankajam said sadly.

'Why are you so afraid of your husband? Sometimes you should just do what you like,' Ayesha said. 'Women have to go up a few notches to force men to come down a few.'

'That may well be. But maruthani is not a matter worth fighting about.'

'So, what will I do with so much paste?' Ayesha wondered.

'I will apply on my palms,' Zaheer interjected.

'You?'

'Yes, me.'

'But maruthani is so feminine.'

'Do plants have gender?'

'But boys don't use ...'

'Why not? Muslim men don maruthani during their marriage. Hindu gods put it all the time.'

'Are you a Muslim or a Hindu?' Ayesha asked him.

'Are you a Muslim or a Hindu?' Zaheer retorted.

'Why can't I be both?'

'Why can't I be both?

Ayesha laughed.

'We both are sometimes saffron, sometimes green, like a chamaeleon. Isn't that a beautiful way to identify with your environment?'

When they awoke the following morning, Anandhi and Zaheer stuck out their hands to compare the stains on their palms. The orange dye had deeply penetrated Zaheer's skin. Anandhi's had turned out a few shades lighter.

'Your hands really look beautiful. Especially, the dark orange disk on your fair palm,' Anandhi said.

'Same paste, but we have different shades on our hands,' Zaheer said.

'They say, if you have an innocent mind, the dye doesn't take deep root,' Ayesha said.

'Just as I thought,' Zaheer said. 'All the gods sport strong colours on their palms, and they are by no means innocent.'

'Nor are you,' she said. Zaheer understood that Ayesha was referring to his dalliance with Kalaivani.

Kalaivani swam into his mind. Her eyes looked kind and innocent.

That was to change later that day.

Kalaivani's home was close to the school. Since she and Zaheer walked to school from opposite directions, their paths had never crossed. When Kalaivani had stopped coming to the orchard, Zaheer had felt the urge to accost her on her way to school, but had held back because he knew that Kalaivani always walked with two or three friends, she at the centre, half a step ahead, and the others like bridesmaids, following her with a mixture of awe and awkwardness. He also knew that, in company, Zaheer didn't exist for Kalaivani. The intimacy with Zaheer, while it lasted, was like a costume that she hung up on the branches of the straggler trees lining the outskirts of the orchard. Zaheer, to her, was a stranger in the world beyond. Zaheer was also a willing accomplice to the unspoken rules of this game, though he was not happy about it.

'That only means she has no respect for you,' Anandhi cautioned Zaheer, adding one more arrow to her quiver of attacks on Kalaivani.

Zaheer was surprised when he saw Kalaivani and a couple of girls walking ahead of him as he was hurrying to the school.

'Kalaivani!'

Zaheer was surprised to hear himself calling out to her.

There was a slight deflection of her head, with just a mild betrayal of recognition—but she didn't turn.

'Kalaivani!'

It was no longer a call that came involuntarily.

He was now closer.

The two other girls—he recalled that he had seen them both in the school—turned around. One of them, a plump girl with a mischievous smile, said, 'Oh, you!'

He had now caught up with them.

Kalaivani looked at him, with her eyebrows more steeply arched. Those eyes. They flashed a new, sharp signal that he had never seen earlier.

Zaheer wanted to say something beyond her name, but those eyes froze him in his tracks.

There was an awkward pause.

Impulsively, Zaheer put out his hands. The outstretched palms opened like a pair of large flowers.

'How beautiful!' the plump girl cried out. She took Zaheer's hands and looked at the painted palms appreciatively. 'Such deep colour!'

Zaheer could see Kalaivani on the verge of acknowledging his presence when the other girl exclaimed, 'But a boy wearing maruthani? Isn't that weird?'

The plump girl now joined her with a giggle, her appreciation quickly melting away.

'I have watched him, and he has always looked strange to me!' the other girl said, looking at Zaheer, as if he were a strange specimen of the species.

'Sissy?' the plump girl giggled more.

Zaheer felt a fountain of fury rising within him.

'He dances,' Kalaivani said tentatively.

'Dances? What dance?'

'Dances like a girl. He even dressed like a girl!' Kalaivani's voice was stronger now, as she had fully joined forces with the rest.

'Really? Dresses like a girl?' The plump girl was closing in like predator on prey.

'Kalaivani!' Zaheer screamed. 'You have the gall to mock me after hanging on to my arms?'

'You, hanging on to this guy?'

Kalaivani looked at Zaheer. Those eyes had flames of anger that scorched him. 'You betrayed our secret,' they seemed to scream.

'He is a liar! *And* a sissy!' Kalaivani hissed.

Zaheer felt an implosion within him, a force that swallowed all his esteem.

thirteen

Zaheer was devastated. And Anandhi sighed with relief.

Anandhi felt Zaheer's anger when he kicked the stool beneath the mirror, or when he shouted at her for over-salting his sambar. She felt his crushing agony, watching him sulk and miss his classes.

It took a few days, despite her shrewdness, to piece together precisely what had transpired. When she was fully convinced that Zaheer had summarily been jettisoned by Kalaivani, Anandhi silently thanked Mariamman. Her prayers had been answered.

'Aatha, you saved this boy. I won't forget to fulfil my offer of two pots of cow milk,' she promised.

But there was a challenge.

Anandhi, after becoming Ayesha, had managed to keep her Hindu gods firmly locked in her mind. She of course conversed with them frequently, especially when she was under pressure or stress. Like the time when Ahmed's shop was under siege by some neighbours, who woke up one day to find that the butcher's shop was an affront to their religious beliefs. News reached Anandhi that there was a mob pelting stones at the shop and that Ahmed had disappeared from the scene. Ahmed didn't show up that night, nor was there any news of him. The following morning, Anandhi opened her shop earlier than usual, restless with anxiety. The Tamil newspaper, that was published from Salem, carried local news on page 3. The elderly reporter had dutifully stuck to an obsolete code of conduct, and euphemistically observed that 'members of one community allegedly caused damage to property belonging to members of another community, amidst unsubstantiated rumours that there might have been physical assaults that could potentially lead to death'. The worldly wise customer who read out the news to Anandhi, opined somewhat insensitively that it meant Ahmed was probably dying, if not dead already. Anandhi swung immediately to face Mariamman across the compound wall that separated her from the sanctum and held a high-intensity dialogue with the goddess: 'There is no way you can harm my husband, not after having accepted my daily offering of appams to you over the last several years,' she beseeched.

Ahmed returned later that evening, hale and healthy. The mob had bypassed his shop quickly, as they couldn't stand the gore for long.

There were many such occasions of Anandhi's purposeful engagement with various Hindu gods, but those conversations never slipped through her lips. She had never visited any temple after her marriage, although Pankajam was scripting many plans for her. Nor were there any artefacts of her earlier faith, including pictures at her home. The house was sanitized of all traces of religion, partly in acknowledgement of the promises she had made to Ahmed, and partly to avoid compounding her already confused identity.

Anandhi was undecided how she would carry out the promise of anointing the goddess with two pitchers of milk, now that Aatha had kept her part of the deal by delivering Zaheer from evil.

One option was to request Zaheer or Selvi to be her proxy and visit the temple to make the offerings. But she rejected the idea, as she feared that the goddess wouldn't compromise on the terms of the prayer …

Pankajam settled the issue.

'Remember: Mariamman didn't hold it against you that you converted to another faith, and she granted your prayers. So, why would you not reciprocate?' she argued.

'But, you are sure that Allah would not mind if I visited the temple?'

'*That* I won't know,' Pankajam said earnestly. 'In any case, you didn't think of it when you prayed to Mariamman.'

Thus it was that Anandhi decided to visit the temple on a Friday morning, armed with the pitchers of milk.

As she neared the temple, she couldn't shake off the gnawing fear that she might now be committing an Islamic sin. Imam had taught her that Islam did not permit idol worship. She had no trouble praying to Hindu idols at heart. That way, in her mind, the lines hadn't been crossed. Yet, going to the temple and offering *abhishekam* was clearly an act of transgression. She couldn't recall what the punishment prescribed in the Quran for this sacrilege was. In any case, she didn't want to take chances and decided to offer two *rak'ah*s in *Salaat al tawbah* for repentance. 'Let me also offer two pitchers of milk to the poor children at the *cherri*,' she mumbled to appease Allah. 'That should take care of everything,' she noted with satisfaction.

The priest at the temple was astonished to see Anandhi. He knew her well, never failing to chat with her every day or drink some tea when he wasn't busy with devotees. He was witness to her daily offering of appams, but had never invited Anandhi to come inside, respecting her restraint.

'You finally decided to thank your protector!' the priest exclaimed.

'No, I do that every day,' Anandhi said. 'This is a special thanks for a special favour done.'

As she walked back home, Anandhi's mind pieced together the story that she would tell Ahmed about her visit to the temple. While she had never lied to Ahmed as far as she could remember, it wasn't as if she had always spoken the whole truth. Her mind was busy excising and editing the events. It wasn't necessary to mention about Zaheer's infatuation for instance, but she would disclose her visit to the temple; it was fine to say that she had prayed, but she needn't get into the pots of milk …

She wondered what made her uncomfortable about sharing her dual faith with Ahmed. After all, he had never been very particular about religion. He had simply wanted the inconvenience of Anandhi's vermilion colour to remain invisible, from a practical point of view.

At the very thought of Ahmed, a cool shower of excitement rose from within that drenched her mind and body. Despite the growing years, her love for the man had never diminished. Aatha had been kind to her. Or, was it Allah? Subhanallah …

Anandhi was lost in thought when Selvi ran into her on the street. When she came face to face with Selvi, words were no longer necessary. Selvi had instantly transmitted her panic to Anandhi.

'Ahmed Periappa is writhing in pain. Severe chest pain,' Selvi said breathlessly.

'What? Why?' Anandhi shook her.

'Don't know. Zaheer is trying to help him. He wanted me to fetch you home immediately.'

'Allah!' Anandhi instinctively held out her palms.

As she hurried home, *tawba surah* spluttered through her lips.

The miasma of death wafted to her even before she entered the house.

Ahmed lay lifeless inside.

fourteen

Ahmed's death felled Anandhi.

Like the inaudible cry of the tree that is sawed off, Anandhi's grief screamed inside her while she sat motionless beside his body. She had falsely believed that she had stood tall and strong all by herself. But she had only twisted herself around Ahmed, like a hapless creeper over a mighty tree, and now she had fallen, cut and savaged, along with the tree.

Her feeling of utter vulnerability came as a shocking revelation to her.

'That's the thing about women,' Pankajam had told her once. 'We are zero, and we should simply accept that. We acquire value only with our men.'

'Nonsense,' Anandhi had said, dismissing the thought, 'that's simply slavishness.'

Now, at this moment, Anandhi felt that Pankajam was perhaps right. The integer was lying on the floor, and there she was, a heap of useless zeros ...

Neighbours were trickling in.

Unhinged faces and wailing voices began to float around her. Anandhi made no effort to connect or comprehend them.

A few ladies came and sat next to her, their copious tears flowing effortlessly as if a tap had been turned on. Job done, they quickly got up with dry eyes and made way for others. Anandhi did not hear them or see any of them. She was receding into herself, circling down into a black hole.

Zaheer was petrified at the sight of the lifeless body of Ahmed. He had seen dead bodies, but had witnessed for the first time, someone dying. Zaheer saw the mighty frame of Ahmed slowly grow limp and cold, while he kept shouting for his Periamma. He had been alone with Death. He saw Life getting drenched in sweat, fighting a losing battle with Death.

Zaheer wanted to unburden to Anandhi every detail of those dying seconds …

But Anandhi had not even looked in his direction.

Not since she entered the house to find Ahmed dead. When Zaheer ran to her screaming, she shook him off. Like swatting an irritating fly. That was the only movement from her in several hours. Zaheer could sense that she somehow held him responsible for the cruel twist of fate that had taken Ahmed away from her.

He felt crushed with that realization.

The stone-faced woman before him was not the loving aunt in whose sari folds he buried his face and smelt her sweat; not the one who could read hunger in his eyes and rushed to feed him; not the woman who dreamt his dreams.

This person was a stranger.

Zaheer felt suffocated. He wanted to cry until he had exhausted his anger and grief.

He moved to the front of the house and sat in a corner of the steps.

A dead fly lay on the floor, with one wing missing. Red ants were gathering around its carcass with a serious sense of purpose. The pall-bearer ants were conversing in small and big groups, finalizing their plans to transport the feast home. Watching the theatre of the ants was somehow soothing to his tortured mind.

Zaheer noticed that his parents and Ahmed's first wife had already arrived. He didn't know who had carried the news to them. The village was always very efficient in spreading news, rumours and scandals. Anandhi's tea shop was often the news desk but not the only one. Death was always high on priority, and trumped even adultery. The more unexpected the death, the higher its importance in the chain of gossip. People spoke about others' deaths with great curiosity and excitement, suitably cloaked in sorrowful words. Ahmed was an important man in the village, and his death was sudden. The news had spread with expected speed.

Ahmed's first wife had edged out Anandhi and had taken a position closer to the dead body of Ahmed. Her loud wailing was in sharp contrast to the motionless silence of Anandhi. She seemed keen to wrench back her claims on Ahmed's death, which she had lost during his life.

Zaheer's father completely ignored his presence.

'Yes, he was all alone at home ... it must have been a massive heart attack,' he heard his father say to someone.

No, he was not alone, Zaheer wanted to interject, but an odd and gnawing anger silenced him.

Ever since Ismail and his wife had moved to the adjacent village to look after the family farm, Zaheer had rarely seen them. He was virtually living in Anandhi's house. On the few occasions when he ran into his father at Salima Bivi's home, both felt as if a thick wall stood between them.

Zaheer could sense the minacious air around his father.

Someone said, 'You shouldn't delay the burial ... the dead have to reach *jannat* quickly.'

Zaheer had not witnessed any burial, and didn't wish to.

How do bodies buried under the ground travel to jannat, the Paradise, he wondered. He imagined Ahmed rising above the grave, like a slow rocket, his legs dangling in the air.

Would Ahmed Periappa be taken to jannat? Zaheer was doubtful. He was a good man, although he was a butcher, but he had never done namaz.

Zaheer remembered that Wazir Periappa had once described jannat, where delicious food was served in beautiful gardens. 'Ahmed Periappa will be clothed in green silk and brocade, but that can be boring, wearing the same colour every day, like a school uniform ...'

People he barely recognized were streaming in. He peeped in.

Anandhi was still motionless, but some life had returned to her eyes.

Ahmed (the living, and not the dead) was the only thought that filled Anandhi's mind. Despite nearly two decades of life together, it was the memory of her union with Ahmed at the orchard that kept coming back to Anandhi. In the recurrence of that memory, the mind was airbrushing the details, and sweeping away the darkness of the night.

A smile crossed her lips.

'Some people seem to *rejoice* in Ahmed's death,' Ismail said sharply, looking at Anandhi. He said this loudly.

There was a confused pause in the wailing.

With Ahmed gone, Ismail's animosity towards Anandhi (he could never accept her as Ayesha), which had always remained bottled up, now burst forth unchecked. Ismail had always considered Anandhi's entry into the family a pollutant, an affront to the family's imaginary pride. He was not impressed with Anandhi covering herself with hijab or her proficiency with the surahs. Her vermilion colour was always visible to him. More importantly, he held her squarely responsible for Zaheer's 'waywardness'. 'That was a big mistake, this marriage to that woman,' he would tell Salima Bivi. 'You should have never consented to it.' He and Salima Bivi found increasing affinity for each other (despite Ismail disappointing his mother on the religious department), given their shared dislike for Anandhi. Yet, Ahmed's care for the family and his financial contributions had effectively ensured that their critical view of Anandhi remained confined to them. Now, there was no need for any restraint.

Ismail got emboldened with the silence.

'Your sins ultimately catch up with you,' he said to someone.

'Yes, especially when you betray your religion,' the person replied. Anandhi looked up to identify the person, connect the sarcasm-laced voice to a face, but her tired mind gave up.

'He was a strong man, but his marriage was his undoing.'

There were more murmurs, but the details were no longer important. The mourners seemed to be arriving at the conclusion that Death had visited Ahmed only to punish Ahmed and Anandhi for their religious transgressions.

Anandhi felt the milky sentiment of sorrow, even if some of it was pretence, rapidly getting curdled, after Ismail showed the way.

Anandhi looked at Ismail blankly.

She was not surprised that the same people who had been respectful, even in fear of Ahmed when he was alive, were now discovering a new sense of courage to speak against him. She knew that her protective shield lay broken and lifeless next to her. She would now have to face the world alone.

As the thought sank in, curiously, she felt a strange sense of liberation.

Ayesha died.

The hyphenated existence of Anandhi–Ayesha collapsed like a tower of thin cards.

Anandhi silently prayed to a god who was beyond religions for her husband's soul to reach the heavens. Ahmed would of course take an Islamic journey and she drew comfort in the knowledge that Wazir would perform *Salat al janazah* with all sincerity. Anandhi knew the *takbirs*, which she had heard at every funeral of relatives in the family. But her god was no longer trapped in any identity.

Zaheer did not go to the mosque for the burial.

He stayed back, hoping to snatch the attention of Anandhi. In the relative privacy, he hoped she would explode with her agony, hug him and sob loudly. Zaheer had never seen her cry, but now he wanted her to cry aloud, so he could too.

But Anandhi had no such fancies. She continued to ignore Zaheer's presence. The vacant look had, however, given place to a hint of defiance. The journey with Ahmed was over, and along with it the green carriage to which she had hitched herself.

When Ismail returned from the mosque after the burial, Zaheer noticed a menacing swagger in his walk. He came with Wazir Periappa, but without Zaheer's mother.

Anandhi looked at Ismail from where she sat, with disdain.

Ismail's burst of bottled up anger had still not subsided.

'I hope you will learn not to meddle in others' families,' Ismail said, facing Anandhi.

There was no response from her, which only irritated Ismail further.

'You are a blot on our family,' Ismail carried on, 'a family that has always had noble traditions.'

Zaheer wanted to spit on his father. He had no right to offend Anandhi Periamma at this hour.

'That's a cruel thing to say,' Wazir Periappa interjected, 'Ayesha has always been a faithful member of the family.'

'If she had any respect for our family traditions, she wouldn't have snatched away my son and spoilt him.'

'I am not spoilt,' Zaheer spat out.

'You are following me,' Ismail said to Zaheer sternly. 'You no longer have a connection with this house.'

'No, I'm not coming, I hate you!' Zaheer shouted.

Zaheer looked at Anandhi with hope. She would push Ismail back … His Periamma knew him, his desire, his dance …

'You can take him,' Anandhi whispered slowly, still not looking at Zaheer, 'he is your son.'

fifteen

'That must have been a traumatic moment for you,' the Diva whispered, shaking her head gently, her eyes focused on the horizon, as if she were watching a tragic movie clip.

'Yes,' Zaheer nodded. 'I never imagined that Anandhi Periamma would cast me away like that!'

'Tsk tsk ...' the Diva clicked her tongue.

'So, you were returned to your green cage?'

Zaheer nodded.

'*Ghar wapasi*! Your father got you back under his control?'

'Yes, absolutely.'

'And your grandmother decided what to make of you?'

'I now wear a skullcap.'

'That must have been a double shock—losing the empathy of your Periamma, and reverting to the suffocating environment of your home. How did you manage during the last three years?' the Diva's expressions and the modulations of her voice were a classic lesson in communicating sympathy.

'I didn't know if I was alive or dead. There has been some respite since I joined college a few months ago.'

'And you killed your desire for dance?'

'No,' Zaheer said. 'I buried my desire. Like a treasure. To be retrieved when I can.'

The Diva nodded with understanding.

'And the knowledge of the hidden treasure consumes all my thoughts,' he added.

The Diva shifted her focus to polishing her toenails. Stroking each nail delicately and lovingly with the tiny brush of scarlet paint, she seemed to be silently conversing with her toes.

Job done satisfactorily, she lifted her gaze. She kept looking at Zaheer for a while. Her large sharp eyes seemed to penetrate right into his soul.

'And you feel it's now time to redeem your treasure?' the Diva asked.

'Yes,' he answered.

Zaheer was talking to the Diva, one of the shining stars of Bharatanatyam, at the hotel in Salem where she was staying.

The Diva was visiting Salem for a dance performance for SPIC-MACAY, an institution that was struggling to promote classical arts amongst college students, whose interest in the subject was almost nonexistent.

Zaheer's college, which hosted the event, was plastered with posters of the Diva. To Zaheer, there was always something mesmerizing about dancers in posters. They invariably grew a third dimension and came alive with movements, like a movie trailer ... *zaheer,* who had been hibernating for a while now, sprang into action at the very sight of the posters. 'Find a way to go and meet her,' *zaheer* urged, 'it could change your life.'

That wasn't difficult. The cultural secretary of the student body of the college, having secured the said position with the sole purpose of gaining legitimacy for skipping classes, was more than happy to let Zaheer attend on the Diva and bring her to the college. 'Just make sure that she mentions my name when she comes up to thank people at the end of the show,' he had said.

When Zaheer set his eyes on the Diva, as she descended from the train at the Salem station in the darkness that was lazily lifting at dawn, he felt the place being lit up suddenly, as if with a sparkler. The Diva, although short in stature, had a commanding personality. As if she had been especially made by the Creator to fulfil an order for supply of a Queen for the planet. And she seemed to know it. As Zaheer stumblingly introduced himself, the Diva acknowledged him with a half smile. 'Show me the way,' she said.

'Actually, *she* might show *you* the way!' *zaheer* whispered with excitement.

The performance was to take place later that evening.

By noon, Zaheer had managed to snatch enough time with the Diva to pour out his passion for dance, his struggle to pursue his dream and his resolve to become a dancing star. He had not quite planned it that way. The script was composing itself and squirting out whenever the Diva's attention turned to him. He wasn't even sure why he was narrating his story to her. The Diva was an indifferent listener, and she was being frequently distracted with the preparations for the evening.

'I want you to practice the upper octave well. Full-throated,' she instructed the musician in her troupe. 'Remember, music is meant to amplify emotive movements.'

'And make sure I get five rounds of jasmine strings latest by three in the afternoon, and they better be fresh,' she told someone who looked like her assistant.

'I can fetch the flowers,' Zaheer courteously volunteered.

'No, thanks,' she dismissed his offer. 'Only my assistant knows the blooms I like.'

Zaheer was happy he would have more time with her.

'Is this all really true?' the Diva asked sceptically, referring to Zaheer's story.

Zaheer felt irritated.

'It's the truth.'

As he was recounting his story, Zaheer realized that truth had many colours. He had to paint truth in the colours most appealing to the Diva.

He had told her proudly about his first public performance in his classroom, but felt too embarrassed to mention the subsequent humiliation from the school bullies; about the prize he won at the dance contest, and the thrashing from his father that came with it, but not his escape to Munoor; about Anandhi Periamma's inexplicable rejection, but not his own odd feeling of estrangement.

He told the Diva that the next three years, back with the parents, meant being returned to a family-prescribed lifestyle, but not the fact that he felt comfortable with his religion.

He told her that he accompanied his uncle to the mosque every day for his namaz, but not that *zaheer* was busy composing dance movements to suit the metre of the surahs. He told her that his father had insisted he do a diploma course in plastic engineering at the Salem college, but not that he was skipping on his meals, saving money to take secret dance lessons from a teacher that he was trying to find in Salem.

He hoped that the Diva would be sufficiently impressed to guide him.

The Diva got up to go.

Zaheer was disappointed. He wanted desperately to prolong the conversation.

At that moment, the Diva flashed a condescending smile.

'You may join me for lunch,' she said.

'No, thanks,' Zaheer said. 'This is the month of Ramzan.'

The Diva arched her eyebrows in surprise.

'Are you a devout Muslim?' she asked.

Zaheer asked himself the same question.

'I fast, but I don't eat meat!'

Did that make him a devout Muslim or not?

Fasting during Ramzan had become a habit by now, a ritual, like the namaz or the daily bath, but was this founded on faith?

In the past three years, he had inhaled unadulterated Islam at his home. Salima Bivi had passed away, but her presence still hung in the air. The family pretty much went about doing things exactly the way she would have demanded, even in her absence. Even the Urdu channel in the radio was turned on and off at the same time that Salima Bivi would have, when she was alive. Religion had grown over him like moss, and Zaheer had no doubt taken its colour.

'We don't choose our religion,' the Diva said, as if reading his mind. 'We are born infused with the religion of our parents.'

'You can meet me this evening after the event,' she added, and left.

The Diva's observation hung in his mind.

Religion was not one's choice. It was an inheritance. Was it a right, a hereditary right, like property? Was it a benediction, a blessing that one ought to feel grateful for?

'To shed the religion that you are born into, is to sin,' Pankajam had categorically told Anandhi, hinting that her friendship was actually an act of forbearance.

If it was a sin, what would you make of the Prophet and Christ, who had forsaken the faith they were born into?

'It is called Bharatanatyam, because the sage Bharata codified this dance form nearly eighteen hundred years ago. Now, why would a sage spend his life writing about dance?' the Diva paused for effect. 'Because, every movement in this art form has a spiritual connotation. "Natyam" means expressive dance,' the Diva elaborated, after presenting her first piece which, she said, was a prayer to Lord Ganesha.

The audience consisted predominantly of girl students, with a smattering of boys, who, Zaheer feared, had gathered there just to heckle. Bharatanatyam, to the young students, was incomprehensible and boring. 'Why couldn't these SPIC people get a good-looking actress?' the cultural secretary had exclaimed in anguish when he saw the programme schedule. On an earlier occasion, a classical musician who was once a leading artiste, had to abandon the concert and leave, not able to face the humiliating catcalls of uninterested students.

Zaheer looked anxiously at the group of boys hanging at the fringes. Almost every boy had a hungry look grazing on the girls, a few making progress with some meaningless mime.

Zaheer felt relieved that there was no sign of any trouble. He needed the Diva to be in a happy frame of mind when he would meet her after the performance.

'Bharatanatyam is not merely a classical dance form. It is a way of worship. Like offering flowers, like prostrating ... In fact, that's how the art developed and flourished in ancient times. At some point in history, almost every temple had a dedicated female dancer, called a devadasi, who remained married only to the Lord and not to any human. She danced in front of the Lord during the daily prayers. And, it was this community of devadasis, or *devar adiyals,* who preserved and developed this art form,' the Diva was rolling her eyes and moving her hands as though she were performing the narrative.

Zaheer quickly looked around on hearing the word 'devar adiyal'. He could relate the word, a colloquial and derogatory term denoting a prostitute. That statement could have easily been a trigger for some wolf whistles. Luckily, the distracted boys had not picked on the cue.

'But, then, the ritualistic dedication to the temple degenerated over the years,' the Diva continued. 'In some places, it was no more than a veneer to provide cover to a community of concubines patronized by wealthy landlords. The British, with their Victorian morals, thought it fit to ban the practice of dedication of devadasis, but it was only in 1947 that a legislation was passed in Madras state to ban the devadasi system. With the overhang of the threat of legislative ban, the art had begun to face extinction. Until it was brought out on public platforms, by Rukmini Devi, Balasaraswati and others.'

'How can a venerable art decay to such a state?' Zaheer asked the Diva, when they met later that evening.

'Art never decayed. Artists, just some of them, did,' the Diva clarified.

'Are art and the artist separable?'

'No. In fact, in the context of Bharatanatyam, even the divine is not separable from the art and the artist. But if they do separate, it is certain decay and death to the artist. Art, like the divine, is eternal,' the Diva replied.

The Diva's dance wasn't the kind that Zaheer was familiar with.

It wasn't like the fast numbers that he had watched in the movies. The glamour and glitter were surely missing. The art of dance in the movies had been like a noisy little fountain. The Diva's dance, on the other hand, was like a mighty river that embraced you with its cool, strong arms. When you surrendered to it, by the force of faith in its power to cleanse you and elevate you to another world, the sparkling waters simply rose up to prove your faith.

Zaheer felt overwhelmed by the majesty of Bharatanatyam.

As the Diva progressed with her performance, the students were getting drawn into the beauty of her expressions.

When the Diva, as a harried mother Yashoda, cajoled young Krishna to sleep, or when, with a quick swirl, she turned to being a mischievous boy stealing butter, the spectators could relate to those familiar themes, while being awed by the power of her communication. When she performed the *thillana,* the end piece, the complex rhythmic patterns of her tapping feet were breathtaking.

She took a bow with a standing ovation from the crowd.

Zaheer felt a sense of fulfilment he had never experienced earlier.

The Diva was back at the hotel.

Zaheer had to spend almost an hour in the small, crowded lobby waiting for the Diva to come down from her room. He was unconcerned, because *zaheer* was occupying his mind fully, trying to replay the intriguing beats of the thillana they had just witnessed.

There were a few others in waiting too, including, curiously, a lady police officer, a deputy superintendent of police. Her presence was perplexing. Zaheer had seen her photographs in the local newspapers and remembered that she had recently been posted as the DSP for the district. There was great excitement about a lady donning the post, and even more so, as she looked like a movie star who was *playing the role* of a police officer. She had a pretty face with carefully trimmed eyebrows. Her tight uniform defined a sculpted physique. She was an impossible mixture of grace and toughness that evoked a sense of wonder and awe.

The hotel manager, a picture of deep respect, was fawning over the police officer. The manager eventually uncovered the riddle of the officer's presence.

'You people might not know that DSP madam had learnt dance from the Diva before she joined the police force,' the manager proclaimed to the crowd in general, confident that the officer would be pleased with that announcement. And she was.

'That's a strange combination of interests!' Zaheer exclaimed. A few others joined in surprise.

'A police officer *and* a Bharatanatyam dancer?'

'Why? Is it not allowed by law?' the DSP asked mischievously.

'Generally, only some type of girls take to Bharatanatyam!' someone said hesitatingly, leaving the definition of 'the type' to imagination.

'And I am not a Brahmin, if that's what you mean,' the DSP chuckled. 'You expect to see only Brahmin dancers and non-Brahmin police officers!'

'Why does it have to be so?' Zaheer wondered aloud.

'*Because society favours stereotypes.* Probably, casting stereotypes made it simpler to manage a society in the past, but it makes no sense now,' the officer said. 'Mercifully, our gods are anything but stereotypes! Goddess Durga is a warrior woman, who relishes fine clothes and jewellery! And she isn't a Brahmin!' There was defiance in her voice.

'But, madam, isn't the order of gods different to that for humans?' This was the disturbed voice of a temple priest, who was also waiting to meet the Diva. He was carrying a plate of garlands, a broken coconut and a stainless-steel container.

'Are you from Tiruchengode temple?' the DSP asked the priest. This did not require great police intelligence, as the priest was carrying a cloth carry-bag with the temple name written all over it.

Tiruchengode was not very far from Salem. Zaheer remembered that Anandhi Periamma had wanted to take him to the temple there, but the trip had never materialized.

'Yes,' the priest confirmed. 'The Diva is very devoted to Lord Ardhanareeswara. I am carrying *prasadam* from the temple.'

'Ardhanareeswara is half male and half female, a very profound concept,' the DSP observed, 'And, by the way, not a stereotype.'

'Indeed! It symbolizes the union of *Purusha* and *Prakriti*; the union of the creative energy, the female power, with the all-pervasive space of the universe, the male power,' the priest said. He followed this with a rapid recitation of some verses in Sanskrit, which, of course, nobody understood.

'It's more than that,' the DSP said. 'In every living being, there is something of the masculine and something of the feminine. We are classified as man or woman based on the dominance of the proportions, but the Creator, and on the whole, the universe, is evenly balanced.'

Zaheer felt a new door swing open in his mind.

Like everyone else, like the DSP, he too was a mixture.

They all sprang up as the Diva sailed into the lobby.

Everyone who had come to meet the Diva had left. Except the DSP and Zaheer.

Zaheer noticed that the Diva and the DSP seemed to talk in two different languages: the Diva formal and polite, the DSP warm and respectful.

Zaheer was happy that the Diva chose to keep him till the last, along with the DSP.

'That was a splendid performance,' Zaheer said with genuine admiration.

'As always! Nothing less can be expected,' the DSP added.

'I am glad you liked it,' the Diva told Zaheer, ignoring the DSP. 'The whole purpose, as you know, was to get our youth to discover the beauty of our ancient art.'

'I feel more excited than ever to throw away everything else and take to Bharatanatyam!'

The DSP turned a surprised eye at Zaheer. Till then, she had believed that Zaheer was just doing his duty as a host for the function.

'Have you had your dinner?' the Diva asked Zaheer.

'No. I was waiting to see you.'

'But you are fasting. Aren't you supposed to eat by dusk?'

She opened the stainless-steel container the temple priest had left behind.

'Eat this, you must be hungry,' she held out a spoonful of sweet kesari.

Zaheer eagerly took it in his palms. The DSP politely declined when it was offered to her.

'Ramzan fast being broken by the holy offerings from a Hindu temple!' the Diva chuckled. 'Do you see a contradiction?'

'No,' Zaheer said. 'I see a connection.'

'Well, it's an extraordinary demonstration of inter-faith respect!' the DSP noted. She spoke, no doubt with the experience of having to deal with sporadic sparks that flew on inter-faith matters within her jurisdiction.

The Diva nodded. She waited silently until Zaheer finished eating.

'How do you want me to help you?'

Zaheer had not thought this through. The Diva had appeared to him as someone from the 'other world' who could show him the way, perhaps, give him the key, perhaps hold his hand and lead him to that other world. He realized he was unprepared for the question.

'Do you see a problem in my aspiration to be a dancer?' Zaheer asked.

'A Bharatanatyam dancer?'

Zaheer paused for a while.

'To be honest, I did not have any knowledge or clarity on this, until I saw your performance this evening. Now, I know I want to be a Bharatanatyam dancer. Desperately ... Do you think it's a problem because I am a man?' Zaheer asked.

'No, not at all. Every male god is an inveterate dancer!' the Diva laughed. 'Can we forget Siva, who dances all the while? Krishna dances on the head of a serpent; Vishnu dances to seduce Siva.'

'Yes, I know. But the laws for gods and humans appear to be different!'

'That could be a statement born out of sheer confusion or profound clarity,' the Diva laughed again. 'You are at an age when it's difficult to make out!'

'There are many male dancers, even now. Many famous ones, like Dhananjayan, Narasimhachari,' the DSP assured Zaheer.

'Like Kamal Haasan.'

'Well, he is primarily an actor. I am naming those who are dedicated stage performers.'

'So, what's the problem?'

The Diva looked at him straight.

'The problem is—you are a Muslim,' the Diva paused, perhaps feeling awkward with her own truthfulness. 'A practising Muslim, who observes the Ramzan fast. I like you for respecting your religion. But, to me, Bharatanatyam is a form of worship. When you are singing and dancing in praise of Krishna, you are not acting. You are simply emoting your devotion in public.'

'That might be true of the artiste, but not the audience,' Zaheer said. 'How can it be a worship if the audience doesn't participate in it?'

'The true purpose of this art is to lift the observer to experience the divine.'

'So you dance only to a Hindu audience?'

'Ordinarily, yes, perhaps that's why the art form has never managed to cross religious lines.'

'That's not true! Everyone watches a movie and they enjoy the dances.'

'But that's not Bharatanatyam. Not the pristine form anyway, and it doesn't meet the objective of the art form.'

'You are saying that Bharatanatyam is an exclusive Hindu property?'

'At least, it was originally so. Have you been to Srirangam?'

'No,' Zaheer said. 'I've always wanted to go. I believe the god there is very fond of poetry.'

'He is even more fond of dance; the priests sing and dance to the Lord as part of their worship.'

'Male priests dance?'

'Yes, as I told you, dance is a form of Hindu worship.'

Zaheer kicked a protest inside Zaheer.

Dance had always fascinated Zaheer. His love of dance had occupied the core of his being. Religion was no more than a costume to him; Hindu, sometimes in the company of Anandhi Periamma, and Islam, when he was at his parents' home. Was he required to choose one religion over the other, because of the art he had chosen to pursue?

'There is, of course, no law that non-Hindus can't do Bharatanatyam,' the Diva said, 'but, *a non-believer can't connect to the soul of the art, and that will show.*'

'Will there be teachers willing to teach me?'

'Yes, for sure. But a Muslim dancing Bharatanatyam will look fake.'

'Fake?'

'Sorry, that was a wrong word,' she retracted. 'Let's just say that it's not the most appropriate thing to do.'

Suddenly, Zaheer felt his respect for the Diva melt away. He got up to leave.

'But you should learn Bharatanatyam. Because, even for dancing in films, it's useful,' the Diva called out after him.

Zaheer was surprised that the DSP offered to drop him at his hostel. He was in a sombre mood as he sat silently beside the DSP who was now driving, after instructing the driver to take the rear seat.

'I can relate to your passion for dance,' the DSP said.

'Thanks.'

'What did you think of the Diva's advice?' the DSP asked.

Zaheer thought for a while. 'Dance—and now, specifically Bharatanatyam—is a such a consuming obsession, no obstacles cross my vision, and no argument against it enters my ears,' he said.

'But what fascinates you? The grace of the movements, the art form, the feminine beauty or just being under the arc lights on stage?'

Zaheer had not searched deep into his interest. It was perhaps all of what the DSP listed.

'Do you really need to clinically analyse every emotion?' he asked.

'No,' she conceded. 'Emotions need not be subject to rational scrutiny, but if you can analyse, it might make choosing easier.'

'I am scared to unwrap this passion, break down this beautiful feeling, as if it were some chemical compound.'

'Very well! Just follow your passion then,' the DSP said. 'That's all that matters.'

Zaheer felt relieved.

'You don't consider a Muslim man dancing Bharatanatyam "fake"?'

'Nonsense!' the DSP said. 'Look, I greatly respect the Diva, her mastery over the art and, indeed, everything she has achieved. But I don't agree with some of her conservative views.'

'You don't think that Bharatanatyam is a form of Hindu worship?'

'It has also been an expression of female sexuality sometime in its history.'

'The Diva might disagree.'

'Well, the art form has been used to convey Hindu prayers. Like a language. Like Sanskrit has been used for Hindu prayers, Persian for Islam. But that's just the medium, not the message.'

'Isn't Sanskrit a Hindu language?'

'It's a language extensively used in the Hindu religion, yes, but I can't agree that it's *owned* by any one religion. No faith can own a medium. Some of the most scathing atheist literature is in Sanskrit,' the DSP said.

'Can you help me find a guru in Salem?' Zaheer asked hesitantly.

The DSP did not answer directly.

'I heard you say that you will give up everything for the sake of Bharatanatyam. Does that include your education?'

'Yes. I am not in the least interested in becoming a plastic engineer.'

'Hmm … Does this disinterest extend to your family?'

'Yes.'

'You would pursue Bharatanatyam even if your parents opposed it?'

'Most certainly!'

The DSP turned to him, astonished by the resolve in his voice.

'You obviously don't have a very happy home!' she remarked with amazing shrewdness.

Zaheer did not respond.

'I can see the depth of your passion,' she continued. 'I suggest you go to the very best teachers, provided you can afford them.'

'And who would they be?'

'I can think of a couple of names. But the guru has also to accept a disciple. And that's not easy. You might need to try your luck with a few.'

'I am ready.'

'I think you should learn from someone who's liberal-minded ... Someone who sees beyond the societal boundaries of the art form. Have you heard of Sivakami Kameswaran?'

Zaheer remembered the posters. The three-dimensional, dancing posters ...

'I saw some announcements that she is coming to Salem for a performance soon.'

'Yes, she could be the guru you are searching for. But she lives in Madras.'

Madras.

To the young in the villages, it was the Promised Land, a place where a myriad dreams became real, where illusions and reality were inextricably intertwined ...

They rode silently until they reached the college hostel.

sixteen

'Young's modulus is the stiffness of a solid material. It defines the relationship between stress, that is force per unit area, and strain proportional deformation in a material in the linear elasticity regime of a uniaxial deformation ...' the lecturer was droning on.

It was the day following the dance event.

Zaheer was hearing the lecture.

'Linear elasticity of a uniaxial deformation ...' Zaheer slowly repeated the words to himself. The words rolled sensuously on his tongue. Nice phonetics. He didn't know what any of it meant nor did he care.

'Li-ni ar ..., Li- ni -ar ... Tak kita, tak kita.'

'El -aas - ti- ci-tee ... el -aas - ti - ci-ty ... Ta-laan- gu- taka, Ta-laan-gu- taka.'

Zaheer smiled with satisfaction. *Tak kita ... Thalangu taka ... Tak kita ...* The rhythmic syllables were weaving themselves into every word that the lecturer was uttering. Zaheer was now notating the lecturer's words almost simultaneously. And he could watch *zaheer* executing dance movements in lock step with the rhythm. He was enjoying the fascinating game ...

Zaheer was discovering rhythmic patterns in every noise that he heard around him. In the thumping of the rubber slippers of the man walking down the corridor, in the cawing of the solitary crow on the tree outside the classroom window, in the cough of the boy behind him …

As the day progressed, *zaheer* was beginning to get restless. 'What are you waiting for? You don't belong here.'

The next class on algebra and trigonometry was reinforcing *zaheer*'s message: 'Think, think … Has quadratic equation brought joy to anyone, ever? Is there any romance in cos theta, sine theta?'

The decision was rapidly and clearly coming together.

No fuzziness. None.

Decision to cast away plastic engineering. Like an ill-fitting, useless shirt.

Decision to take to dancing … to become a world-famous dancer, no less …

At times, he was weighed down by fear of the decision; at other times, he felt a surge of energy …

Zaheer had played out in his mind the scene of the prospective meeting with his father. His mother would continue to be in the background, like a stage screen. The sort of painted canvas screen that had patiently witnessed several plays, overheard many anecdotes, with no role to play.

The meeting would have to be brief. Business-like.

Zaheer would allow no small talk. Not that his father was a great conversationalist—in any case, not with him.

Zaheer would announce that he had decided to quit the diploma course, bid farewell to his college (would he have to disclose that he had kept back the semester fees, sold all his books, collected some more money?), and intended to move to Madras and earn a living there.

'Doing what?' his father would ask.

He would have to concoct a story about a friend ('You don't know him, he is my senior'), promising a job in Madras ('His father runs a pharmacy, no, no ... er ... a textile business'), because he was very impressed with Zaheer's sharp mind and business skills ('Yes, yes, he is a Muslim, very rich and respected'). 'Abba, you have been so kind, and I don't want to be a burden to you any longer,' he would finish off with this difficult but necessary statement.

He had to get it all out in one breath. Better to tackle the force of his father's reaction summarily, rather than in instalments.

He would make the announcement in a humble, but confident tone ('should remember not to overdo, lest the lie shows').

'I am proud of your confidence, son, that's what is most important.' Zaheer tried to imagine his father saying those wonderful words, but the image eluded him. He suspected that his father's facial muscles did not lend themselves to a happy smile or a kind expression, nor his eyes designed for love.

The announcement was more likely to turn his father violent. The usual thrashing could follow. Would he use his belt, like the last time? Well, that would depend on the time of day. When his father was at home with his lungi tied around his waist, just below his large protruding belly, he managed his modesty deftly even without a belt.

Zaheer wouldn't attempt to dodge the blows. He would receive them stoically, like a man.

He would pause for a day or two, and when things calmed down a bit, he would bring up the subject of money. He needed to work out his strategy carefully.

Zaheer did not want to encourage any thoughts towards the probability that he might fail to convince his father about his course of action. He needed his father's money to support him until he became a star—which he had no doubt he would.

There was simply no other option.

Except Anandhi Periamma.

In the years that followed Ahmed's death, there had been no contact with her. She was no longer running her shop. The village news that trickled down to him was that she had gone to the neighbouring village to live with her sister.

'If Periamma is the only option left, should I not make peace with her,' he said to himself.

But he also knew that he would not be able to bear another act of rejection from her. Anandhi Periamma would have to remain a closed chapter in his life.

It was when he was about to leave the college for the bus station that Zaheer came across the letter.

He had gone to check the mail board in the pigeonhole earmarked for him. Even though he had never received a single letter, he checked anyway, out of habit.

Today, a postal envelope, with the address in his father's handwriting, awaited him.

Zaheer opened the envelope with curiosity.

It was a short letter.

... I have a few former students of mine, who are your seniors in the college. I understand from them that you were seen in the company of some dancer woman a few days ago.

I want you to know that if you ever attempt to return to your waywardness, I'll be very angry. I have spent a lot of money to educate you at the college and I want you to concentrate on your studies, become an engineer and make a decent living. You owe this to your family.

Affectionately,
Abba

P.S. By the way, I have married a lady, a very nice person, in a simple nikah last Friday. I did not want to disturb you from your studies. When you come during your vacation, you will meet her and find her a very loving person.

Zaheer immediately sat down to reply, even as he crushed his father's letter in anger. His reply was even shorter:

I am determined to be a dancer. I propose to leave college to pursue my interest. You will hear of me when I become famous. Until then, don't come after me and waste your time.

He didn't sign the letter.

He read it again. He scored out '*propose to leave*' and wrote '*I have left*'.

He read it once again, underlined '*don't come after me*' and folded the letter.

~

'One ticket to Madras,' Zaheer told the clerk at the ticket counter at the bus stand.

PART II

The Faith of Dance

I am *zaheer.*

Yes, you know me. I am the spirit inhabiting Zaheer.

The dancing spirit. Or, the spirit that dances.

The 'spirit': '*That which is independent of the body, and unpossessed by thought, that which is unscorched by heat and unfrozen by cold, that which is neither substance nor nothing, that which is neither past nor future, that which is ...*' Let's cut it out.

That which knows only dance. O N L Y D A N C E.

At the very moment when Zaheer boarded the bus to Madras, shedding his troublesome past like moulted skin, when he was fully de-tethered from his relationships, when there was no force to suppress my being and no compulsion to deny my existence, I was finally out.

And, at that very moment, the need for the dual existence of Zaheer and *zaheer* ceased.

I, *zaheer,* have fully subsumed Zaheer in me, and, quite naturally therefore, taken control of this story. As I fluttered to launch my flight into the blue skies from my constricting cocoon, I was in awe of my own splendorous wings.

seventeen

'*You stand no chance,'* Kumar told me emphatically.

This, he said, as he dissolved into the darkness of the stationary railway carriage, which we had both boarded to spend the night in.

Sorry, I am getting ahead of myself... I should begin the story at the beginning, with title credits—screenplay, actors, et al.

I should first introduce Kumar properly.

I should also explain why you'd find me sleeping in a *railway carriage,* when I had boarded a *bus* to Madras (Yes, it was still Madras, hadn't yet been indigenized as Chennai), if you recall, when we met in the last chapter.

Well, I omitted to tell you that, before I left the college, in a rare flash of smartness, I had chosen to write to Karimullah (also called *Kari* or *Curry,* the etymology of which might have had reference to his dark colour or his craving for meat curry), my classmate from school, who was now studying at New College in Madras. Anyone who went to study in Madras had already climbed a few steps in the ladder of esteem in the minds of the village folks.

I had shared a desk with Karimullah for a couple of years in school and I assumed that he owed me a debt of gratitude for all the roasted groundnuts stolen from Anandhi Periamma's shop that I had fed him over those years. I must record that at the time this was an entirely voluntary act of kindness, with no expectation of return of any kind. I also hoped he would remember that, sitting next to me, he had copied my maths answer paper substantially, which act of crime had enabled him to pass his seventh class, although he had chosen to trivialize my contribution then.

Despite these acts of magnanimity, Karimullah was not particularly close to me, but he was the only one I knew who lived in Madras. Or rather, the only one in Madras who knew me. I had warned him that I was going to depend on him to support me for a few weeks, until I found a job and a place to live (I hadn't yet shared with him my desire to pursue dance). I gave him no time to respond and no option to consider. Moreover, I had heard that Karimullah's uncle was an important functionary of the ruling party, and that, I assumed, placed him in an unassailable position of influence.

I had a hundred and twenty-three rupees on me (savings from my monthly allowances + the term fees that I had not paid + proceeds from the sale of my textbooks—remember, they were relatively untouched). I had counted it so many times that the sweaty smell of the currency notes had penetrated the skin of my index finger and came through my nostrils. But I had no idea how long this wealth would last me in an unknown city, nor how I would find a guru or fund my dance lessons.

Karimullah turned out to be just the crutch I needed.

He was lodging at the BC Students' Hostel in Kodambakkam, the BC standing for Backward Classes. It was a government-run hostel, intended to provide subsidized hostel accommodation to students belonging to Backward Classes, which were government-notified caste groupings. (It was never clear to me how some Muslims were considered backward and others forward, and whether I was backward or forward.)

The hostel consisted of a large hall, where students slept on their own beds on the floor, an open yard with several taps for people to wash out the dirt (if your bathing spot was closer to the drain, your feet were licked tenderly by the soapy river from the lucky bathers upstream) and a few toilets that were condemned to remain filthy forever. Every brick and piece of wood in the crumbling structure appeared to ensure that the students were left in no doubt that *they were truly backward.*

Karimullah reluctantly agreed to let me stay with him at the hostel for a few days, provided I would 'take care' of the warden.

The warden was a natural entrepreneur. He was running his own enterprise, letting unauthorized boarders like me (who often outnumbered the authorized ones) to stay in the hostel. He had unpublished tariffs for night stay, for buying food from the canteen and for use of the common toilet. He kept reminding us that he believed in honesty, even if we thought he was bilking. 'Even if you break the rules, you have to do it honestly,' he would say righteously. (To prove his point, he even returned two rupees fifty paise to me that I had paid in excess for my meals.)

There was one piece of nuisance though. There would be periodic 'surprise' inspections of the hostel by a government official, (who understandably gave adequate notice of such surprises) and whenever such notices arrived, we, the warden's customers, were required to vacate the premises immediately and spend the night elsewhere.

It was in one of those nights, that I met Kumar, a fellow stowaway.

Kumar was an adult of uncertain age. He had an emaciated body that betrayed several years of malnourishment but had a young face with sharp eyes. He was an errand boy at a film studio in Kodambakkam, the Kollywood town. (Everyone in Kodambakkam seemed to work for the film industry.) Kumar didn't talk about his family, but one got the impression that it wasn't a pleasant story. He was enormously well informed. Not merely about films and film stars (of which he was an encyclopaedia unto himself), but just about everything. For example, he knew how to adulterate coffee powder with ground tamarind seeds without any adverse effect to the taste. He could lucidly explain the complex economics of lottery schemes. He even knew what punishments were given by the courts for various categories of cheating.

Kumar was the one who took me to the Egmore railway station on one of those 'inspection nights' when we had to make ourselves scarce from the hostel. He knew which carriages were left unlocked in trains that were parked overnight at the station.

'The last rake in this train, Thoothukudi Express, is the best, because the compartments have Rexine covers on the berths, and we can sleep without any disturbance,' he explained, as he executed a deft manoeuvre to climb on to the train, filmi style.

'We have to wake up at 4 a.m. though. That's when the cleaners will get in. If you still feel sleepy, I'll show you where to go, but I suggest you finish your toilet business, because the public toilets at the station are cleaned just about that time,' he said.

Kumar seemed like a perfect guide to navigate the way forward with my life.

Have you ever seen the Railway Guide? The thick book with thin yellow and pink pages that has the schedule of all trains, departure and arrival times, stations, etc.? Kumar looked to me the human equivalent, who could tell me how to reach my destination in life.

I enthusiastically described to him my dream.

'Bharatanatyam?' he asked incredulously. 'Why, why?'

Instead of answering him directly, I let my silence convey that the subject was not up for discussion. 'Just tell me how I can get to learn,' I snapped.

That's when he made the declaration: '*You don't stand a chance*!'

We both had settled on the berths of a sleeper-class carriage. He took his berth in the compartment next to mine. ('Think big. Have the whole compartment to yourself.') The bogey was stationed far away from the platform, and had doors with broken locks. Unlike the BC hostel, where you couldn't stretch your hand in the bed without striking your neighbour, here you were the king of all you surveyed, although you couldn't survey much in a dilapidated third-class compartment, even less in semi-darkness. But, quite honestly, I found the place immensely more comfortable than the hostel. In fact, I wondered why this couldn't be a permanent arrangement.

The eyes were slowly pulling out the contours of objects from the blinding darkness, when Kumar spoke again, through the compartment partition: 'You don't stand a chance, because you fail on *all three* counts!'

'What three counts?'

'You should be a *female* or *a Brahmin* or *rich*. You fail on all three.'

'Who has laid this rule?'

'No one has. But that's the way it works.'

'About time someone breaks this rule!'

Kumar remained silent for a while. I thought he had gone to sleep.

Suddenly, he broke into a torrent of words, spoken in the sing-song tone peculiar to the orthodox Brahmin community.

'You don't sound authentic,' I said.

'Now you see?' he said. 'You can make out that I don't get the Brahmin lingo correct. That's what will happen when you attempt to dance Bharatanatyam. Because Bharatanatyam is the language of the Brahmins. Like Carnatic music. You will never get it right.'

'I have heard this before.'

'And think about the money. Do you know how much the costumes alone cost? At least two thousand rupees! Is that forty times the cost of your Deepavali dress? Yes, something like that … And you need at least two per show. Then there's the orchestra … I am told you also have to pay the Sabhas to get a slot to perform. Huh! And you are aspiring to be a Bharatanatyam dancer? My friend, this is a sport for the rich!'

His words hurt, although my ears were shut.

I stayed quiet for a long time.

'So, what do you suggest?' I asked meekly.

I heard a light snore in response.

I repeated the question to Kumar at five in the morning, when we were sipping tea from paper cups.

'This is the best time to have tea from this tea stall,' he said, ignoring my question. 'Till four, its old milk and old tea; between four and five, it's old milk and new tea, and at five, it's new milk and new tea,' he said, as he slurped the syrupy liquid noisily.

It was when we were travelling back to Kodambakkam in the local train (ticketless; the railways didn't have enough inspectors to deploy this early in the day), that he chose to reply.

'Listen, you are very young and getting everything mixed up in your mind,' he said. 'Have you considered that you have to eat, sleep and live first?'

I didn't respond.

'Be practical. You need to find a job first and earn some money, and a place to sleep, before you can even dream of Bharatanatyam.'

I nodded. He had paid for my tea.

'I will take you to our film studio today,' he said in a condescending voice.

'I'd love that! But what has that to do with my getting a job?'

'Well, every day there are several group dance shoots. Sometimes one or two artistes don't turn up. If you are lucky, you might land a chance to be recruited on the spot.'

'Thank you, that's wonderful!' I said. 'You mean I could appear in some movies?'

'Don't assume anything. You have to be a member of the Film Dancers Union to get a place in the group. I am just hoping there is some temporary work, so that you can earn something!'

Periazhwar was furious.

'If you need to host the Lord in your heart, first sweep away unsuitable tenants like jealousy, anger ...' Sukhi sang, despite knowing that she was not a good singer.

'Will you stop your stupid song?' Periazhwar screamed.

He held out the garland of tulsi leaves in front of him, his hands shaking with fury.

'Every day, at dawn, I go straight after self-purification, to the sacred garden and pluck the tulsi leaves chanting His name, so that the leaves joyously and effortlessly separate from the stem, at the exciting prospect of adorning His shoulders and nestling on His chest! And then a mere sinful mortal has the temerity to seize the garland and wear it? How much more debased could this sinner be?' Periazhwar's voice choked.

'Godha, were you asleep when the sinner sneaked into the house? Were you in a trance when the sinner flung it on his ugly chest?'

'What is the problem, Appa?' Godha asked calmly, as she stirred the pot of milk.

'Problem? This is a disaster! Look at this, look, look!' Periazhwar held out a strand of hair.

Godha came close and examined the hair.

'Oh this! It's only a stray hair from my head, not from any stranger!' Godha said casually.

'I've always warned you—girls from good families never leave their hair loose,' Sukhi chimed in.

'You mean, you mean, you wore the garland, before you gave it to me?' Periazhwar was aghast.

'Yes, of course!' Godha said with surprise. 'Every day I wear it first to make sure it is soft on the skin and has a good fall. Actually, today the garland came out beautifully!'

Periazhwar collapsed on the floor.

'Oh! My Lord, I know You'll never, ever forgive me for this sacrilege. Not even if I roll on the rough floor around Your sanctum a hundred times,' Periazhwar sobbed uncontrollably.

'Appa, you make it seem as if Krishna is a conceited, arrogant tyrant. It only means you don't yet know Him! You are not a true bhakta.'

Periazhwar looked at his daughter with awe and shock.

eighteen

Anonymity is a great liberator.

Madras proved to be my place of liberation.

The BC Hostel felt like my kingdom. I ate awful food (tastebuds, pampered by Anandhi Periamma, remained in revolt), I slept breathing the malodour of my neighbours and I closed my eyes and held my breath in filthy toilets.

And yet, I was savouring the sweet taste of independence. My mind was singing the song of freedom. My dance was my language of liberty.

But creative artists can't be confined for long to the pleasures of singing privately in their bathrooms. Nor can freedom be their only need. There is something even more critical to their nourishment: approbation. Artists crave it. When a few hundred pairs of eyes are fixed on you in admiration, the energy it imbues you with is beyond measure. A stage actor had said as much in an interview: 'If I don't get under the arc lights on any evening, I suffer withdrawal symptoms.' Yes, the stage is an addiction.

~

I kept replaying the question the DSP had asked me: What was it about dance that held a fascination for me?

Initially, it was just the beauty of the artiste. When Vyjayanthimala or Padmini danced, I was mesmerized by their looks. Beauty didn't come to me, tagged to a gender. That sense of beauty I felt was plucking at my spiritual chords, not my senses, not my body.

With more exposure, I realized that the art form was also beginning to make sense to me, then it had me intrigued, and soon, without me being aware of it, had me totally captivated.

Then I began to experience a new desire. When the Diva stood onstage with folded hands, bending with humility and grace, acknowledging the ovation, I desperately wanted to be her.

It was Beauty and it was also Fame. And I needed the Freedom to be what I wanted to be.

I did not think these thoughts when I entered the film studio with Kumar.

~

It was an untidy and chaotic hall under a tin shed. Far from my image of a film studio.

A bulky, uncouth man sat overflowing from a small leather chair. A rickety pedestal fan stood beside him, spewing wind on his face, with angry sounds coming out from its bowels of worn-out bearings.

'This is the dance master,' whispered Kumar. I later learnt that he had been a successful dancer in his heyday, morphing into a dance master after he amassed weight around his waist. 'He is lucky. Most older dancers get ejected in a few years and end up as sweepers,' Kumar said.

There were about twenty dancers, male and female ('extras' they were called, leaving them in no doubt about their dispensability), standing in rows facing the dance master. While the females seemed to answer (more or less) to a standard template of body contours, the males came in all shapes and sizes, their eyes betraying their failure to realize their original dream of becoming movie heroes.

There were at least twenty others on the sets, who didn't appear to have any defined role. ('Extra extra,' Kumar called them. 'That's where you'll begin if you are lucky.')

'Where are the cameras?' I asked.

'This is just a rehearsal. Shooting is not due for another three hours,' he said.

That explained why all the dancers were in their everyday clothes.

'One, one two three. One ...' The dance master was tapping his feet and swinging his arms, without moving his huge bottom from the chair.

'What is he doing?' I asked, although I almost knew the answer.

A younger, leaner specimen of the dance master was translating the numerals into dance movements through some mysterious communication. 'His son,' Kumar whispered.

'Start!' the master's son commanded.

The dancers executed the manoeuvre with utter boredom and with synthetic smiles.

'Once more,' he shouted.

More boredom and more synthetic smiles.

In between the several 'once mores', and between several pauses for no obvious reasons, the dance master got up laboriously and walked into the formation. He held a male dancer with an obstinate paunch by the collar. 'Just as I suspected,' he hissed. 'You are reeking of last night's cheap liquor! Get lost!'

The dance master kicked the man in the shin, as he staggered and rolled on the floor.

Instantly, an extra extra jumped in his place, graduating to being an extra. Though he looked no less drunk.

'You!' the master shouted at another woman in the back. The unspoken, obscene word that moved his lips following the 'you' was effectively communicated. 'If you make another mistake, you are out. Forever,' he shouted.

'One, one two three, one. One, one two three, one. One, one two three, one ...'

'Where's the music?' I asked.

'No music. That will be superimposed later,' Kumar replied.

'That's like our PT class in school,' I said. 'At least, we didn't have to smile.'

After an hour or so, the master appeared satisfied. The mechanical motions (with the synthetic smiles, now wider by command) had been mastered.

'I think some of them still haven't got their steps right,' I ventured.

Kumar looked at me with amusement.

'How many movies have you watched?'

'May be fifty or sixty?'

'And seventy to eighty group dances?'

'Yes, of course.'

'And can you remember any one face from the group from any of those dances?'

'No.'

'When the leading lady is dancing, do you watch her or the extras at the back?'

'Well, of course the leading lady!'

'That's it. Beyond a point, nobody cares. These people provide just the backdrops for the leading lady or man, an animated screen, if you will.'

It was easy to understand the reason for their lack of enthusiasm.

Kumar had a strong network of contacts, as became clear to me watching him talking to a number of people on the studio floor for a long time. A couple of times, he would point towards me. It was evident that he was canvassing for a place for me. When he returned from his confabulations, he looked very pleased with himself.

'Everything arranged,' he said triumphantly. 'You will need to pay some money upfront, but that can be arranged as a loan. Somewhat high interest, but that's all right.'

'Arranged what?'

'Extra, extra.'

'*I'm not interested,*' I said.

Kumar was confounded.

'But you have to begin there. Eventually, you could get to be a member of the union. And you could really become an extra.'

'I'm not interested,' I repeated, this time more firmly.

'But why?' Kumar asked with unconcealed anger.

I did not know why. But I knew that what I witnessed wasn't anywhere near the colour of my dream.

'Can you dump your goddamn idea of Bharatanatyam, that elitist, rubbish, snobbish sport?' Kumar shouted.

'No,' I said.

'No?'

'No!'

Kumar stormed away.

He was a survivor who had learnt the skill to ride the ferocious waves of the world and stay alive. He was a combative rat that knew its place was in the hidden corners of the gutter, away from the glare, celebrating triumph with survival.

He did not understand the mind of a mad man insistent on swimming against the current, dreaming of riding the wave on his own terms.

nineteen

I don't know how Kari fixed it, or even why, but the job of a bill clerk at the Farhan Hotel (actually a restaurant) was arranged within a week after I disclosed to him that I had been skipping breakfast to save money.

Karimullah acted promptly.

No doubt, he rushed to have me fixed on a job (I presume his powerful uncle had a benevolent hand in the matter), entirely out of self-interest. To protect himself from a potential parasite.

'I don't understand you,' Kari shrugged his shoulders. 'Which mad guy will run away from the comfort of a home hoping, of all things, to be a dancer with no idea how?'

After a pause, he said with uncharacteristic firmness: 'But, that's up to you. Don't expect me to help you anymore.'

With that, he signalled that he had squared off his schoolday debt of gratitude for the groundnuts and copying.

I grudgingly admitted to myself that my passion for dance would have to concede to my hungry stomach for now: a job, any job, was urgently needed.

~

People who came to pray at the Mubarak Masjid never failed to show up at the adjacent Farhan restaurant for their favourite biryani or paya curry. They came before the namaz, after the namaz, and they always came with king-sized appetites. It was difficult to say what held the primacy of interest for them—masjid or the restaurant.

The tables, with green laminate tops, that carried turmeric stains and printed designs of yellow flowers in one indistinguishable pattern, were always full. It was perfectly normal for total strangers to share a table, silently conducting mini territorial wars with their plates and cups. On busy Fridays, people waiting for their turn to get a table would stand in clusters just outside the restaurant on the busy Mount Road, with their white '*sangu mark lungis*' tucked deep into their crotch, skullcaps radiating in the bright summer sun, casually exchanging notes about police harassment in Burma Bazaar where they sold contraband and spurious goods with paid-for-impunity. While they conversed, their predatory instincts remained alert. The moment they noticed through the corner of the eye, anyone licking his fingers in that unmistakable finale of a feast, they would dart in to grab the place at the table, abandoning the conversation in mid-sentence, and forsaking all civility.

The restaurant owner kept raising the prices periodically, but the customers paid their bills with just louder curses, without ever slackening their patronage.

But, that was at the forecourt.

Behind the kitchen door, ironically, the cooks complained about the poor quality of food. They knew that the delicious biryani concealed the cleverly transformed stale meat. The 'servers' and cleaners complained about poor cooking, since they got to eat the cold leftovers which were suitably diluted or adulterated. Everyone complained about the customers not complaining.

But everyone gorged. Except me.

My job was from 'two to two': in other words, twelve hours from 2 p.m. to 2 a.m. I had to write up the bills, as conveyed by the servers, who, for some reason had the annoying habit of shouting the details of the food served, with their backs to me. The son of the restaurant owner sat at the cash till.

Mine was a simple job. It demanded only elementary knowledge of multiplication and addition. The owner was mightily pleased that I made no errors on either.

My meals were on the house.

During the initial days, it was difficult to scrounge a meal that was not cooked with meat. I had to carefully pick out the meat pieces or the chicken shavings from the curry or the rice to make myself a meal. Egg curry was staple diet.

Moeen Bhai, alias Bhai, was the head cook. I learnt that Bhai had been especially imported from Hyderabad for his culinary skills. 'My father and grandfather would have killed themselves rather than cook with this wretched quality of mutton,' he would mumble in Tamil, making sure everyone around understood his exalted pedigree, and would proceed to silently pray to his illustrious ancestors (who were rumoured to have cooked for the Nizam himself) for pardon.

A tall man with a beak-like nose and henna-dyed hair and beard, Bhai looked like a flamingo that was suspicious of its surroundings. He divided his time equally between overseeing the chicken broth and reading a carefully folded copy of the Urdu newspaper.

'Eighteen Muslims killed in Coimbatore last year, and now eighteen bomb blasts! Mistake, mistake!' he would shake his head and mumble to himself, now and then, referring to recent news reports of violence in the state. Nobody asked him what he considered the 'mistake', the original killing or the retaliatory blasts.

Moeen Bhai never failed to hop across to the mosque to do his namaz and I would be one of the very few from the restaurant to accompany him. I went up in his esteem a few notches, when I chose to display my patchy Arabic knowledge.

'Your parents have brought you up well,' he certified.

'Bhai, is there not some way to get vegetarian food here?' I mustered the courage to ask him after a few weeks.

'I could keep aside some plain rice and a spicy gravy before I cook the meat,' Bhai said kindly, and asked me with a penetrating look of suspicion, 'are you a vegetarian?'

'Well, I eat eggs, and chicken sometimes, but no beef, no mutton. And no pork,' I added.

Moeen Bhai nodded. 'Well, food is your personal choice. But Islam does not support this habit of vegetarian food.'

I chose not to argue with Bhai. His friendship was important to secure the food of my choice.

He would never forget to keep aside my 'unpolluted' gravy before the cooking proceeded as necessary.

On some nights, I slept on the kitchen floor (as did a few other bearers who had no place to go), amidst buckets filled with rotten fish heads and entrails of slaughtered lambs and the clanging noise of vessels being washed. (Don't believe anyone who tells you that creativity gushes out only in the stillness of a mountain lake or with the embrace of gentle breeze. Rubbish. Lying on the kitchen floor, with eyes shut and ears closed, I was happily composing new dance movements in those delightful minutes before sleep enveloped me.)

On Sundays, business was brisk; families streamed in to celebrate a birthday or an engagement. The owner sat at the cash counter, not wanting to miss out on the feel of soiled currency for more than a week, demoting the son to man the billing counter in my place.

That meant that I was free to discover Madras on Sundays.

twenty

Let me tell you, there is no better way to discover a city than to walk its streets.

I eagerly awaited Sundays, and I would set out to explore the city, ingesting every sight, from its suave exterior to its dark underbelly.

I roamed on the sands of Marina, that socialist construct of Nature, where rich and poor kids built sandhills not far from each other, scratching the wet skin of the beach with innocent hands; I made friends with Lazarus, the kite seller, and followed him to his dilapidated apartment at the Slum Clearance Board tenements at Santhome, to discover that his school education was being funded by the church, while his widowed mother prayed to Kolavizhi Amman, the city goddess of yore.

'All gods are good. Some, like Jesus, help you immediately, and others, like Amman take longer, sometimes until your next birth,' she explained, 'but, believe me, you need them all!'

I rode up and down the elevator in Devi Theatre, even managing to buy myself a softy ice cream from the soda fountain in the foyer, while feeling amazed at the confidence of young boys and girls who behaved as though they owned the city.

I marched on Mount Road, gaped at the newly reconstructed Spencer Plaza, ascended the escalator with a nonchalant look, casually enquired about the price of an expensive (I thought) ruby necklace from the display window, while the shopkeeper kept glaring at my worn-out rubber chappals contemptuously.

I treated myself to the world's cheapest and tastiest samosa sold from a food cart in the by lanes of Sowcarpet, where the city coyly covered its head, chewed and spat meetha paan artfully and spoke in a localized dialect of Hindi.

I was beaten up and my nose bled, when I had unwittingly walked into a drunken brawl in the slums of Chintadripet.

I became sufficiently seasoned not to be shocked by the swear words that permeated everyday conversations, especially among women, in the backyards of the city.

I saw the city dressed in its finery in the malls at T Nagar, and lying naked and ugly in its dark corners.

Wandering around the city, I was in awe and wonderment, but as it turned out, that was all a complete waste of time.

It took a few weeks before I discovered Mylapore.

The epicentre of music and dance in the city.

The sanctum of scholarship, the ultimate destination for all those seeking nirvana in classical music and dance. Or, so the Mylaporeans believed.

I don't disagree.

There is something in the air in Mylapore that gets the autorickshaw driver to sing a devotional song in the midst of chaotic traffic. Something that gets mothers to help their young daughters skip school on false pretences in order to attend a dance event.

When I walked down the crowded Ponnambala Vadhyar street and the narrow lanes around the Chitrakulam tank, my ears filtered out all noise to listen to the sound of music (*varnam*s and *alankaram*s, I learnt to identify much later) wafting from the houses—the innocent, tentative music of novices (all presumably young girls) practising their daily lessons, often with teachers (all presumably elderly males).

In later years, I've heard liberals argue that it's the concentration of Brahmins in Mylapore that generated the critical mass of interest, engendering the ownership of the classical arts by this community, and in turn perpetuating the incestuous relationship between the two.

But we might just be stepping on the minefield of politics in art. Let's leave that aside for now.

It was again entirely accidentally, and somewhat belatedly, that I stumbled on the many Sabhas of Mylapore. A prosaic description of a Sabha might be a platform where purveyors of music and dance meet with connoisseurs of creative art, but that would do no justice to its true character. Sabhas are wrestling rings where the slugfest of power in the world of performing arts is decided. A place where the relative strength of the artistes, the organizers and the sponsors of the events is continually put to the test; where the conquest of the stage is an all-year-round endeavour for any aspiring artiste.

If that sounds like a war theatre antithetical to art, you are badly mistaken: art flourished famously in this very environment.

Within a few weeks, my mental map of Mylapore was lit with locations of auditoriums, often confusingly referred to as Sabhas.

Mylapore became my hunting ground on Sunday afternoons.

I soon befriended the owner of Nehru News Mart at the southwestern corner of Luz Circle, who, at three in the afternoon, would let me sneak a glance at the 'Today's Engagements' column in *The Hindu* newspaper, which listed the music and dance events for the evening. I learnt to look for the 'All are welcome' mention in the event advertisement, which meant free admission. I found it a good bet to drop in at the Mylapore Fine Arts or at the smaller auditorium of the venerable Music Academy, as the chances were that there would be an *Arangetram*, an inaugural performance of a dance student, who was signalled to be ready for ascending the stage. You were certain to be warmly received by the eager parents of the debutante, thrilled at the rare sight of an uninvited stranger. If you were lucky (that is, if the parents were rich), you might even be presented with a packet of sweets from Grand Sweets, a token of deep gratitude for your presence and a symbol of their desperation to attract audiences for their dear daughter's dance exposition.

I would watch a debutante perform *alarippu* and *jatiswaram* in the cosy auditorium of Bharatiya Vidya Bhavan, and then dart across the road to the legendary Rasika Ranjani Sabha to watch a senior dancer execute an incredible *suddha nrittam.*

I must confess that I couldn't for many weeks distinguish between any two dancers: they all looked fluent and impressive on stage.

While I didn't understand most of what I watched, the sheer visual beauty of Bharatanatyam held me in its thrall.

I was charmed by the heavily bejewelled female form wrapped in colourful costumes, particularly the deep coloured skirts that opened like a fan when the dancer bent her knees. I loved the joyful swing of the *jhumki*s, the beautiful eardrops of the dancer. I was also fascinated by the grace of fluid movements that amplified the notion of beauty.

The art form was gradually beginning to reveal its secrets to me and drawing me deeper into its bosom. I began to notice familiar patterns of the foot and the geometry of hand movements, to make sense of the rhythm and to understand and interpret the meaning of this artistic communication.

When the mist of ignorance lifted slowly, I could differentiate the sharply sculpted postures of a senior performer from the loose approximations and the mechanical execution of a poorly taught debutant.

I yearned to paint my eyes with collyrium and colour my lips like the beautiful dancer on stage. I lost my sense of gender.

I craved to be under the arc lights.

I was a village boy from the hinterland, awed by the mightiness of the ocean that welcomed me with its thousand arms of spectacular waves.

The ocean was threatening too, with its unfathomable depths and unfamiliar inhabitants.

'Our sense of beauty comes with our birth,' Kumar observed, reminding me of Anandhi Periamma. Perhaps, like Periamma, he also derived his wisdom from the movies. After all, he was fully ensconced in Kodambakkam, the movieland.

'People like me, born in a lower class, cannot appreciate Carnatic music or Bharatanatyam, because we are not intelligent people,' he said.

'Nonsense,' I replied. 'It's all about what we are exposed to.'

'You've been to so many Bharatanatyam performances. Have you seen anyone from my class?'

'No.'

'Not even when it's free admission?'

'No.'

'Has any dancer appeared in dark skin?'

He was right. Every dancer was painted the same pale pink. It hadn't occurred to me that this had any class connotations.

'This art form is not for us, the working class! It is for the elite, by the elite!'

'And of the elite, you mean,' I said, completing his sentence. Kumar wouldn't have read about the Indian Republic.

'I suggest you keep away from these,' he said.

'Perhaps, you feel intimidated by people connected with the art?'

'That too ... but it's the art itself that's intimidating.'

'How can it be?'

'That art requires intelligence to understand. And we from the working class are not intellectuals.'

'But what about the movies? You relate to the same art when P. Susheela sings or Jayalalitha dances in the movies?'

'Yes, cinema is the common meeting ground,' Kumar agreed. 'Common language of the aristocracy and the hoi polloi, Hindus and the Muslims, Brahmins and the pariahs ... But make no mistake. Beyond the cinema theatre, the doors are firmly shut to each other's worlds.'

'Every art form brings people together. Art does not divide,' I said.

Kumar shrugged his shoulders.

~

It was yet another Arangetram ...

With an audience dominated by women.

It became a habit for me to look around and count the number of young men present at any performance, and usually, it was no more than a handful.

Again, the same familiar class of people, a class that I hadn't ever encountered in my village, speaking a sort of varnished Tamil that sounded strange.

In the early days, I would creep into a seat in the farthest row, somewhat timidly, with the auditorium and the occupants calling out that I was a trespasser. No one explicitly said so, but I could hear the auditorium warning me. Loud and clear. Even your skin curls, when you know, you don't belong to a place. Like the way the farmhands would pile themselves self-consciously in a corner to take the last serving at the wedding feast of the landlord.

Gradually, I picked up the courage to progress to the middle seat in the middle row: the perfect place to watch a dance performance, neither too far to miss the expressions of the ringed eyes, nor too close for comfort. (The thing about Arangetram is that rarely is the auditorium full.)

I had reached early. The hall was still sparsely filled.

'My granddaughter's Arangetram is on Thursday next, please note to attend,' a heavily dressed-up lady in the front row was telling the equally dressed-up lady seated next to me. With that unmistakable Brahmanical intonation.

'Congrats! That's pretty quick! Didn't she start only four or five years ago?' my neighbour asked in surprise.

'Three years!' the front-row lady said with pride. 'That's the thing about her guru. She guarantees Arangetram in three years flat!'

'How much does she charge?' my neighbour asked.

The front-row lady opened and closed her palms thrice, gesticulating thirty.

'Throw in the orchestra, the auditorium and everything else, it's more than half a lakh,' she clarified, intending no doubt to duly invoke jealousy.

'Good art doesn't come cheap!' my neighbour nodded in agreement, the diamonds in her ears and nose illuminating her words.

I had not till then understood the *business* of dance.

It was becoming evident that the ticket to this world was indeed highly priced.

Kumar was right. I was neither a female, nor a Brahmin nor rich. Those months at Mylapore had made it clear that I failed on all three counts.

I sought out Kumar. He had thawed, after the cine studio episode. I was grateful for his softened attitude.

'So, be sensible,' Kumar said. 'Be content to stay this side of the stage and just enjoy the dance.'

'But this side is dark. The lights are switched off when the show begins.'

'Take it from me,' he said, 'I watch people in the spotlight all the time, and I know they are more miserable.'

'If that's true, I need not have run away from home.'

'Yes, precisely that. Now, make peace and go back,' he said firmly.

I began to fear that I might get convinced by Kumar's practical wisdom. I had to chase away the ghost of fear each time it reared its ugly head in my mind.

In the dreariness of adding the cost of two biryanis (two rupees thirty paise) and two cups of tea (sixty paise), (sorry, I do these sums involuntarily), when I couldn't break into a jig, the ghost tenaciously kept returning, and started playing out the scary scenarios of returning home.

In the battle between Agony and Ecstasy, the former was beginning to gain ground.

Until I went to watch *that* performance.

The performance by Sivakami Kameswaran. At Narada Gana Sabha.

Yes, SIVAKAMI KAMESWARAN. One of the triumvirates of Bharatanatyam. The artiste who was credited with infusing a breath of fresh air into the ancient art. The dancer whose name was always spoken with awe and wonderment in the art world. The dancer that the DSP had spoken about.

That performance made everything that I had seen until then look truly pedestrian. It was a revelation, a profound experience.

There are moments in life when a new vista unexpectedly opens up. When you discover a new purpose.

After that performance, I stopped watching all other artistes; it was only Sivakami Kameswaran from then on. I kept track of all her performances and missed none. Including the ticketed ones, even if it meant watching from the last row, which was all I could afford. Sometimes I stood and watched. Once, I even took an overnight bus to Bangalore to watch her dance.

Bharatanatyam had till then been a mysterious but utterly enchanting script to me, whose symbols and figures needed to be deciphered. Like an ancient inscription. Whenever a code suddenly revealed its mystery to me, I felt enthralled, as if I had unexpectedly secured access to a treasure trove. In contrast, Sivakami's dance was an easily relatable language of human emotions. Such as the unremitting love of a maiden, of milky affection of a mother, of the naked fury of the wounded. These emotions required no complex keys to understand. They needed no introductory narrative in convent English. Her communication was lucid.

Watching various dancers, I had thought that rhythm was the boundary of a musical expression. I imagined that it served to contain the dance movements into an order. But Sivakami's art revealed to me that rhythm amplified, rather than limit, the creative outpourings. Rhythm added a necessary additional dimension. I was mesmerized by the beauty of the kaleidoscopic patterns.

I had never in the past, paid attention to the stage, as my focus was always riveted on the performer. I now realized that space was another force that Sivakami commanded to serve her art. She filled the space of a stage the way a painter would fill the canvas.

Kumar was utterly wrong on this count: she was far from being miserable under the arc lights. She was the very embodiment of bliss.

As I watched Sivakami, my mind cried out: My place is on the stage.

I could actually see it.

twenty-one

A cyclonic depression had been hovering over the Bay of Bengal, unable to make up its mind whether to make landfall in Madras or Cuddalore. Madrasis were stoically preparing to face the cyclone, an almost annual visitation, the city swiftly retreating into its protective shell.

I was crossing the Adyar bridge, walking towards Alwarpet, under an overcast sky.

The Adyar river below had swelled after remaining dormant all year, all the filth that had desecrated its waters was being spewed up to the surface in wounded fury. The slum dwellers near the riverbank were hurriedly packing their homes in plastic bags, ready to take their customary shelter in the nearest Corporation School building when the waters overflowed.

It was against this sombre backdrop that I was going to have my first meeting with my idol. While the skies around me darkened, I was filled with elation and in high spirits, for I was on my way to meet Sivakami Kameswaran!

It was the resourceful Kumar, again, who got me her home address.

He was outright dismissive when I first approached him for help.

'Why would she at all meet you?' he demanded to know.

'Of course, she doesn't need to meet me,' I said. 'God doesn't need devotees; the devotees need him.'

'Actually, that's incorrect,' he said. 'Without devotees there can be no god.'

'And no guru without followers,' I added.

'Yes, but it doesn't somehow seem appropriate in this context,' he said.

When, after a few days, I was about to give up hope, Kumar surprised me with Sivakami Kameswaran's address. With road map and all.

('The smartest species live in the deepest oceans and hottest deserts,' Anandhi Periamma had once observed, not necessarily understanding its meaning.)

'It doesn't mean you will get to meet her,' Kumar cautioned. 'You will likely be turned away at the gate.' He had pointed out how busloads of people were taken on a guided tour to the homes of movie stars, only to return after reverentially touching the tall iron gates that remained locked from inside.

(Kumar, being the smart pragmatist, was impressed with my job at the Farhan Hotel.

'If you improve your English, who knows, you might even land up a job as a bearer in the Connemara Hotel,' he would say. That was, to him, the ultimate measure of success for a runaway kid.

'I know enough English to be a Bharatanatyam dancer,' I would retort.

'You are beyond redemption.'

'No, actually dance is my redemption.'

Kumar would throw up his hands in exasperation.)

After all this time in my company, he still couldn't make sense of my adamantine will to meet Sivakami Kameswaran.

'Do you realize it will cost you two times your current salary just to learn dance from a mediocre teacher, to say nothing of a superstar?' he asked.

'Yes, and a hundred times my monthly salary to stage an Arangetram,' I said.

He was trying hard to knock some sense into me.

'And you are not even clear what to ask of her, assuming you get to meet her,' he said.

'I don't know yet,' I admitted. 'I just know that a step in the right direction will eventually lead to the right destination.'

'Nonsense,' Kumar retorted. 'You don't know if the direction is right, unless you know your destination.'

'I know my destination,' I assured him.

It was Tuesday, and I had to wait four interminable days.

During those four days, my mind kept oscillating between various clever ideas to win over the watchman and on what I would seek from Sivakami Kameswaran.

I asked Kumar for his advice if I should carry some biscuits for the dog, if there was likely to be one at the gate.

He ignored my question. I persisted, despite his annoyance.

'This is the first and last attempt. If I don't succeed in getting to be her student, I'll join the cine extras,' I assured him.

'Sure?'

'Sure.'

'Extra, extra to start with,' he corrected me.

'All right! Now you tell me,' I said.

He thought deeply and advised that it was more prudent to spend my scant resources to buy some fruits for Sivakami than biscuits for her unverified dog.

'Dry fruit,' he clarified.

'What's that?'

'Almonds, pistachios, walnuts … that's what you are supposed to carry when you go to meet big people.'

'In our village, we take a lemon.'

He sneered at the very suggestion.

'No point talking to you about dry fruit,' he said dismissively. 'Take some bananas and oranges. And apples, if you can afford it.'

I sought Kumar's expert opinion about what I should wear for the visit.

'Obviously, a white dhoti,' he said. 'That's most aligned to the cultural world that you are seeking to enter.'

I didn't have one. Kumar offered to arrange, if I insisted, but he pointed out with great insight that dhotis had a certain class issue. Super-white cotton dhotis with thin black or red borders that were silky to the touch were favoured by the upper political class ('that's how they whitewash their black souls', he said), but that would have been grossly inappropriate; dhotis with red and green zari borders were decidedly Brahmanical ('you'd look fake in that'); and ones that carried the dull stains of long washings in contaminated water were dead giveaways of the lower classes …

'You can't mess up this opportunity from lack of sartorial sense,' he said, before lending me his only polyester shirt and dark blue terricot pants, a suitably vague and neutral choice of clothing, under the circumstances.

The storm had now picked up full force. Trees whose roots had been imprisoned beneath the pavement stones were now displaying their pent-up fury, swaying their heads and flinging branches and leaves on the deserted roads. It seemed like these trees were 'possessed' by the spirit of Aatha.

'There are no goats in Madras, Aatha,' I cried out to the skies teasingly. 'You can't demand a sacrifice!'

The trees, I thought, shook even more.

The gusty winds were playing games with an old man on the road, who was struggling to choose between folding back his umbrella that had turned up like a cup, and his dhoti, that was violently dancing with the wind.

The sky opened up just as I neared Sivakami Kameswaran's house.

(Have you heard about the Hindu belief that showers are direct blessings from the heaven, that rains are a good omen? Cyclonic downpour might not be on the list, but you get the idea ...)

Just when the city was in danger of going under water, the wet pathway opened up for me in Sivakami's house, like the Red Sea for Moses and the Yamuna for Vasudeva.

God is a master showman. He can curate life to be a super thriller.

Black paint of the new moon night. Menacingly viscous with the heavy downpour. A vulnerable Vasudeva holding aloft infant Krishna in a flimsy basket, struggles to find his way through the swelling waters of Yamuna. Vasudeva despairs. How will he cross the river to reach Gokulam, the village of the cowherds, to leave the infant and save him from the sword of Kamsa, the demonic uncle? And then a miracle happens. The river parts to show a way for Vasudeva to cross.

(We had staged a play on the annual day function of our school where the scene was enacted with two cardboard props painted navy blue, representing the Yamuna River, being pulled away by two boys hiding in the wings. Thus the Yamuna made way to thunderous applause, for Vasudeva to walk through to Gokulam.)

No less drama, even when it comes to saving his devotees from the brink of disaster or blessing them with a largesse for their devotion. Remember Kuchelan, the childhood friend of Lord Krishna?

His story went something like this:

Kuchelan is in penury with twenty-seven children (a super-large family is an unmistakable sign of poverty), his wife nags him to go to his childhood friend Lord Krishna, who is the King of Dwarka, to seek some alms. She gives Kuchelan a handful of beaten rice tied in a piece of cloth (another sign of poverty) as a gift to Krishna. Kuchelan is very embarrassed with his humble offering but goes to Dwarka nonetheless. The sentry at the royal gates turns him away (the poor have an unmistakable identity of their own), but Krishna comes out, embraces him and devours the beaten rice with great relish. As Krishna eagerly swallows his favourite food, Kuchelan's hut turns into a palace, his wife finds herself clothed in finery and expensive jewels and so on ...

(In the school play in another year, this turned out to be a disastrous scene: as Krishna swallowed the beaten rice in slow motion—'come to the front of the stage!'—the lights were to go off, and the wife and twenty-seven children, richly costumed, were to quickly take the stage in the rear. It wasn't easy to marshal twenty-seven kids in utter darkness, and there was chaotic shouting and kids screaming, with a bunch of them still fighting and pulling each other's hair, when the lights finally came on.)

Mythology is always high drama.

The backdrop to my meeting with Sivakami was dramatic. That alone led me to wonder if this was a divine intervention ...

I am too frightened to pry open the memories of my meeting with Sivakami K. I do not even wish to scratch the verdigris of that beautiful happening. That memory is far too precious to play around with.

So, pardon me, I am not going to describe the meeting in any detail.

'So, there were no watchmen?' Kumar asked.

'No.'

'No dogs?'

'Only terracotta elephants!'

'You just entered and met the lady?'

'Yes. She was sitting in the patio, enjoying the rain.'

'And, just like that, she agreed to take you on as a student?'

'Well, not exactly. She wanted me to dance a small number. By the way, those pants of yours were so tight at the crotch, I could barely flex my legs.'

'And she was impressed with your dance?'

'Actually, she couldn't control her laughter. There were a few other girls and they laughed too.'

'And still she took you on as her student?'

'It's all god's design,' I said.

'Which god?' Kumar asked pointedly.

That question continued to be confounding. I must admit that I had not prayed to any particular god for success. I wasn't sure that Allah would have volunteered to bless, not for Bharatanatyam, in any case. Nor was it likely that Aatha or any other from the Hindu pantheon would have jurisdiction over a Muslim boy. So, who indeed was my guardian angel?

'Is that important?' I asked, trying to distract him.

'No,' Kumar agreed. 'Except that this is unbelievable.'

'I have heard from my aunt, that the meeting of the *shishya* with their guru is always by divine design.'

'Did she get your name right?' Kumar asked after a while.

'I think so.'

Kumar mumbled some words.

'She couldn't have mistaken Zaheer for, let's say, Sekar?'

'Well, I hope not.' I was beginning to get a little doubtful.

'Well, what with all the noise of the rain it is possible, isn't it?'

'If that's so, I'll change my name to Sekar.'

'Well,' Kumar said, 'that might just be the beginning. You need to destroy yourself, your name, your religion, your family. You need to be born again to be suitable for this art!'

I made my first mistake in multiplication.

'What are you constantly daydreaming about?' the owner's son said, giving a knock on my head.

'I am not dreaming anymore,' I replied. 'It's for real now.'

He gave me another knock, ignoring what I'd said.

'Two biryani, two chai,' one of the servers shouted.

This is my world:

Biryani, paya curry, brain soup, fish curry, masala omelette, chicken soup, mutton cutlet, fish cutlet, beef biryani …

This will also be my parallel world now:

Alarippu, Jatiswaram, Ganesha kauthuam, Padam, Javali, Thillana …

One foot in one world, the other foot in another …

twenty-two

The dance lessons were nothing like what I had dreamt of.

They were just more of the 'One two three; One two three' drill.

The same drill that I had watched at the film studio. Well, almost the same, because here the numbers had been replaced by rhythmic syllables: *Thai yum tha tha, Thai yum tha ha ...* repeated ad infinitum. Here, the dancers weren't tired adults selling their exercise for a price, but young girls with eager eyes and nimble legs. And here, the air wasn't polluted with swear words; everyone spoke in polite English even though everyone knew Tamil.

Impatient mothers, who watched over their young daughters with admiring eyes, were as dismayed as I was, since they were convinced that their wards had already mastered the onetwothree, onetwothree regimen. Each day of unnecessary training was another day of delay in their journey to the coveted destination of Arangetram.

I wasn't taught by Sivakami Akka (Sivakami was an affectionate and much respected 'Akka'—elder sister to every one). I was naive to even think that might be the case. She taught only the senior students—the dance postgraduates, if you will. Beginners like me were taught by one of her senior students. And yet, Sivakami Akka seemed omniscient, knowing and controlling every occurrence in that house.

I rarely saw her.

Kumar was curious about my dance lessons.

'All our friends are gathering on the terrace after dinner tonight to watch you perform what you have learnt so far,' he said, just two weeks into my training.

By then, I had been taught to flex out my knees in a semi-standing posture. And stomp my feet rhythmically. And flip my neck. And move my eyes. 'Right, left, right …'

'You're in for disappointment like I was,' I said. 'What I am learning is not dance; its physical exercise. Yoga asanas at best.'

'Bharatanatyam is yoga's first cousin.'

'Can you imagine, for three classes, we were merely being taught how to fold our elbows at a perfect right angle.'

'Is it that difficult?' He tried the posture to judge for himself.

'You also have to plaster a smile permanently on your face!'

Despite his deep misgivings about my 'misadventure', Kumar comforted me: 'You'll have to begin with lifting the bricks and mixing the clay, before your mansion takes shape,' he said, 'and it takes time.'

After some thought, he added, 'But you could just end up being a bricklayer forever. An underpaid one at that. Someone else will get the trophy for building the mansion and someone else will live inside.'

He did not believe that the world had a fair side.

While I was impatient with the pace of the tutorials, I was enchanted with the vibrancy at Sivakami Akka's home.

When I breathed the air of her home, my body cells resonated with the rhythm of dance.

With the incessant tintinnabulations of the ankle bells, the wooden beats of the tapping stick and the mild vibrations on the floor, the house itself seemed perpetually to be in dance.

Girls, who all looked distractingly beautiful to me, streamed in and out like bees at a hive and, in between, went through their lessons with varying levels of interest and expertise. It was fascinating to watch them. As they gracefully executed the *araimandi* and spread their arms, dainty flowers seemed to blossom in a garden.

I was charmed by the sparkling torrent of *sollukattu*s that poured forth from the mridangam artiste, which I kept trying unsuccessfully to repeat.

I was awestruck by the footwork of a senior disciple, who responded syllable by syllable, the rhythmic patterns being played on the tabla.

I was mesmerized by the sonorous music of Kameswaran, Sivakami's husband, who cracked sharp jokes when he was not singing.

On days when there were to be stage performances later in the evenings, the whole household went into a frenzy, with last-minute rehearsals going on in one room, make-up kits and jewellery in another, some girl sobbing for having misplaced something or the other, the musicians strumming their instruments in a corner of the dining hall, and the kitchen churning out a stream of delicious snacks and steaming cups of coffee for the floating crowd ...

It was like being at a chaotic wedding.

I was so overwhelmed by the swirl of activity around me that it took me awhile to be even aware of my being the only male student amidst a bevy of girls, most, much younger to me. While we danced in the class, I was right in the middle. But, it soon dawned on me that *I wasn't being placed at the centre owing to any distinction.* Not even because I was the only male amongst female students. I began to realize that the girls were actually pulling themselves away from me, towards the arc. Was I repelling them? (*What was it called—centrifugal? Centripetal? The force that pushed things away from the centre? Was I that kind of force?)*

I soon discovered that the force was a man called Neelakantan Sharma.

Sharma was a musician. He was a part of the troupe, an integral part of Sivakami Akka's training classes, but seemed to be also a key member of her household. Since he was always present at her home whenever I visited, I wasn't sure whether he lived in the same house or if he even had a family of his own. He was a handsome man, in his mid forties, and looked like a male god from the paintings of Ravi Varma, who had stepped out, changing into everyday clothes. He wore his religion on every part of his body. I wouldn't have been surprised if someone divulged to me that Sharma's mother delivered him with the three thick lines of *vibhuti*—the sacred ash—on his forehead and forearms, the single *rudraksha* around his neck and the thin tuft that hung from the crown of his closely cropped hair. He also sported ruby ear studs, for good measure.

Singing the same line infinite times, to ensure that an errant student learnt to get her *abhinayam* right, was his primary responsibility. But Sharma seemed eager to occupy every vacant job slot in the classroom and household. He answered telephone calls with an elaborate 'Hello' that was almost a mini song; performed as the substitute if the cook failed to turn up; and advised anxious mothers and grandmothers where they could get their silk saris dry cleaned safely.

Sharma made no secret of his intense suspicion and dislike for me.

'On whose recommendations have you joined?' he confronted me on the very first day, clearly irked by the fact that he had not been taken into confidence by Sivakami on the epochal decision of admitting me as a student.

'None,' I said. He was intrigued. Since Sivakami was beyond reproach in his mind, he was sure that I had some undisclosed diabolical intent.

He was determined to get to the bottom of the mystery and launched into a long conversation, without attempting to hide his irritation.

He was deeply offended that I stonewalled all his questions on my parentage, my father's income (which information, in fairness, was sought in a roundabout way), where I lived and so on. I fed him much innocent information, such as the depth of water in the lake in Yercaud, the approximate price of a cow in our village and the like.

'You must be wanting to make a career in films!' he said, after failing to uncover the riddle.

'No, I intend to stick to Bharatanatyam,' I assured him.

'Ah! This is not an art that can be mastered by anybody,' he said. 'You need to have earned the blessings in your previous birth!'

'Well, I haven't kept an account of my deeds in my previous birth, but I intend to master the art,' I said.

'No doubt, in your previous birth, you were born in a ...,' he trailed eloquently without completing the sentence. He was seeking to somehow legitimize my interest in the art.

The classes took place in the floor above the ground level, in a large hall that was kept bare—except for a beautiful bronze statue of Nataraja, kept in a well-polished teak-wood shrine, at the rear of the hall—to provide space for dancing. I noticed that Sharma was particularly possessive of the shrine, just a little short of claiming ownership of the god himself—decking the idol with flowers, lighting the silver lamp and arranging the incense sticks on the wooden platform below. Students would go first to the shrine, bow down in prayer with a short dance movement and then assemble for the classes. I too followed this routine. I would also spend a few minutes, when possible, to have a close look at the Nataraja idol. (He is an enigma, this Nataraja! Tiger skin and coiling snakes as costumes, dancing in gay abandon, hair flailing in all directions, his left half supple, graceful and decidedly feminine!)

Sharma entered the hall, when, on one of my early days, I was bending close to the idol, lost in admiration of the beauty and precision of the sculpture.

'Don't touch, don't touch!' he cried, as he rushed to me.

I pulled myself away, taken aback by the aggression in his voice.

'You know, it's not a showpiece. It is *our* very own god,' he said. He was clearly agitated. I could recall other students touching the idol, but I could imagine the reason why he restrained me.

I turned away.

On the following day, I was confused if I should offer the prayers as others did, or skip the practice. I decided to continue, keeping a safe distance from the Lord.

I did not fail to notice that Sharma had also taken upon himself the responsibility of protecting innocent females from me. He would not let any girl be left alone with me in the class room. He would sniff any such eventuality and promptly creep in to stand at a corner of the hall or pull away the girl from the hall.

I suspected that he might have even spelt out his warnings to some girls.

When the girls were not dancing, they would chatter like sparrows and I tried in vain a few times to inject myself into their conversation, even though I didn't understand much, as they always spoke in that wretched form of English that sounded as though it was severely clipped at the edges. I could find no entry to their world.

I was alone.

I was an aberration.

More than a couple of months had passed since I had started the classes but I had still not had any one-on-one time with Sivakami Akka, other than formal greetings. Her frequent travels didn't help either. While she was at home, she always seemed under siege from anxious parents waiting to enlist their children under her tutelage, Sabha secretaries scrambling for her dates, eager musicians wanting to be part of her entourage or sundry other people seeking an audience with her. Everyone seemed to have many things to discuss, but no one managed to have enough time with her.

Yet, Sivakami's presence could be felt all around the house. Like the pleasant smell of incense.

'I cannot believe that you are taking lessons from a superstar without paying any fees,' Kumar said.

'Well, no one has said anything about fees so far.'

'Perhaps, the secretary has bungled.'

'Isn't it possible that Sivakami Akka is just being kind?'

Kumar looked at me quizzically.

'That's an alien word in our kind of world,' he said. 'We are used to paying for even our entitlements. For everything. Birth certificate, caste certificate, ration cards, school admission, hospital care ...'

'You doubt this world, I trust this world.'

'Perhaps. But that's what makes me more prepared for this wretched world than you!'

I began to feel that it would perhaps be wise to have the matter about fees clarified.

I was, however, determined not to let go the opportunity of continuing my tuition, even if I had to pay for it. Perhaps I was foolish to think so. I had no idea what the bill would be. It would no doubt be steep. The girl students appeared deliriously rich. It was evident, not merely from the cars they came in, but from every detail—the chappals they wore, the way they spoke, their smooth skin, their clipped eyebrows, and from their heels and nails. Yes, heels and nails, the most telling social signatures.

I had to find some way to raise the money.

While I searched for the answer, there wasn't even a fleeting moment when I considered returning to my father. He had not made any attempt to contact me since I had left. Of course, I had warned him not to cross my path, but aren't parents supposed to ignore such tantrums and show their love and support to their children? Not that I would have returned home, even if he had asked.

Anandhi Periamma?... Yes, I could revive my contacts with her ... She would be very pleased with the news that I was learning from Sivakami Kameswaran. She might discount Sivakami's celebrity status a bit, in the absence of any connection with movies. It was worth trying to contact Periamma.

I also felt angry at the very thought. Why was I still struggling to come to terms with the fact that I had been banished from her world forever?

I could never understand my own emotions when it came to Anandhi Periamma.

'Kumar!' I nudged him, as he lay in his bed next to me.

'Hmm ...'

'You said I could get a bearer's job at the Connemara Hotel?'

'I never said that.'

'All right, you didn't. But how much would that job pay?'

'Forget it! You can't get past the chowkidars at the gate!'

'Why are you always obsessed with chowkidars?'

Kumar turned to face me.

'They are an interesting species: they are "us" who guard "others" from "us"!' he said.

The following day I took time to loiter around the Connemara Hotel. It stood majestically bearing its imperial heritage and maintaining its elitist distance.

Kumar was absolutely right. We had no right of entry into that world.

And then, the long-awaited meeting with Sivakami Akka happened.

That day I had reached Sivakami Akka's home earlier than usual.

The previous night was an inspection night at the hostel, and I had to shift my address to the railway station. Kumar was doing night shift at the studio and I didn't have his expert guidance at hand. I tried unsuccessfully to snatch some sleep on a stone bench at the farthest end of the platform, after chasing away a stubborn mongrel who was understandably upset that a foreign aggrandizer had usurped his kingdom. I made peace, buying him a biscuit, and he coiled underneath my bench with great contentment. However, soon I gave up any attempt to sleep, surrendering to the swarm of mosquitoes. When I returned at dawn to the hostel, I found the legitimate lodgers still in bed, no doubt enjoying the breath of less polluted air, as all the unauthorized ones were yet to return.

I chose to leave early for my classes, taking a shorter bus ride to save some money. Perhaps, I could meet Sivakami Akka and have the matter relating to my fees clarified.

As I entered, I saw Sivakami Akka in conversation with some visitors.

I went up to the classroom and was duly lost in reverie, looking at the statue of the Lord of Dance.

Soon, other students began to arrive. Sivakami Akka was still with the visitors.

There was a new teacher that day, a young woman, whom I had not seen earlier. I could tell she was also a senior student, as some of the older students greeted her familiarly.

She appeared taken aback to see me, a man amidst the girls, as she stepped into the hall.

'You ...?'

It was obvious no one had briefed her about my presence.

I introduced myself and greeted her.

'Zaheer?' she repeated by name, her tone betraying her discomfort.

'Yes, Zaheer,' I said.

She looked at me in confusion.

There was a lot of friendly chat between the new teacher and the students for a while, and I could make out vaguely that she had returned from America after a successful tour.

It was an unusually long class. For the first time, I felt tired.

While I tried to concentrate on my steps, I was slipping up and made many mistakes.

I was sweating with exhaustion.

I could see my young teacher was visibly irritated, though she said nothing.

When the class got over, it came as a relief to me. The teacher and the girls, my fellow students, went down the stairs chattering. I neither understood what they were talking, nor was I inclined to participate.

I sat down exhausted, for lack of good sleep coupled with the rigorous practice.

A few minutes later, Sharma peeped through the door, quickly announced that Sivakami Akka was looking for me and ran down the stairs.

Had the teacher complained about my mistakes? Panic gripped me.

If that was the first report Sivakami Akka had of me, it would indeed be very unfortunate. If I was to be thrown out for that reason, I could run through all I had learnt so far, and demonstrate to her that I could dance a thousand times better than those dim-witted girls whose brains could talk either to their arms or legs, never both.

Maybe it was about the fees? In which case I would have to plead for some time. One more month? Perhaps, two would be safer. There had to be a way to raise the money. Even Periamma, as a last resort …

I went down. My legs were weak, in fear or exhaustion, I couldn't say.

Sivakami Akka was seated, surrounded by my fellow students. Sharma stood alongside, unmistakable contempt in his eyes. The youngest in my class, a girl of seven or eight, upon seeing me, pinched her nose and ran out. A few others laughed, some cupping their mouth, feigning modesty.

Sivakami Akka motioned for all of them to leave. Sharma alone hung around.

Sivakami Akka waited for a few minutes in silence.

'Did you take a bath today?' she asked.

'Yes,' I stammered.

'When?' Sharma interjected.

The bathing place at the hostel was always crowded in the mornings. The boy next in line would always hang over you menacingly while you bathed, and if he was bigger than you (which was often the case), you'd be rudely pulled out, even before you had washed away the soap suds from your thighs. Since my dance classes were in the forenoon, I preferred to return to the hostel after the classes, and take my bath in relative privacy, before I left for work, a little after noon.

'Girls are complaining that you smell!' Sivakami Akka said, looking me straight in the eyes.

'Stink, stink,' Sharma corrected.

STINK? Did he just say 'stink'?

I hadn't been aware of my body odour till then.

Was I stinking? Instinctively, I smelt my palm.

Was I stinking like a filthy rag? Like rotten fish? Like a sewer? Like shit? ...

I cowered in fear.

Would I be expelled because I stank?

I was close to tears.

I had always fancied that I was mentally a strong person. I was discovering that I wasn't.

Sivakami Akka must have sensed my crushing humiliation.

She motioned for me to sit down closer to her.

I hesitated. I feared that if I took another step towards her, she might be assaulted by my malodour.

'It's the non-vegetarian food that causes the stink,' Sharma said. 'You cannot get rid of that!'

'Neelakantan!' Sivakami Akka raised her voice. 'You can go from here,' she dismissed Sharma with a wave of her hand.

At another time, I might have gloated at the treatment meted out to Sharma, but just then, my spirit lay in tatters, as I believed my dream was unravelling.

Sivakami Akka waited while I sobbed.

It was a long wait.

'Tell me, what do you do for a living?' she asked gently, when I had recovered.

I must confess that I was tempted to lie.

I don't know, whether it was my creative mind, or people generally get imaginative for self-preservation—I was ready instantaneously with a story about being a bearer in the Connemara (I can't explain why I didn't choose being a plastic engineer, which would have certainly sounded more impressive), that I lived with my rich uncle in Egmore (I had seen big houses there) … 'You know, I used a new soap this morning, neem, I think, very, very, pure, it's great for skin, as you can see, it usually smells a little bit after the bath but disappears after some time, actually I would recommend …'

But I said none of that.

I told her the truth.

Including the truth about Farhan Hotel, mutton biryani, chicken soup, long walks, dirty bathing place, filthy toilets, railway platform, mongrels and mosquito bites. I had suddenly slipped into a complex web of self-pity.

Hearing myself, I felt repulsive. I glanced at Sharma who had managed to hang about and saw sheer contempt in his eyes.

Why should anyone put up with me? … I was certain that I would be asked to leave. I had always known I did not belong here. It was foolish of me to have chased an impossible dream. I should have stayed back in college, completed my studies, taken up a government job … maybe as a factory inspector … Married and…

'Can you resign from your job this afternoon?' Sivakami Akka asked.

I stared at her in incomprehension.

'Can you give up your job today?' she repeated.

'What … what will I do for—'

'We'll find a way out,' she said.

'I cannot afford to pay any fees, as it is,' I mumbled. I thought it was an appropriate time to clarify the matter.

'Who is talking of any fees?' she snapped. 'I took you in because of your passion for dance, not for fees.'

I cried, this time not out of fear.

As I stepped out of the house, Kameswaran called me.

I turned back.

He was holding out a canister.

'What exactly is this "deodorant"?' I asked Kumar, as I pressed the nozzle of the can Kameswaran had handed me.

'A magical spray that transforms the stinking poor to the perfumed rich,' he said.

'Do the poor always smell bad, and the rich pleasant?' I asked.

Kumar smiled.

'Everyone, rich or poor, has the same stinking shit,' he said. 'I should know. For generations, we have been clearing human shit.'

twenty-three

It was another week before I mustered the courage to inform Kumar that I had quit my job at Farhan.

'Why?'

Kumar's question was simple, straight.

In that one innocent word, there were sharp spikes of dissent, disillusionment, anger and angst.

'I have another job,' I said. I found my voice a tad meeker.

'What job?'

'To look after Sivakami Akka's library.'

'Library?'

'Books. She has a large collection …'

'What is there to "look after"?' Kumar asked.

To someone who had barely been to school, understandably, it didn't sound like a job.

'And do odd jobs,' I said, trying to put some more substance to my job description.

'So, a plastic engineer doing household jobs!'

'I'm not a plastic engineer!'

'Nearly one.'

'And it's not household jobs.'

'That's what you think now!'

'Kumar, I trust her,' I said. 'This is my dream coming true, and I'm not going to give it up for anything.'

I began to see less of Kumar in the succeeding weeks.

While I worked at the hotel, I would return to the hostel late at night, after work, and that's often when Kumar would also return from his work. The movie industry in Kodambakkam had the habit of working late into the night. ('Movies are dreams. So they can be put together only at night,' Kumar would say.) Kumar and I would chat, sitting on the unlit terrace, munching boondi mixture or kara sev that I would bring from the restaurant (free allowances, within strictly enforced limits), Kumar blowing perfect smoke rings in the air (which, at that time, was a popular habit of movie heroes), and narrating interesting episodes from the studio floor, mostly recounting the idiosyncrasies of popular stars. He would mimic the sloppy manoeuvres of an ageing hero in an action scene. He swore that he caught a young assistant director in a 'compromising position' with the middle-aged mother of the leading lady, in the lady's make-up van, while she was busy shooting. He was contemptuous of some well-known producers and directors, as he was convinced that their primary interests were sex and black money, in that order. Movies were merely means to that end.

In the mornings, we would both go to bathe at about the same time. Kumar always used Mysore sandalwood soap, a rather expensive choice, while I used the cheaper Lifebuoy, the carbolic soap. I was curious about this, as Kumar was otherwise very spartan in his habits.

'Comes with heredity,' he said with a deadpan expression. 'Every adult male in my family has done sewer cleaning sometime in his life. Perfumed soap is to erase that memory from the skin.'

~

Since I was now on an 8 a.m. to 6 p.m. schedule, there were fewer occasions to meet Kumar. For many continuous days, I found his 'bed' (if one could describe that lifeless pillow and worn-out sheet, thus) remaining rolled up. It was evident that he was often not using the hostel.

Many weeks passed by, and I hadn't met Kumar.

I learnt that the cinema studio where he was working was facing financial difficulties and they were laying off many workers. His friends at the hostel hinted that he might have lost his job.

~

One of the privileges at Sivakami Akka's house was my access to newspapers (mostly English) and magazines (mostly Tamil). Though my attention was still on the 'Today's Engagements' column in *The Hindu*, to check out the music and dance programmes in the city, my eyes grazed on other subjects, political and social. That's how I came across the news that the studio where Kumar worked was 'locked out'.

'That's what industry owners do to tame violent workmen,' my senior explained.

'Lock out violent men like locking in violent animals?' I asked.

'Yes, it's essentially the same,' she added, before proceeding to shape her eyebrows.

More news followed.

A few days later there was a report that a few demonstrators had been taken to police custody. The trade union leader alleged wanton victimization. There was a photograph of a man, presumably an agitating worker, with half-closed eyes and a bloody nose. There was also a brief quote from the owner of the studio, that, given the deteriorating law and order situation, he was contemplating shutting down the studio.

I worried about Kumar. I hoped that, given his strong survival instincts, he would find a way out of the difficulties. But his continued absence from the hostel was concerning.

I kept telling myself that Kumar deserved to succeed.

I prayed to a nameless, formless god that he would.

twenty-four

Paya curry was a signature dish at Farhan.

Having watched the preparation amidst the grisly environs of the kitchen many times, I became a vicarious master chef. I knew how to chop the sheep trotters at the exact time when the fat would separate (after patiently simmering the meat for an hour or so), what ingredients went into the masala, and how much garlic and cumin to add (some pure cow ghee doing wonders for the taste).

My palate that had been nourished by the explosive ginger chutney of Anandhi Periamma and the aggressive paya curry (sans the meat) of Farhan, was thoroughly unprepared for the passive pudalangai koottu and poricha rasam, when I was invited to join the lunch table at Sivakami Akka's home.

Any one, students or visitors, who happened to be present at lunchtime (which was often unpredictable), was invited by Sivakami or Kameswaran to join the lunch, often throwing the cook into total panic, being left with insufficient food.

It was on one such occasion, when eight people sat around the table, while the cook had prepared only for five, that Sivakami Akka summoned me to help her out at the kitchen.

(I had heard that most Brahmin households wouldn't let anyone outside their caste into their kitchen, nor share their dining table.

'It's not about Brahmins at all,' Kumar had explained. 'Every caste in the hierarchy looks down on every other caste lower in the ladder as pollutants.'

'Isn't it their right to decide who they wish to open their doors to?' I argued.

'When every individual in a community decides to keep away every other individual in another group, it's not about personal choice, it's called societal discrimination,' he retorted.)

I had not entered the kitchen till then and was hesitant.

'Neelakantan is away shopping, and I hope you won't mind my taking the liberty. Can you please cut some fruits, as I assist the cook?' Sivakami Akka asked.

I was thrilled at the request, as it signalled, that I had been fully assimilated into her home, and more importantly, it confirmed her liberal values.

I threw myself enthusiastically at the task.

'Can I quickly prepare some tomato chutney as well?' I volunteered.

Sharma was appalled, when he noticed me at the kitchen on his return. He skipped lunch that day.

~

'Curdrice (curd and rice are inseparable) defines us Brahmins,' Kameswaran once said. 'If you could eat curdrice twice a day continuously for a week uncomplainingly, no further proof is required of your Brahmanism.'

I couldn't.

I wanted the pungent juice of raw onions to irrigate my mouth. I craved for the sting of the green chillies firing up my tongue.

I craved for paya curry (without the meat).

Thus it was that I landed back at Farhan one afternoon.

Rather unusually, I was wearing a white dhoti (my wardrobe was undergoing changes), the trademark Hindu costume, and not a lungi like a Muslim.

Moeen Bhai didn't appear pleased to see me.

'I had always suspected this,' he said, not taking his eyes off his copy of *Musalman.*

'Suspected what?' I asked.

'Betraying the cause of Islam,' he grunted.

'Is there something in the newspaper?' I asked.

Moeen Bhai made a low, guttural sound.

'I missed your super-tasty paya curry,' I said, trying to divert the conversation.

He kept reading *Musalman,* obviously gaining time to make up his mind, whether he should entertain me or not. He slowly got up from the stool that he was perched upon and ambled to the kitchen counter. He heaped a massive spoon of rice on a plate and dipped the ladle into a cauldron of curry that was boiling on the stove.

'Without meat pieces?' he asked, turning to me.

'If you don't mind please!'

'Tch, tch,' he shook his head and pushed the plate towards me.

There was a tiny piece of meat that had escaped his shoddy filtration. I picked it carefully and threw it out.

'So, you are working in a Hindu household?'

'No, I'm learning Bharatanatyam.'

'Do you do your namaz?' he asked.

From the time that I started lessons at Sivakami Akka's, I had more or less given up on my daily prayers. It was simply inconvenient to slip out during prayer time, and in any case, the nearest mosque was at least two kilometres away. With Neelakantan's intimidating presence, I could not consider doing namaz anywhere in Sivakami Akka's house, not even in the uninhabited terrace. It did trouble me initially, but I had soon gotten over my feelings of guilt.

'No,' I was honest.

Moeen Bhai was silent, obviously reassessing me.

'So, you sing?'

'No, I dance. Someone else sings.'

'It's all the same,' he concluded. 'And are the songs about Hindu gods?'

I was irritated. 'Yes, about all the Hindu gods. Thirty-three crores of them.'

Moeen Bhai grunted.

He went back to the *Musalman.*

He read aloud a report of a minor communal clash in Nagercoil. The report referred to a religious procession as being the trigger.

'Our respective worlds *are* different, Hindus and Musalmans, we have to come to terms with that. Very different, like milk and lemon. Mix them, you have spoilt both. Why can't we live in peace by leaving each other alone?' he mumbled.

'So, will we see you soon in movies?' Rahim, one of the cooks, an old colleague, asked eagerly, as he was de-feathering a headless chicken.

I shook my head.

'This has nothing to do with movies,' I said.

'Not movies!' Moeen Bhai cut in. 'They dance Bharatanatyam in temples.'

'Very nice, very nice,' Rahim said.

'What's nice about dancing in a temple?' Moeen Bhai wanted to know.

I didn't finish the meal. It tasted different.

Was I slipping between paya curry and poricha rasam, laying claim to neither?

Things changed.

Do you recall the way you relate to fellow passengers in a long train journey, initially suspecting, then advancing cautiously, then more courageously, and ending up sharing intimate personal details? Well, my familiarity with the Brahmanical cuisine was advancing somewhat like that. It wasn't long before I found myself salivating at the very thought of the fare that awaited me at lunch.

More than the delicious food, I looked forward to the delightful company of Kameswaran at the lunch table.

'What is the significance of Nataraja's dance posture, with one leg lifted up?' he would ask with great seriousness.

The first time, I struggled with many theories:

'Maybe, that represents the earth and sky? ... Perhaps, it symbolizes the living and the non-living ...?' (By now, I had gone through many reviews by art critics who wrote such wonderfully vacuous stuff.)

'Simple,' he would say dismissively. 'If poor Nataraja puts both legs up, he will fall!' he would roar with laughter, enjoying his own joke.

It became a habit for me to smell my armpit every time I entered Sivakami Akka's home. The deo was doing its job. Actually, I need not have bothered. Perhaps because I was beginning to get endearingly included in the household, thanks to Sivakami Akka and Kameswaran, the barrier between me and the rest of the students had substantially melted away. Neelakantan Sharma notwithstanding.

'You make the best chai in the world,' was a compliment that I often received from my fellow students.

'That's just to get me to do the job for you lazy girls!' I would retort.

I danced with a variety of students, some very talented ones, some who were in the classes only because they had been pushed into it by wealthy and eager parents.

We danced together. We chatted together. We gossiped together.

We talked about other dancers, movies, costumes. They also talked about many other things—restaurants in London, Burmese rubies, perfumes, *Star & Style, Femina* and chiffon saris. I could not relate to any of that, but I no longer felt diminished.

Meanwhile, I had taken to voracious reading, utilizing my responsibility to 'look after' the library, which had an eclectic collection of books. Charles Dickens jostled for space with Swami Vivekananda. Kalki's *Parthiban Kanavu* rubbed shoulders with *Srimad Bhagavatham.*

I was like a bee in a flower garden. I sat down with an armful of books, flitting from one to the other, never having enough of any one book.

'Does Kaliya, the dreaded snake, get killed by baby Krishna, after he danced upon the serpent's head?' one of the students asked Sharma, while she was composing a dance sequence based on the famed mythological anecdote.

'Yes, he is killed by a single stroke from baby Krishna. That should be the climax, we could have a loud bang of cymbals,' Sharma responded enthusiastically.

'No, Kaliya surrenders, and the Lord forgives him,' I said.

The student looked at me in surprise.

'That story is told in the sixteenth chapter, tenth canto of the *Bhagwata Purana,'* I pointed out, having gone through the heavy tome recently.

I could see sparks fly from Sharma's eyes.

twenty-five

It was sultry April.

Madras, having lost, like an inveterate gambler, all the water from the monsoon rains to the sea, was now pauperized, scrounging around for the smallest traces of the liquid anywhere. Rich residents and avaricious traders drilled deep holes into the ground and sucked, like leeches, water accumulated centuries ago. The less fortunate ones were marking territory with plastic pots in front of geriatric water lorries that were ambling around the city roads day and night, peeing with incontinence.

The hot weather was punishing everyone, while the oppressive humidity made things much worse.

Madras was sweating and it stank.

It required a strong deodorant. Imported, no less.

This was my second summer away from home.

Faced with the water shortage, the warden had moved with speed, rationing one bucket of water for each resident, both legitimate and illegitimate. A civil war of sorts was brewing as some of the legitimates were protesting the eligibility of the illegitimate lodgers for the scarce water. Since the warden was privy to the illegitimate habits (such as liquor and then, some more) of some of the powerful legitimate lodgers, the protest was a bit muted. As the summer progressed and the water scarcity worsened, no doubt the war would escalate.

Water was not the only issue.

I wasn't able to sleep in the hall, what with the walls regurgitating the heat absorbed during the day. The two fans in the large hall groaning with age had been declared 'operational' by the inspector and had hence been denied retirement. The legitimates, the 'truly Backward class' of the hostel, claiming priority right over the limited space on the terrace (after water tank, broken handpumps, tarpaulins, mouse traps, asbestos sheets, etc., taking the pride of place) were enjoying a decent night sleep.

When I slept, I dreamt of gleaming white Western toilets. The kind that I had seen at Sivakami Akka's house. Where sitting and shitting was a pleasurable experience.

And there were more sights around me that began to assault my sensibilities:

I was being overcome with revulsion at the sight of the unwashed undergarments of my neighbours, defiantly coiled over their rolled-up beds.

I began to wash my plate a second time before I ate at the canteen, to get rid of the residual grime.

Why were these things not even visible to me in the past few months?

Why had the hostel suddenly ceased to be the horizon of joy that I thought it was?

I wondered if I had become conscious of my deprivation only because I had been exposed to a new seductive world of comfort. But that's where my art lived.

As if she had read my mind, Sivakami Akka broke the news to me shortly.

She had spoken to a few of her friends, who had all agreed to give me a monthly stipend, for a few years, so I could live in a 'decent' place and pursue my classes. I was to meet Viswanathan, a business tycoon, Arni Chettiar, the silk baron, and a few others. These, I came to know, were really big names in Madras society.

'What job should I do in return?' I asked, perplexed.

'Nothing. They are generous patrons of art.'

'You mean that I simply receive a monthly allowance from them and do nothing in return for them?' I repeated incredulously.

'Why don't you believe that there are kind-hearted people in the world?' she asked with a short laugh.

'Yes, I do, I do!' I said.

'Actually, I was wrong,' she said. 'You do have to do something in return.'

'Anything,' I said.

'You have to *thank god*, for it is his will that you should become an accomplished dancer! And, you have to dedicate yourself fully to learning this marvellous art.'

'You should *thank god* that you have been blessed with an outstanding guru,' said Viswanathan, as he handed over an envelope with my first month's stipend.

'It's all *god's design*! He is showing you the path to glory,' said Arni Chettiar, as he assured me that I could count on him for any support, as long as I was a student of Sivakami Akka.

I was pushed back into my confusion. I had not prayed to any god. Why was he hell-bent on helping me? Anyway, which god was this, who was taking so much trouble?

Perhaps, Maha Baba had read my letter?

It was an oppressive Saturday evening.

I went up to the terrace of my hostel to catch some fresh air.

The gentle breeze from the sea must have lost its way by the time it meandered to Egmore. It was hot even in the open.

I was surprised to see Kumar crouched on the parapet wall.

He was smoking a beedi. I looked for the smoke rings. There weren't any.

His left cheek was badly swollen and bruised. As a result, the left eye had taken a crooked angle that made him look like an angry eagle. His left arm was bandaged and hung in a sling. From the dirt on the bandage, the damage appeared a few weeks old.

'What happened?' I rushed to him, perturbed about his state.

'Are you still in this hostel?' he asked, without answering my question. He didn't smile at me, perhaps he couldn't have, given the swollen cheeks.

'Did you get beaten up?' I asked without answering his question. I put my arms around his shoulders. I was struck by his body odour. (I had become very conscious of this.)

'Isn't that obvious?' he asked.

'By whom? The police or the studio people?'

'Aren't they all the same?' This time, he smiled. Yes, he could smile, except it was very ugly.

We sat in silence for sometime.

'How is your new home?' he asked.

'It's not my home, but it sure feels like my home.'

He nodded his head and removed my hand from his shoulders.

'We celebrated Tamil New Year at Sivakami Akka's home a few weeks ago,' I said, hoping to cheer him up with some happy news.

'New Year in April?'

'That's when the new year begins as per the solar calendar. This year is called Pramodhuta. This year will give prosperity to everyone, there will be a record harvest, it's going to be a victorious year. That's what the priest read out from the new *Panchangam,* the almanac,' I paraded my newly acquired knowledge.

'Victory over what?'

'Victory of Good over Evil. We celebrated with dance and music.'

'Oh!' Kumar looked at me sarcastically. 'So, Good will win over Evil in this world?'

He ran his fingers slowly over his swollen cheeks.

I understood what he meant.

'Have you changed your name to Sekar?' Kumar asked.

I ignored his 'question'. He had never believed that my Islamic faith would remain unaffected by the pursuit of my art.

'We had some delicious wheat halwa and badam payasam,' I said, attempting to change the subject.

'I had a bun and tea,' he said. It wasn't jealousy. I thought he just wanted to make me feel guilty.

'If I had known it was the glorious New Year, I too would have celebrated by taking another spoon of sugar in my tea. That doesn't cost extra, you see,' he added. Again with an ugly smile.

'We all enjoyed the celebrations.'

'Who is "we"?'

'I mean, Sivakami Akka, her family, students ...'

'Oh!' he said, with unmissable hint of sarcasm. 'And family includes errand boys like you?'

'You are prejudiced,' I said, annoyed. 'I am not an errand boy. I organize and manage the library, I get to read plenty of absolutely absorbing books, I watch all the dance classes, learn and practice without any constraints, interact with and learn from some wonderful people, take part in their festivals, and by the way, look after Sivakami Akka's travel arrangements, dance costumes and ...'

'Good. Enjoy your new status!' he said sharply, cutting me short. 'And, by the way, isn't this place unsuitable for you now?'

I could sense the alienation when he spoke those words.

In his mind, I had crossed over to 'the other world', become a part of 'them'. I had ditched the world of the underdogs and had parachuted into the world of the privileged.

In his mind, I had inexorably and hopelessly been 'converted'.

I felt suddenly irritated by his attitude.

'I have begun to enjoy my dance classes,' I said to Kumar. 'You were right, it takes time to build the mansion.'

I tried to enlist him as an accomplice, quoting his own words.

'It's not the dance, but the company of the rich and the powerful you are enjoying,' he said, now looking at me straight.

'Not true. Even if it were, is that a crime?' I was riled by his accusation.

'No,' he said. 'You can choose your poison.'

'You have a very negative view of the world.'

'Comes from one's life experience!'

'Right,' I agreed. 'I have experienced both good and bad. If my father assaulted me for who I am, there was my aunt to encourage me. If one Diva of dance turned me down, there was another superstar who took me in. There are the patrons of art, well, there has been Kari, there has been you. I see goodness all around. And I am at the doorstep of my dream! I don't think it's right to suffer from the delusion that the entire world's only job is to plot against you.'

'Why are you still in a Backward Classes hostel?' Kumar asked. He sounded as though I had forfeited the right to stay, because I had crossed over to the 'other world'.

'I will be leaving this place for a lodge in T Nagar. My patrons have agreed to fund my living expenses until I can be on my own,' I replied.

'Oh, patrons!' Kumar said sarcastically. 'I thought only beggars need patrons; because they are lazy, they don't like to work to earn their living.'

Infuriated, I stormed out of the place. That was the last time I saw Kumar.

twenty-six

It was the best bed I had ever slept on. In fact, this was the first time I had ever slept on a cot that had a mattress, having always slept on the floor.

(Only Salima Bivi had the right to a cot at home. The cot, which was from her dowry, also doubled up as her throne during daytime, from where she held court, overseeing supplicant daughters-in-law and errant sons.)

My cot was placed along the wall with a window, from where I could see the terraces of neighbouring houses like a minor god from a low heaven.

I hummed a tune that was haunting me since I first heard it during my classes. The rhythmic sound from the ceiling fan neatly kept the *talam* to my music.

God (whichever) had chosen to smile on me.

I thought I was going to sleep like a baby in my cosy bed. But sleep eluded me. My mind was too excited.

I must have somehow slipped into a dream, though I thought I was awake.

She was ageless ...

At times she was a charming young girl with spring in her step and at other times, a mature woman, with a royal gait. Her form kept dissolving into myriad patterns, and it was exhausting to keep pace with her morphing.

'Why do you need to assign an age to me?' she asked in astonishment.

'Even if I don't, how can I even know you, if you keep morphing like this?' I asked in exasperation.

'You need to know me exactly this way: I am formless, ageless!' she smiled, as she scampered through lush fields.

'I need to know you, because I sense that you have fully possessed me!' I cried. 'Your name, your age, your lineage ...'

'I will be what you want me to be,' she turned and said coyly.

And at that very moment, she became a beautiful peacock.

'Strange! At your age, you should be thinking of a beautiful young girl, not this!' the peacock protested.

'Sorry, I don't want you to be a peacock! I want to think of you as a goddess, a Hindu goddess, four hands and flowing hair, shining crown and shimmering clothes, twinkling nose rings and tinkling anklets ... yes, anklets, very important ...!'

She stood there in the dark precincts of the inner sanctum.

'Why would you fancy me this way?' she asked teasingly.

'Since you are a goddess, shouldn't you know?'

She nodded. Strange! The idol nodded! The diamonds scattered a hundred stars.

'I willed you to will me this way,' she said.

'I still need to know your name! Even if you are THE goddess,' I insisted.

Did I hear her say Nrithya? Was it just what I heard, but she didn't say it?

I remembered Nrithya meant dance.

Dreams are very imprecise ...

'Krishna nee Begane Baro ...'

That was the thirteenth time that the line was being repeated by the singer.

'Listen, girls! Understand the meaning, the context, the emotions,' Sivakami Akka was exhorting us. 'Don't move your limbs like a robot.'

(I didn't at all mind being included in the collective noun of 'girls'.)

We nodded.

'Now, let me see if you all get the context right. Tell me, who are you beseeching to come quickly?'

'Lord Krishna!': Voices in chorus.

'As a boy, or as a young man?'

'As a child! Isn't this song addressed to Udupi Krishna? The idol of Krishna in the Udupi temple is that of a child!'

'But, Rukmini, the consort of Krishna, gets Vishwakarma, the celestial architect, to make that idol. Like the way you girls ask for the childhood photos of your boyfriends. Is Rukmini calling the adult lover or the child Krishna?'

'Akka, perhaps, this is not Rukmini's song, could it be of some other devotee?'

'But the call is to come and dance. Who is the one calling him?'

'Why couldn't a young girlfriend—and Krishna had thousands—be the caller?' one of the girls suggested.

'Perhaps, Devaki, Krishna's mother, who never got to experience the joy of his childhood, is calling him,' another said.

'Girls, think! There are a thousand ways to imagine your god! You just have to fully believe in your vision ...' Sivakami Akka said.

In a flash, I remembered the myriad ways that I had experienced religion.

The innocent faith in an Aatha who manifested in a human, and carried out commercial negotiations with you; the blind faith in a Baba who challenged the duality of god and humans, and presented himself comfortably as a combination of both to his followers; the proud, aggressive belief of Salima Bivi, that drew its strength on being exclusive; the amorphous and inclusive faith of Anandhi Periamma—weren't they all equally real and valid to each of them?

'Girls, think! Imagine! Create! Emote!' Sivakami Akka said. 'There are a million ways to convey your belief. You will get it right only when your identity is fully subsumed in the caller, whoever you imagine it to be, and when you actually see Krishna in front of you, in whichever form you imagine him to be. Girls, if in your young minds, Krishna is indeed the romantic, do you truly and desperately want Krishna, his Vyjayanti garland swaying as he walks? Girls, do you notice the twinkling anklets on his feet and sapphire bracelets on his hands …? Do you smell the sandalwood paste on his body? Do you want to embrace him tightly, lick the honey from his lips? … Do you, do you? …'

I need to fall in love with Krishna. Quite urgently.

'My dearest Lakshmi, let me take leave of you! I will miss the calm gaze of your black eyes, the leathery feel of your pink tits and the sage-like wisdom of your mind ... but I have to go to join my Lord!' Godha said, gently stroking the loose skin of the cow's neck.

'I am coming with you!' Lakshmi said, trying to break free of the tether.

'No, you are not! Lord Vatapatrasayee in the Srivilliputtur temple needs to have His favourite milk from you every morning!'

'If you are so concerned about Vatapatrasayee, why didn't you marry Him, instead of running after Ranganatha who looks to me a lazier person, preferring to lie forever on His bed, on an idyllic island? In any case, aren't they both the same Narayana?'

'Of course, they are the same Narayana; they are also different. Like this Universe. Everything is different, and yet everything is the same. You can love the differences, yet be conscious of the sameness!'

'Your usual clever statements!' Lakshmi turned her face.

'Let's hurry up,' Sukhi urged. 'We have a journey of three nights!'

twenty-seven

It was more than four years since I had started my dance lessons. I had already been pickled and seasoned in the oily broth of Madras. I knew most of the bus routes, had mastered the fine art of bargaining at Pondy Bazaar and knew exactly where in the city you could buy the cheapest slippers. I spoke Madras slang with autorickshaw drivers as if my family had lived five generations in the city.

Memories of my village had already acquired a tinge of sepia.

It was entirely by chance that I ran into Anbarasan at the T Nagar bus stand.

'Zaheer!'

That familiar, gruff voice was followed by a hard tap on my shoulder.

I was about to board a bus to Mount Road, one of my favourite destinations on weekends. Mount Road always vied with Mylapore for choice: *Farhan restaurant ... or Karpagam Mess? Amitabh Bachchan? ... or Arangetram?*

Like a man with two wives, I had learnt to share my soul.

In truth, Mount Road was in atrophy, rather like an ageing actress, rapidly losing out its status as the most happening place in the city. Shops were losing customers because the clientele considered their cars more important than themselves, and there was no more parking space left on the road. Pavements were all being swallowed up by street hawkers, who, ironically depended on the patronage of the pedestrians whose space they had usurped. Theatres on Mount Road which had once boasted of the most modern facilities were now having their vitals nibbled away by rats, which were running angrily around as they couldn't forage enough popcorns from the dwindling crowd.

Yet Mount Road held its charm for me.

An old Padmini film was being screened at the iconic Shanti Theatre, as a part of some sort of retrospect, which I was keen to watch. As usual, I had planned to round up my evening with a dinner at Farhan restaurant after the movie.

I was not pleased to meet Anbarasan. He now had more white on his head and less black on his shirt, and was less presentable on the whole.

'Your father is still very angry with you,' he said gravely.

'I don't care,' I replied.

'You abandoned your course at the college.'

'I am learning different things.'

'You have run away to learn dance,' he continued, as though he was reading out from a charge sheet. He spat out the word 'dance', as if it were a dead fly in the mouth.

News didn't seem to have lost its velocity in the village, despite the absence of Anandhi Periamma and her appam shop.

'Not run away,' I corrected, 'I *chose* to learn dance, which is my passion.'

'Anyway, I am so pleased to run into one of our own people in this large city,' he added rather incongruously.

He boarded the bus without any invitation from me.

Anbarasan had come to Madras to attend a rationalist conference, which, for lack of enough financial support, was being held at a dilapidated marriage hall in a low-income suburb.

'It's a mammoth conference,' he said.

I couldn't recall seeing any wall posters or news reports about the event.

'We can't raise enough money. It's all because of upper-caste conspiracy,' he explained.

'What conspiracy?'

'The high-voltage marketing campaign on religion that these fellows do. Religion is the opium of the poor, and fodder for the rich,' he said. It was evident that he had repeated that statement a few thousand times in his life.

'You see, people have become hopelessly god-intoxicated. They don't care for logic or reason anymore,' he said ruefully.

'If the poor find solace in religion, isn't that all that matters?'

'Yes, but it's like the way drugs give you a high. They both snare you into a make-believe world that keeps you from recognizing the miserable reality!'

I suddenly remembered the drug addict in our village.

Unlike liquor, drugs were not easily available in the village. Yet there were a few addicts, and one of them was an artist, who made beautiful charcoal drawings of unseen temples and strange gods and sold them to clients in cities. Some people thought that he could have risen to greater heights but for his addiction. Others believed that his mystic art flowed directly out of his drug-induced hallucinations.

'You remember Muni in our village?' I asked.

'Yes, of course, the drug addict!'

'Yes, was he not always saying that the only problem with drugs was that it dumped you back to reality sooner than later?'

'Not in recent days. Muni is on his deathbed.'

The news did not disturb me. Muni was someone who had always seemed to be waiting to die.

'Religion, even if it's an addiction, is at least not temporary like drugs,' I pointed out. 'If your make-believe god stays with you until your very end, and perhaps even beyond, isn't that all you can ask for?'

'To those determined to cheat themselves, it might be so. You remember the hallucinations at the temple festival at the village? After the high of the festival, didn't they get back to the painful reality of their grinding poverty?'

'Yes, but their pain is more bearable when they imagine it to be the punishment of a just goddess, and their hope is stronger when they believe in a merciful god.'

'I've heard that bullshit for long,' he said dismissively. 'It's an elaborate fabric of deception, spun around an illusory god!'

'To a non-believer like you, it might be an illusion. To believers, their religion is more than just a belief. It's a cultural bulwark, the only thing that binds them together as a society. Beyond class divide and beyond caste differences.'

'No, it's the Indian Constitution that binds us.'

I tried to remember the lesson on the Constitution that we had to study in our eighth or ninth standard. 'We the People,' the Constitution began, I was sure of that, but couldn't remember anything beyond ... Yes, of course, I knew that Dr Ambedkar had authored the Constitution ...

Is that the document that keeps us all together with the shared values of a nationhood? Does it have a story, a legend, a history that we all relate to? Does the Constitution say something about a father's responsibility to allow freedom to his child? Does it explain the shared experiences of dusty roads, pig-shit odour and noisy classrooms that had brought Anbarasan and me together today?

Come to think of it, which chapter of the Constitution dealt with art and music and dance and Bharatanatyam? ...

'I think an abstract thread of values, beliefs and experiences is what binds us. If the Constitution is not a product of that belief, I'm not sure how that could be relevant,' I hesitantly suggested to him.

'But you agree, religion is just a belief, a self-deception?' Anbarasan annoyingly persisted.

'Won't societies fall apart to anarchy, if it weren't for faith, a belief in a god who lays down the rules, a god who oversees us, a god who knows everything? Like the law and police?'

'Yes, provided everyone believes in the same super god. Not if each person has his own god and claims that his god is superior to his neighbour's. That's why the attempted orderliness of reality is constantly threatened by the militant chaos of beliefs!'

I remembered my visit to Munoor. The thousands of devotees who witnessed Maha Baba's 'miracle', that wasn't just a belief, it was their reality.

'For all of us, isn't our belief our reality too?' (Now I sounded like Anandhi Periamma.)

'There is one reality, which is the same to everyone. Beliefs are not the same for all,' he said.

Anbarasan was right.

I could not imagine that the sophisticated lady with ringed fingers and the deerskin bag, a staunch believer of Maha Baba, would have easily connected with the oracle of the possessed goddess man of the village. Each one's belief was a product of their class and personal history, each unique, even within the 'same religion'. Yet, each one's belief was as real as the other.

'What's your belief? Are you a Hindu or a Musalman?' Anbarasan asked, looking straight into my eyes.

The bus stopped at the station near the theatre.

We got down and walked towards the theatre silently.

It occurred to me that all who went to watch a movie, were in fact rushing to lose themselves in a make-believe world. At least for a while. Is this urge to live in beliefs, temporarily or permanently, in the very nature of humans?

'You haven't answered my question,' Anbarasan reminded me.

'I am surprised that it is even relevant to a non-believer like you!' I said.

'It is relevant to a believer like you.'

The answer to that question came to me in a flash, when we were standing in the foyer, waiting for the doors to open. It was a motley crowd, young and old, rich and middle-class. Some stood alone, trying to save themselves from the contaminating contact of human skin, while other restless people were pushing their way past us, as though they were escaping from fire. It was interesting that the movie appealed to such a diverse audience.

As I was being ushered into the theatre, I turned to Anbarasan, who was behind me.

'*My dance is my religion. My very own. And that is broad enough to assimilate many streams from different faiths,*' I shouted to him, over the excited crowd.

I could see him shaking his head in disapproval.

When we were seated, he returned to our conversation.

'No one can help you, if you choose to wallow in your self-deception, but you will have to choose your product, sooner than later.'

'What product?' I asked.

'Religion is the most aggressively promoted product. Through festivals and myths. Through fake gurus and rich mutts, and through music, movies and ... and ... dance!'

'Dance?'

'Yes, the kind that you are in love with!'

I did not respond.

The movie was a typical Padmini starrer. I had hoped to watch some dance, at least in the customary dream sequence, but it turned out that the protagonists were too poor even to dream. Padmini was the forsaken lover, abused wife, punished simultaneously by god, women, men and, most of all, the movie director. She looked ethereal whenever she cried, which was during most of the movie. The women in the audience, vicariously suffering all the pain of Padmini, shed enough tears to fill a pond, while the men struggled to pretend that they didn't care.

Anbarasan was critical that the movie glorified the husband worshipping/god-fearing character of the heroine and romanticized pain and suffering.

Farhan restaurant was unusually quiet. There were just a few old customers who came customarily to the masjid, so they could come to Farhan to gossip about philandering men, and then go to the masjid to atone for the gossip. They usually talked loudly, as they always presumed their friends were deaf, given the average age of the group. But today they were talking in low voices. I could see them huddled together, like a pride of lions over fallen prey. They turned to look at Anbarasan and me, as we entered. It was a look of unease. Probably because Anbarasan was a stranger to the restaurant. Although Anbarasan was the target of their suspicious look, I could feel some of that suspicion sprinkling on me too.

'*Salaamalikum*,' I greeted the son of the proprietor, who was seated at the till.

There was a fleeting nod of acknowledgement. The usual warmth and cordiality were missing. I had been visiting the restaurant periodically and had maintained a friendly relationship with him till then.

I got Anbarasan to sit at a corner table and attempted to go towards the kitchen, as I always did.

'Sit there!' the son ordered in a tone that took me aback. The passport to enter the kitchen, even after I had left the job, was proof of my citizenry of the restaurant and I was secretly proud of that privilege. I had always enjoyed the banter with the cook and waiters at the kitchen, besides ensuring that I got my vegetarian curry.

The son was a very friendly and courteous person, and I had never heard him raise his voice in the past. I sat down at my table and attempted to converse with the few waiters whom I had known, but strangely their response was also cold.

A new waiter, unfamiliar to me, came to our table. At least he had a pleasant smile.

'My favourite paya curry. Without the meat. Moeen Bhai knows how I like it,' I said enthusiastically.

He looked at me quizzically and took the order silently from Anbarasan.

'You seem to be a well-known customer here,' Anbarasan said.

I had not disclosed to Anbarasan my past professional association with Farhan, and I was pleased that Anbarasan was led to believe that I was an influential customer. At the same time, I was disappointed that I couldn't show off my importance with a visit to the kitchen.

Actually, it was more than disappointment.

I felt, for the first time ever, the awkwardness of an unwelcome stranger despite those familiar environs.

I could sense the walls, the old ceiling fans, the flickering tube lights, the silver-framed Arabic calligraphy on the wall, the uncleared plates on the neighbouring tables, all looking at me strangely and exchanging glances.

When the waiter brought the food, I saw that meat pieces were mocking at me defiantly.

'Didn't you tell Moeen Bhai?' I asked the waiter with irritation.

'Moeen Bhai is not here,' he said in a low voice.

'Is he on leave?' I asked. I remembered that when I was at Farhan, Moeen Bhai had made a short trip to Hyderabad to visit his son.

The waiter looked around him.

'The police took him away,' the waiter whispered, eager to share the sensational news.

'Moeen Bhai arrested?' I must have been very loud. The old men seated at the far end of the hall turned towards me.

The waiter nodded.

'Why? Why?'

The waiter shrugged his shoulders. 'They say his son was involved in communal riots in Hyderabad.'

'Why would they arrest Moeen Bhai, even if it's true that his son was mixed up in some riots?'

The waiter again shrugged his shoulders, this time less vigorously.

'A deeply religious person, a kind man I'd say,' I said, not particularly directed at anyone.

The waiter scurried away, worried that he might have spoken too much.

'Strong belief and bigotry are like dusk and night,' Anbarasan said, 'a very diffused dividing line!'

'Did Bhai hide a dark side?' I mused aloud.

It was at this point, that one of the old customers, who was sitting at the far side of the dining room, ambled towards me. He was a regular; I had seen him many times, had even talked to him. I remembered that he was a retired teacher from a madrasa in some part of Madras.

'You are talking about Moeen Bhai?' he growled, as he came closer.

He was obviously not deaf, as he had heard me across the hall.

'What happened?' I asked.

I was petrified to see in those small watery eyes of the old man, a sharp flash of anger.

'He has been framed. Such a pious, innocent man,' he said slowly, fiercely.

The old man shook his head in despair. 'If Moeen Bhai can be arrested, how are we all supposed to feel safe?'

'This is a perfectly safe place for all law-abiding citizens,' I said.

The old man stared at Anbarasan, who had an inappropriately bemused look.

'Who is this man?' the old man asked. His tone was offensive and I was riled.

'He is a customer, like you. Do you need to know more?'

'I asked because Hindus don't usually come to this restaurant,' the old man said, shaking his head.

'I am not a Hindu,' Anbarasan said with a smile.

'Musalman?' the old man asked doubtfully.

'I am Anbarasan. Do I need a religion to identify me?'

The old man turned to me. There was again that quick flash of anger in his eyes.

'Oh, I heard you had joined a Hindu religious prayer group?'

Obviously, I had been the subject of some conversation at the restaurant, and unsurprisingly, facts were getting twisted.

'That is sheer gossip! In any case, what's your problem if I have indeed turned a Hindu?' I retorted.

The proprietor's son who was watching us from his cash desk, came quickly over to the table. No doubt he sensed that a rather challenging situation was developing.

'Zaheer, did you get your food?' he asked me rather brusquely and immediately turned to the old man. 'Ustad, let's go to our table,' he said and led him gently back to his friends.

It was clear that the son was signalling that I ought to eat, pay and leave.

Your citizenship is hereby revoked, he seemed to be saying.

I felt small and humiliated.

We ate in silence.

When we finished, Anbarasan insisted on paying the bill.

'You are not even earning,' he said.

I didn't like that he pointed it out, although it wasn't far from the truth.

'What is surprising about religion breeding extremism? Doesn't drinking almost always lead to a habit, and habit to addiction? Doesn't an addict always end up in a brawl?' Anbarasan asked, as we walked back to our bus stand.

'On the contrary, doesn't religion teach love?'

'Love needs a villain. Think of all the movies you have watched. Lovers fling into each other's arms only at the sight of a villain. You need to create a villain!'

'And who is the villain?'

'The *other one.* The *other religion,* the *other caste,* the *other god.*'

'I am not the other in Farhan!'

'If you are not fully with them, then you are against them. You also become the other. That's the problem with every religion!'

'That's not true,' I said, 'can you remember a time in our village when we felt any kind of communal divide? Do you remember how all communities came together harmoniously for the village festival?'

'That's not harmony,' Anbarasan said, 'that's the amoral equilibrium of a feudal society.'

'You mean, that kind of togetherness exists because people are resigned to their given station in the society and don't challenge it?'

'Exactly! However unfair and unlawful that situation might be!'

Strangely, Anbarasan was beginning to make sense to me. It was as if he was showing a mirror, and what I saw wasn't very pleasing.

We stopped at a tea stall.

Anbarasan turned to me and asked: 'Why don't you try your luck in movies?'

'You approve of that?' I asked, astonished.

'Yes, cinema is mostly purposeful,' he said. 'In fact, it's the only art form that's fully democratized. It's not just a rich person's idle entertainment, like your Bharatanatyam!'

'But cinema is not my goal,' I said. 'Bharatanatyam is. And I can't see why the art form couldn't be used just as effectively to convey a social message, like the way cinema has done.'

Anbarasan shook his head, 'Religion, Hindu religion, not even the so-called spirituality, is the air that fills the balloon of this dance form. You take it away, and the art form will collapse!'

'I am not in it for its religion, and I can stay a Muslim and be a dancer! I can dance about social issues.'

As I said this, I could sense my own words drooping, lacking the strength of conviction.

We walked towards the bus stand in silence. We had to take buses in opposite directions. I stopped at the road crossing.

'It was nice to have met you again. Best wishes for the success of the conference,' I said formally, and held out my hand. Anbarasan ignored my proffered hand. Perhaps, I should have said *vanakkam,* considering that he was once upon a time my teacher.

Anbarasan stood at the crossing looking at me.

'Zaheer, do you sometimes feel that you might have made a mistake breaking off relations with your family?' Anbarasan asked.

'No, not the least.'

He nodded.

There was no doubt that Anbarasan had dealt a few hurtful blows on my thoughts. I needed time to think.

'Zaheer, do you realize that you are on a wrong path, the one-way road of religious art? Worse, you are trying to ride two horses at the same time. There is no dual citizenship when it comes to religion; no middle path, no place for the rational, it's just emotional,' Anbarasan said, holding my arm.

'What's the right path, according to you?'

'Give up all these obscure beliefs and useless art and be a rationalist,' he said. 'This country requires solid economic progress, rational young people, not make-believe spirituality!'

'I don't care what you say,' I shouted.

But I was lying.

twenty-eight

I needed to talk to Krishna. (Or, someone like him.)

Not the God, not the Lover, but the Charioteer.

I know you know *the* book: The Bhagavad Gita. Who doesn't?

You remember, this strange man Arjuna, instead of commandeering his army to charge ahead in the battlefield (as any general should), throws his weapons down, overcome by doubts and questioning the very purpose of the war (a soldier is never permitted to question the ethics of the war—only because, I think, all wars are fundamentally unethical). It takes Krishna, his charioteer, to remind Arjuna of his military discipline and duties.

The Arjuna in me was getting thoroughly confused and confounded: Had I taken the wrong road to my future?

I had no doubts about the road I had left behind, the road that would have taken me towards a life amidst Ramzan fasts and plastic buckets; doubts were only about the road that I had chosen.

I had no regrets about fleeing home.

No, not *fleeing. Leaving home.*

Don't birds fly away when they grow wings? Do animals look to their fathers for advice about where they should hunt and with whom they should mate? Aren't humans supposed to be a more intelligent species?

I remembered a movie where the protagonist, as a young boy, had run away from home, only to return many years later as a successful film star. (Everyone hugged everyone else, and they all gathered together with smiling faces for a concluding group shot.)

And think of all the school dropouts who became celebrities ...

The moral is: running away from home or dropping out of school is not fundamentally a sin; it all depends on the outcome.

Anbarasan's target of attack, I liked to believe, was not me, but Bharatanatyam. Thinking about it this way eased my pain a bit.

Anbarasan's disapproval was somewhat different in nature to Kumar's distaste for this art form: while both despised the art for its elitist character, Anbarasan's scorn was further compounded in his belief that it was a Hindu snare. That it would pull me inexorably into the Hindu faith; Zaheer being converted to Sekhar, leading to irrational bigotry and a purposeless life. In his classless and casteless world, there was no place for god-promoting art.

Could I not be neutral to religion? Did art and music not have any purpose, other than religion? Was poetry a waste of rhymes? Was Mohammed Rafi's music meaningless?

Dark clouds tend to crowd together.

The demons created by Kumar's taunts also now found the chance to dance their way to the centre stage.

It suddenly felt humiliating to think of receiving monthly stipends from the art patrons. Especially to pursue a questionable career. Wasn't a stipend just a name to dignify alms? It hurt to hear Kumar say only beggars receive alms. But wasn't that the unalloyed truth? Should I not be honourably earning my living, working hard like Kumar? If not as a plastic engineer, at least as a bearer in the Connemara? On the other hand, if I did not pursue dance, why would I not continue to remain at home?

I cursed Anbarasan. He had muddied my mind. I cursed Kumar.

I felt alone.

Like a lone boat in the vastness of the ocean. The infinite blue waters showing no sign of any direction. My compass, with the needle of my passion that had so far been unerringly showing me north, was now broken. So I thought. The sea which had been rocking me like a baby was now challenging me with her unconquerable depths. So I felt.

I needed my navigator, my charioteer, my Krishna. *My* Krishna? *My? My?*

When did I join the creed?

Was I slipping into the Hindu faith?

Was I getting 'converted'?

Or, was I already converted, when I danced to the narratives of Rama and Krishna and Siva? When I cupped my palms and prostrated in front of the Nataraja idol, before I started my lessons every day? When I began to devour the Hindu mythological prose? Have I been camouflaged—involuntarily, with my skin turning to the vermilion pervading my environment, without my being even aware?

I am lost.

I need my charioteer. A talking guide.

Parthasarathy!

I remembered hearing about the Parthasarathy Swami Temple, a temple for the Charioteer God. The god Parthasarathy ('Arjuna's driver') sports a twirled-up moustache. Appropriate for a war-zone appearance.

Besides the Mariamman Temple, I had been to a few other temples, accompanying Selvi or other friends, salivating at the prospect of some delicious prasadam. Temples were godly restaurants. God was an excuse, a stone doll, dark and distant.

Those gods at the temples were not the ones that I captured in my mind, when I danced their myriad tales. My dancing gods were alive, colourful and came out of calendars ...

I stood in front of the imposing entrance of Parthasarathy Swami Temple for some time, hesitating to cross the threshold. I wondered if it was the final act of switching loyalties ...

There were people rushing into the temple, no doubt unable to bear the load of their sins. They would go into the temple, as if entering a kitchen sink, and expect to come out washed clean, smelling of soap-like incense. Others, hastening to make deals with the Lord.

That's being cynical. Perhaps there were some who were just surrendering to the Lord ...

I hadn't come to the temple for any of that. Nor for the prasadam.

I had come to the temple on an impulse. To seek answers, directions, guidance.

To have a conversation.

Isn't it bizarre that I should seek out a stranger, even my *potential kidnapper*, for helping me find directions in my life? A dark, dull stone idol to talk to me?

But I had nowhere else to turn.

~

The temple was heavily crowded.

It was the Tamil month of Margazhi, a period, which I knew had special association with Andal, the female Vaishnavite savant, and Lord Krishna.

The Lord had said that he was the month of Margazhi, amongst all months. I didn't quite understand *that*, but knew that this month had the same sanctity for Vaishnavites, as Ramzan had for Muslims.

Except Margazhi was not for fasts. Andal had sanctioned the feast of sarkarai pongal drenched in ghee, that flowed down your arm, as you ate from a leafy cup.

I rather like a feasting faith.

Someone was giving a lecture, sitting on a small stage in a *mandapam* in the outer corridor of the temple. The lecturer's forehead and his bare torso were boldly painted all over, with the white-and-yellow *namam*, the symbol of Vishnu, leaving no part of his own body in doubt about his devotion to the Lord. He was obviously a popular religious leader, as there was a considerable crowd listening to him with rapt attention.

I stood there trying to listen to what he was saying. He spoke in Tamil, for sure, but I found it difficult to follow. (Have you noticed, dialects have caste, even intonations have class?) I had, by now, got familiar with Brahmanical Tamil; I even found my own dialect had begun to get sprayed with the Brahmanical dye, but this man's Tamil was altogether different. There was too much Sanskrit in his language and it made him sound knowledgeable and authoritative. I tried repeating some of his lines, and they did sound sonorous ...

After some effort, some of what he was saying began to make sense, like a mist clearing.

'... It's important you follow *Svadharma* ... Bhagawan clearly says "It's your duty to lead a life that's prescribed for you" ... that's Svadharma ... Don't try to be someone else ...' the lecturer warned.

'Lead a life prescribed for you!'

Stop. That seemed like a message. Was it meant for me?

What was the life *prescribed* for me?

What was my Svadharma? Being a faithful Musalman? Fasting during Ramzan, and feasting at iftar? A loyal son taking care of elderly parents? An engineer, producing plastic bottles every day?

But, that would not be *me* ...

Am I destined to be a dancer, like a worm is destined to be a butterfly? Or, am I prescribed to be a moulvi, because I was born a Muslim?

But, wait… why would I even listen to a what a Hindu god says?

As I moved through the long line of devotees waiting to have a darshan of the Lord, I became restless. I was unsure of why I had at all come to the temple.

It was *my* life's questions. *I* had to find answers.

It was naive to believe that the god was going to discuss my life issues with me. That's irrational faith. What Pankajam said about the talking god was sheer fantasy. Those things don't happen in real life.

I tried to turn back.

The line was barricaded so tightly that it was impossible to squeeze my way back.

'Have I got into a one-way street to the Lord ...?'

If he had to live up to his mythological reputation, he would need to guide me, when I reached him.

As the line snaked it's way to the Lord, I was distracted by the wide variety of devotion that was in display. There were some who were praying with closed eyes, unmindful of the sights and sounds around them. There were others who were loudly calling out to the Lord.

There was one man just behind me, who caught my attention. He was talking to the Lord, in a low tone, as if he was conversing with a trusted old friend.

'… have to help me. I have been asking you to knock some sense into my boss's head … and you are not acting fast … you are the Almighty. The entire universe, the stars, the planets, living and non-living beings, all function, because of your will. I know that's a lot of work, and you are incredibly busy, but you have to find time, because you are the only one who can make my boss agree to transfer me to this new job ... if I continue in this present job, I'll go mad, and I better warn you that you will have to take responsibility for my state ...'

I turned to look at him sideways, without appearing to be listening to him, but he was so absorbed in his conversation with his god, that he didn't seem to bother.

I now knew, how to address this charioteer.

He was not my *god.* At the moment, I expected him to be just a counsel, a guide. I'll address him, *matter-of-factly,* like the man behind me.

I'll decide about him being my god, if I received clarity to the questions in my mind.

I would ask the Lord to show me the way. Not pray, mind you; just ask.

I might have to dream. He could come into my dreams and tell me what he thinks about my life.

As I came in front of the sanctum, I was struck by the majesty of the idol, his commanding posture. He stood there, resplendent with a long golden crown, a bright orange and green (beautiful colours!) dhoti, with zari linings, and a long garland of fresh tulsi leaves. As the tiny flame of camphor lit up his face, I could see his eyes looking down intensely at me. He was not the prankster child, not the flute-playing romantic, not even the energetic charioteer that I was familiar with. With his white, twirling moustache, and deep penetrating eyes, and just a fleeting smile, he could have been a father. *The father that I didn't have.* Pankajam might have been right about the talking god in Srirangam. Well, here he was, a few feet away from me, and he seemed ready to have a chat with me. Like a father would.

That is, *if I believed he would chat.*

But I was not going to lose myself in awe. I reminded myself that he was just a guide.

I said under my breath: 'You look indeed very impressive. Being god, I presume you know all about me. If I have taken a wrong road, let me know quickly. How you would message me, I've no idea. May be you will visit my dream ... Now that I've let you decide for me, I'll blame you if I don't succeed in the path that you show ... And, by the way, don't try and trap me; I am still a Muslim. I might be on the crossroads, but I know how to retrace my steps ...'

The man behind was getting a little louder:

'... and I mean quickly, by tomorrow. I'll see my boss in the morning, so, make sure I get the right response from him ... oh, my god! You are dropping a flower! That means you are acceding to my request! That's wonderful! You have spoken! YOU HAVE SPOKEN ...! Thanks!'

I turned and smiled at him.

He smiled back.

Did the Lord drop a flower for me or the man behind me or for everyone who was praying to the Lord at that moment?

Does god converse in symbols?

twenty-nine

No, he didn't appear in my dream. At least, not directly.

I dreamt, in fact, of a dog with two horns which ran away with my lunch, and I was chasing it round and round ... until it disappeared into a hole in the ground.

I woke up and searched hard for a message in that dream. I gave up.

I went back to sleep, telling the charioteer that if he chose to convey a message through my dreams, he ought to be more direct.

I dreamt again. This time I was urinating into a 'western type' commode, that overlooked a valley full of thorny cactus.

I woke up with my bladder full.

I was angry.

My awakened mind creaked with the weight of tormenting doubts, and I was irritated that I had no one to help clear my mind.

The charioteer had obviously chosen to ignore my advances.

I chose not to go to the classes for more than a week.

'I am unwell,' I said on the phone to Kameswaran Anna. It wasn't a lie. It was mental illness. I felt depressed and unsure of my self-esteem.

'Should we send you something to eat?' Kameswaran Anna asked kindly. I declined politely.

That morning, I had to collect my stipend from one of my 'patrons'. That stipend was absolutely essential to pay my mess bill.

I hated my position: I had no alternative livelihood. Stipends paid for my meals and that was tied to my dance career.

I had truly got trapped in a trench from where it was impossible to climb out.

I gathered myself to make a slow journey to the patron's office.

I never met the patron himself during these monthly visits, as his office manager had instructions to disburse my stipend every month.

The office manager was not at his desk. I waited for a while, looking upside down at the parade of gods underneath the glass top on his desk. The gods looked at me with inverted smiles. I wondered why people needed the constant company of gods in two- and three-dimensional forms.

I was pleased that I could identify most of the gods in the various pictures.

Ganesha. Venkatachalapathi. Saraswati, with her veena. I even knew the story of Markandeyan and Lord Siva at Tirukkadaiyur, whose picture was jostling in the crowd.

I was passing my own tests on Hindu religion.

But why was I even testing myself? Had I slipped into the twilight zone of being both Hindu and Musalman? Can I be both?

I played with the glass paperweight, rotating on its top, but the restlessness returned.

The office manager eventually came back and I greeted him. He went about searching for some papers in the mounds of files that lined the walls, completely ignoring me. I cleared my throat a couple of times, but it was obviously a weak cue. He probably did not succeed in finding the paper he was searching for, and was making impatient sounds. He once again left his place without in any way acknowledging my presence.

I was reminded of the village fakir. This man, who went around the village with a copper cup of smouldering incense powder, would religiously come home every Friday morning and move around the house, waving the cloud of incense into every corner. I had never heard him speak to anyone. After the ritual, he would humbly wait just outside the front door. Every time, Salima Bivi would pretend to be busy and delay giving him his due of fifty paise. She would never forget to let him know that she considered it a complete waste of money as she believed that the fakir didn't do a good job of excoriating the evil spirits that lay hidden in crevices, where entry was possible only for the matterless odour from the incense.

I was perhaps worse than the fakir. At least he drove away some evil spirits and earned his pay.

I left without collecting my stipend.

As I came out, I ran into Rukmini Krishnan.

She was an extraordinary woman, who had multiple talents, as an accomplished singer, composer, an impressive compère and a TV personality.

I keenly watched her programmes on TV, although she would typically address a female audience.

I had met her several times in Sivakami Akka's place, and was always impressed with her intelligence and diverse talents. I wondered why I had not thought of her to guide me and clear my confusions.

'How are the dance lessons progressing?' she asked.

'Not sure I should continue,' I said.

She looked at me curiously.

'What's the problem?'

'I wonder if I am doing something purposeful.'

'Purposeful?'

'Yes, does dance have any use to solve any human problem? Say, hunger?' I tried to sound intelligent, but knew that my confusion showed.

'It's not enough if it solves *your* problem of hunger?'

'Dance, like every other human activity, has to address a human problem,' I repeated what Anbarasan told me.

Rukmini Amma looked at me with astonishment.

She didn't respond. We walked quietly until we reached the sari shop that she was going to visit.

'As you know, there is a dance programme of Sivakami at the Music Academy this evening. You should go. She would be expecting you there,' she said.

I nodded.

~

It was an outstanding performance.

Sivakami Akka had chosen to present the theme of Ramayana in a seven-part sequence, set in seven captivating ragas and seven different *talas*. Her eloquence was incredible with absolute clarity in her communication. As she portrayed the trauma and the triumphs of the hero, spectators became involved participants in the drama of Rama. They cried when Rama was banished from his kingdom, cried even more when his wife Sita was kidnapped by the demon

king Ravana, rejoiced when Hanuman discovered Sita, all the time not failing to appreciate the incredible rhythmic patterns that Sivakami was weaving on the floor with her dancing feet.

An ecstatic audience stood up to give an ovation at the end of the presentation.

I was entranced.

I realized that, in the past when I watched a dance recital, I'd mentally thrust myself onto the stage substituting myself in the place of the dancer. It would always be a tension-ridden excitement. I experienced now, for the first time, the thrill and pure joy of a spectator.

As I came out of the hall, I saw Rukmini Amma coming towards me.

'How was the programme?' she asked.

'I was transported to another world,' I said.

'How do you think the audience felt?'

'I'd be surprised if any individual in the audience did not feel a sense of exaltation. You watched the standing ovation!'

'And, yet you think dance has no social purpose?'

'Well ...'

'Isn't it a unique blessing to humans and humans alone that they can spread joy through creativity?' she pushed her argument.

'You can't bring joy through art to someone with an empty stomach or an ailing body.'

'Of course you can't! Nor can you guarantee peace and joy only through a wholesome meal,' Rukmini Amma said with a short laugh. 'Where is the conflict between two parallel needs of man—the material and the emotional? Or, the material and spiritual?'

'I have too many questions in my mind ...'

'Look,' she said, 'there is only one place that you can find answers to all your questions. That's your art. When you surrender to your passion, all questions disappear. There is not even a need for answers.'

Perhaps the charioteer had spoken. Through my own teacher.

Or, I had become an addict to my art and I needed excuses.

I slept that night without a dream, a deep, restful sleep.

I went back to my classes after a break of nearly two weeks.

I felt like a child rushing back to the warm bosom of the mother, after losing a petty quarrel.

As I entered the porch of Sivakami Akka's home, the sound of the tapping stick filled my ears, sending a shiver of excitement. I hummed along with the music that wafted through the door.

I confidently put my foot past the front door.

I rushed to join the girls who were dancing.

This was my world. My Own.

I had reached where I belonged.

thirty

There was a new voice in the classroom.

A petite lady had taken the place of Sharma.

'Sivakami Akka asked him to go,' was the cryptic message from my fellow students.

'We need to plan for your Arangetram,' Sivakami Akka said simply.

Do a few words have the power to shoot you into the sky, let you kick the moon and stroke the stars? Yes, they do.

Can a mere suggestion of an event brighten your eyes, lighten your steps and fire up your mind? Yes, of course …

I would soon be ON THE STAGE!

I. Zaheer.

On the stage. On a platform, a pedestal. At a higher level than others.

Newly minted and duly certified.

Lusty lights licking me with coloured tongues,
I would ascend the stage to look down on all,
draped in orange and red, like a vain hibiscus,

face painted pink, eyes lined and lips like blood,
the make-up finishing what god left half done;
studded chains nestling on my barren chest,
ankle bells and golden bangles in joyous clamour ...
noisy cymbals speaking from the dark flanks
And a heaving hall of applauding audience ...
I would be on the stage, dancing like the gods!
ON THE STAGE!

I wanted to roll on the floor, jump around the room, run circles and scream with joy.

I wanted to kiss Sivakami Akka's feet. Shower flowers on her.

I did none of that. I hesitated for a full minute.

'Thank you,' I said simply.

There was a reason for my excitement to have had just a fleeting life.

I had of course dreamt of my Arangetram many times in the past.

I would immediately worry about the enormous expenditure that an Arangetram entailed and my excitement would be swept away. That anxiety had again bubbled up in my mind.

'Don't worry about the expenses. I'll take care of them,' Sivakami Akka said precisely at that moment. As if she had read my mind.

'Go, prepare well,' she said simply.

I wept with joy.

The rehearsals began right earnest.

There were endless confabulations with my seniors and fellow students about the choice of dance numbers for presentation.

'You are very good when you are pining in devotion. That comes naturally to you,' my senior said.

Among the songs chosen for my dance was *Sriman Narayana*, a devotional song on Lord Narayana.

'You are not getting it right,' Sivakami Akka said with disappointment.

'I am doing my best,' I said. 'What else can I do?'

'Imagine you are *Andal*!' Sivakami Akka said.

'Why Andal?'

'Because there is just no one else who experienced Narayana as intimately as Andal. I want you to express your devotion with as much passion as Andal.'

'Andal was a girl, and she was madly in love with the Lord. I am a man. Would it be appropriate to act as though I am a girl?'

'Narayana is the alpha male, the Paramapurusha. Every mortal, man and woman, are all the feminine equivalent. Many *Azhwars*, the Vaishnavite savants, have sung in praise of the Lord, imagining themselves to be females in love with Narayana!'

'Wasn't Andal a rebel?' I asked.

Sivakami Akka simply smiled and said, 'Precisely.'

The practice sessions continued.

'Do you see Narayana in your mind's eye?' my senior asked.

'Yes, I do.'

I saw the charioteer.

With fierce moustache and mischievous eyes.

With rocky solidity and flowery suppleness.

With the war bugle and the protective palm.

With gleaming crown and fresh tulsi leaves ...

'Do you see the Lord reclining on the serpent, the thousand-tongued *Adi Sesha,* and being in *Yoga Nidra,* envisioning the unfolding of creation?' my senior asked.

The charioteer obligingly lay down on the serpent bed.

'Do you see the ever-expanding universe, the divine lotus, germinating from the navel of the Creator, the *Kamala Nabha*?'

'Hm ...'

'Do you see?'

'Yes, I see all the stars, the space, the nothingness, and everything, the living and the non-living, all unfolding as a part of One Supreme Being, and I am witnessing the miracle!'

'At whose lotus feet, you bow, your forehead kissing the ground that he stands on?'

'Yes, kneeling on the floor, bent in pure devotion to the One and only Supreme. Allahu Akbar!'

'I am not your devotee. At least not yet!' I told the charioteer. 'Please understand. I am just pretending to be Andal. I just want my dance to come out to be the best, and therefore this relationship is purely transactional. Of course, I see your face, radiant like a thousand suns, your eyes, the very fountainhead of kindness waiting to douse the worldly worries of your devotees. The nectar of your lips flavouring the enthralling music that flows from the proud reeds of the flute ... yes, I see all that, I hear all that, without a doubt ...

'Then you are my devotee!' the Lord smilingly said.

'I am? Oh, I didn't *want* to be!'

'You don't choose devotion. You experience it!'

'Hope you are not suggesting that I am already a Hindu?'

There was no answer.

'Can you please, please confirm that I am not a Hindu?'

No answer.

Actually, I was talking to myself.

Sometimes you mistake yourself for god.

I now conversed with god every day. Like Andal.

As I danced his tales. As I called out to him, 'Narayana, Narayana.'

I kept telling him that it would be utterly unfair to suck me into his devotion, since I was approaching him only for the sake of getting my dance to be perfect. Not through religion.

I heard no voices in my mind. Yet I felt I 'conversed'.

'At least let me know if I could continue to be friends with you, without having to convert,' I told him.

No answer.

The charioteer chose to be stubbornly unresponsive.

'Come anytime when you need a sounding board,' Rukmini Amma had told me.

'I am confused,' I said to Rukmini Amma, as I stood in front of her. She was going through her script for the next show.

'Good. That means you are thinking,' she said.

I sat down beside her.

'Can I not be a Musalman, or just irreligious and yet continue to perform Bharatanatyam?' I asked her.

'Sure, you can,' she said.

'I don't need to convert?'

'What do you do to convert?'

'Going to temples?'

'You are doing that!'

'Wear a namam on the forehead?'

'Aren't you doing so when you dance?'

'Praying to Hindu gods?'

'Well, you say you are conversing!'

'Change my name?'

'Saint Kabir didn't change his name, though he was Rama's devotee.'

'I haven't stopped eating omelette. I actually like it very much.'

'Whoever said all Hindus are vegetarians?'

'I cannot ever be part of a religion that sacrifices goats.'

'Where did you come across that?'

'In my village, there is this festival, where you have animal sacrifices and possessed men being worshipped as goddess! I can't relate to that kind of religion.'

'Don't! There are lots of Hindus who feel like you.'

'Is that not an authentic Hindu practice?'

'Of course it is. Did the village folks not hear the voice of the goddess, through the possessed man? Were there not rains after the festival?'

'Yes. They believe that the rain came as a result of their offerings.'

'Isn't that all that matters? How is their belief inferior to mine?'

'And I don't believe in Hindu godmen. They are tricksters!'

'Purandaradasa, a great devotee of Lord Krishna, who lived five hundred years ago, said, "Don't go to godmen, because you don't need an intermediary, when you can directly communicate to Krishna!"'

'Why do people then throng godmen?'

'Because they see god in them. Their belief is all that is real to them!'

I kept looking at the picture of Krishna on the wall for several minutes. Krishna smiled at me mischievously.

'Are you saying I am already a Hindu?' I asked.

'Does it matter? '

'I am confused,' I said.

Rukmini Amma sang in her mellifluous voice:

Gods, old and young, come in many colours
Character and costumes, shapes and form.
Through the quarrelling gods and loving ones,
Look deep enough and discover their maker—
Your mind, your beliefs, your faith, your hope!
Your reality, your truth, as real and true as you Are!

She went back to her script.

'Am I Muslim or a Hindu?' I asked again. In different words.

'Does it matter?' she asked, and sang again:

Ram and Rahim are the same
To those who believe them so.
They're also the diminished god
Warring with limited reign,
For those who want them so!

'The Lord was emphatic that He would be adorned only with those garlands that you have worn already!' Periazhwar was perplexed as he narrated his dreams to Godha. 'He, the Paramatma, the Supreme One, the Absolute masculine force of the Universe, is madly in love with you!'

'What's there to be surprised?' Godha asked her father, as she milked Lakshmi, who mockingly kicked Godha. 'As the mortal—the Jeevatma—fully surrenders to the Supreme, He embraces her in sublime love. That's what He has done to me.'

'The Lord hasn't graced me with the same intensity of love, that He seems to have for you.' There was a hint of jealousy in Periazhwar's voice.

'I'm surprised you don't understand this,' Godha said, turning to face her father. 'If you stand at a distance from your God in awe, He blesses you from the same distance. I throw my arms around His rock-like shoulders and kiss His nape with passion. He returns my kiss with even more lust. You define and decide your God!'

'You are Andal, the One who has conquered!'

'I'm a symbol, a metaphor,' Godha said modestly. 'All the sixteen thousand maidens, who have laid their naked souls and bodies, with no pretentious coverings, in the service of the Lord are all Andals. And they are metaphors too.'

'I am just Periazhwar, the big devotee, but you are Andal, the One who has power over the Lord!'

'I hope you will now give up any thought of giving me in marriage to an incomplete mortal,' Andal said.

'Well timed,' Sukhi chirped.

Periazhwar looked at his daughter with ecstasy. Tears flowed down his cheeks.

'By the way, I will be leaving for Srirangam tomorrow for my union with my Lord,' Andal informed her father.

'But ... but ...' Periazhwar hesitated.

'What but?' Andal asked impatiently.

'Tomorrow ... tomorrow is not an auspicious day.'

'Time and space are His creations and all His creations are auspicious,' said Andal. 'I cannot wait any longer to be held in tight embrace by Purushottaman, the Supreme Man, and have my lips locked with His, whence the flood of all wisdom and the nectar of all music flows!'

'Tut, tut ...That's not how a Brahmin girl is supposed to talk to her father,' Sukhi said mischievously.

'Oh!' Andal looked at Sukhi with mock surprise. 'When did I ever subscribe to man-made conventions? I define my own faith, my beliefs, my religion and my very special relationship with the Divine!'

thirty-one

'Go,' says my senior.

The first cycle of *jati*s, the sol-fa syllables, is closing ...

The cue for my entry to the stage.

THE MOMENT.

With a burst of sweat and legs folding up like wet cloth, I enter the stage under the arc lights that come hunting, my heart pounding louder than the drums from the music team.

Tham thith tham, Thai thath thai, Tham thith tham, Thai thath thai.

My arms are iron rods, as I jerk them into position. And the legs ... My god, why are they moving around like wayward snakes?

I should remember to move my head and roll my eyes ... yes, I am almost getting that under control, but now I should haul myself to the front by two steps with the next beats ... Why on earth is the stage so small? ...

No ... no ... I need water ... Water! The throat feels like a desert ... !

Tharikita, tharikita ...

The body is at last beginning to move correctly, like a wound up toy. No, like a lathe, cutting and slicing the air precisely. But I, meaning my mind, seem to have nothing to do with the manoeuvres of the body. Machines don't have brains, but don't they move? But machines don't sweat ...

Tham thith tham, Thai thath thai ...

My dear knees, bend more! Urgent!

Oh, holy cow! That landing misses a beat ... No doubt, I'll be pulled up by Sivakami Akka ... And now one more beat missed. Why on earth are my feet suddenly revolting?

The toy is now moving as per design ... well, almost.

Thank god, the first number is drawing to a close ...

'I can't do it!' I tell my senior, as I rush behind the curtains.

'Don't be silly,' she admonishes. 'Just nerves. Happens to all new entrants. Go back confidently!'

Andal is checking herself in the mirror. 'That string of flowers around my hair bun is beginning to darken at the edges ... and may be I should wear a necklace of pearls instead of the rubies ... which are, anyway, not suitable for a young girl like me!'

'Your lover knows you thoroughly! You don't need to particularly dress up for Him!' says Sukhi.

'Hmm ... I can't take chances. He shouldn't find excuses not to accept me, when I present myself at Srirangam ... He is never a reliable lover! ... Besides, He is in the company of His consort, Ranganayaki, who has a reputation of being a tough and unyielding lady!'

'Oh the Courageous One! You are sweating. Just nerves. Happens to all brides!' Sukhi says.

I am able to see the dignitaries in the first row, peering beyond the blinding lights.

Padma Subrahmanyam, the doyen of Bharatanatyam, is right ahead ... What a gracious lady! Did she not take me, Zaheer, a Muslim man to her puja room, her sacred shrine at home, to bless me with *kumkum,* wishing me for the success of this programme? Am I going to disappoint her?

The jatis are cascading like an exuberant waterfall. I've got to get these complex steps correct ... There is only one chance you have in life to land on the moon. A small step on the stage, but a giant step in my life ... Let me concentrate on the *theermanam,* the concluding steps ...

And there is Viswanathan, the patron, sitting with a smile ... but for whose generosity, I could not have gone through my dance lessons ...

No, I can't let them down.

My body is my mridangam, the drum, for my mind to play the rhythms. Yes, I am getting it. No mistakes so far. Precise. Sharp. Thank god.

I am sweating now, not out of stage fear, but because of the exertion, the bright lights, burning like mini suns ...

When I return, my senior towels my sweaty back and says: 'For heaven's sake, don't be conscious of the people in front of you ... You are Andal, madly in love with the Super Man! Just transform into Andal. People around you should disappear ... Only Narayana should occupy your mind! Now go!'

'Oh young girls from the clan of cowherds! Join me in my journey to Srirangam! We shall knock at the doors of that sleeping Lion, destabilizing Him with the torrent of beauty at His doorstep,' Andal is calling out to her friends from the Yadava colony.

'It's too early in the morning. Don't you see the doors are shut, and the girls are still sleeping?' Sukhi points out.

'I want them to see how Narayana throws His muscular arms around my supple shoulders, and how He crushes my tender breast in His tight embrace. Let them feel jealous and yearn for Narayana!'

'No Andal, you are not seeking a union with the Lord for providing a spectacle for others! People around you should disappear from your thoughts. Only Narayana should have room in your mind!' Sukhi says.

I am back on the stage for my main presentation: 'Narayana, Narayana.'

I stand with my mind transfixed on
His lotus-like feet, light shining from within
beckoning the believers to surrender;
His palm, the lines forming a coded design
signalling security to the truly devout
His eyes, half closed, at once looking
at this the visible and that the invisible …
I surrender to that Only One, the Omniscient,
Who is the Creator and all the Created.
One called by many names, worshipped many ways.
It's Srirangam at last.
Andal stands before the Lord. Transfixed on
His lotus-like feet, light shining from within
beckoning the believers to surrender
His palm, the lines forming a coded design
Signalling security to the truly devout
His eyes, half closed, at once looking
at this the visible and that the invisible.
She surrenders to the Only One, the Omniscient,
Who is the Creator and all created,
One called by many names, worshipped many ways.

PART III

The Faith

thirty-two

I am, because you believe I am.
And what you believe of things that lie
beyond what you see, hear and feel
is your Truth. The whole Truth.
I am false, really false,
a mere whiff imagined
To your 'others', who think so.
Your mind is my Creator
And I created your mind.
I have revealed to the researching mind
My super position:
I may exist, I may not,
I am here and I am there
As you observe,
Some Truth is born.
As you believe
Your Truth is born.
As we observe, so we all believe.
As you believe, you alone observe.
In an illusory world you alone are true,
You and your beliefs.

About the Author

R. Seshasayee is a senior business leader. He has held several leadership positions, including as executive vice chairman and managing director of Ashok Leyland Ltd; chairman, Infosys Ltd; chairman, IndusInd Bank Ltd, etc. He is presently vice chairman, Hinduja Group, and independent director, Asian Paints Ltd.

He was president of Confederation of Indian Industry (CII), president of Society of Indian Automobile Manufacturers (SIAM), and has served on several committees of the Government of India, including the Board of Trade. He was also the co-chair of World Economic Forum, Middle East.

Seshasayee is deeply committed to social causes, and is the chairman of Cancer Institute, Chennai; chairman of the executive committee of Hinduja National Hospital, Mumbai; and chairman of Schizophrenia Research Foundation of India. He was formerly chairman of National Institute of Technology, Tiruchirappalli (NITT), and other educational institutions.

He served as chairman, Board of Trustees of Srirangam Temple. He has also received formal training in classical music and was the vice president of the Music Academy, Chennai.

The Dance of Faith is his debut novel.